Underworld

Level Up or Die

Book 1

By Apollos Thorne

ISBN 978-1-7336644-1-7

Beta Readers

PROLOGUE

Her mistress's throne room was decked out just like the pillowed dungeon you would imagine a millennia-old succubus would have. Fabrics and cushions in gaudy reds, purples, and gold warmed up the gray stone walls and floors as much as could be hoped for. What was missing were the hypnotic tones and trance-inducing beat that would be common except on special occasions.

A pearl white throne with blood red fabric was graced by a modestly dressed lady. Her purple Victorian gown had full-length sleeves and didn't even leave any leg or cleavage for the imagination. The odd fashion statement by the otherwise lusty, full-lipped succubus wasn't lost on the Lich.

"Mistress Lilith. If I may be so bold, why are you dressed so…"

"Elegantly?" she interrupted, challenging his resolve, even though she had no doubt expected him to ask.

Having second thoughts, she answered the question on his mind. "Yes, yes." She sighed. "It certainly must be odd to see one of my kind dressed so finely, let alone wearing so much clothing in the first place. After a thousand years I'm tired of males of every race ogling me. How would you feel after daily having every man's lecherous eyes feasting upon you?"

The Lich couldn't help himself. A full belly laugh erupted from his skeletal frame. "Forgive me, Head Mistress," he said immediately, knowing he had crossed the line.

Obviously not happy with him, she demanded, as a threatening cold energy resonated from her, "What's so funny?!"

"You capture and leech the life out of the men who you are accusing of being lecherous. Not only that, you are the queen of leeches. That is why I agreed to our deal."

He could tell she was still upset, but her pride had been invoked. He had wisely stroked her ego enough to hopefully save himself from a headache later restoring their working relationship. Their deal, after all, could grant them both great power.

"And it's the fact that I have grown tired of the act that has led me to our agreement. Leeching energy through magic is a much cleaner and more refined way of growing more powerful."

"On that, we both agree. You do look lovely. It will make our meetings easier to manage."

She nodded at his compliment but picked up on the last part of his statement. "Easier to manage?"

Perhaps he shouldn't have gone as far as he did. She wasn't a lady in a gown after all, but the ruler of all succubi in the west and likely the most powerful one in existence. He had best remember that, even if she no longer desired to round up and feast upon men in the same way that came naturally to her.

"Yes, Mistress. In this attire, I can enjoy your presence, while not undertaking too many distractions."

With a raised brow she pushed him a little further. "So my race's normal dressing habits would distract you. A Lich? How so? You have no flesh."

"Very true, which gives me immunity to some of your more persuasive abilities, but I was and still am a man."

"Noted."

Though she didn't show any indication that this new bit of information affected her, he knew that she would test him later. How foolish had he been? It was time for a change of topic.

"If I may, I have some news that I think might please you."

For the first time, a grin tugged at the corner of her mouth. "Oh yes, please. How is our little project coming?"

"Everything is prepared. We begin tonight!"

With a thought, the shadow-cloaked, skeletal lich turned into a hunchbacked old man in a servant's attire.

Chapter 1 - Kidnapped

Ranch dressing! It's a magically delicious concoction that should be put on everything. Steak. Burgers. Sandwiches. Chicken. More Chicken. Anything with bacon! Bacon? The two most wonderful things in the world... ranch dressing and bacon!

Well not quite, but I, Elorion, was a gamer. Food and gaming went well together, so dreaming about food while logged in on my favorite VR gaming chair was a great way to prepare myself for my next meal. It also helped pass the time while I was grinding or doing repetitive boring stuff to level up my game character. The sacrifice was often fierce, but with enough bacon, anything was possible!

Unleashed hellfire on another Minotaur Sentry; seasoned fries dipped in ranch dressing! Lightning strike from heaven empowering my hammer to forge some epic magic weapons; bacon pizza with extra bacon! Spamming 'ITEMS FOR SALE' in the town square; ranch dressing and applesauce! Eh, wait... Well. I'd try it.

Okay, I'd had enough. I needed food. Logging out, it took a moment before my VR headset gave me the red light that I was safe to take it off.

As I pulled the full VR helmet off of my head, I saw the ugliest flying lizard in the history of the world hovering a foot from my face. My first reaction was to scream like a macholess girly man, and scream I did!

No, wait. It was not a lizard because its snout was human in shape and its skin was green-gray in color.

"Now that's the sound I expect a fat lazy human to make! Congratulations! You have passed the test!"

Test? Why hadn't I hit this flying, obnoxious, turtle-headed thing in the face yet?

Instead of reacting as I should, all that came out of me as I faced a creature that shouldn't exist is, "Uh."

"I'm not an uh. I'm an imp. My job is to kidnap you. So come along."

"You can talk?" I asked dumbly, completely missing what the creature just said about kidnapping.

"No, I can't. You have just wasted your life playing so many video games that you have gone insane. I don't really exist. You are just seeing things. Oh and by the way." He lifted his hand and pointed a single finger at me, then said, "Bind."

A dim gray light extended from his finger. It was quick but slow enough that it could be seen with the naked eye. He was a foot from me so there was no dodging it. Whatever it was.

My arms shot to my chest, one over the other, and my heels clashed together. Something like an ethereal rope bound me and I suddenly found myself fallen off my chair, flapping around like a caffeinated walrus. There was no way of loosening what had bound me.

"Time for your first lesson. You are a weak creature, only level 31. Fairly impressive I suppose for someone so young who is also so lazy, but humans normally get to between level 40 and 70 in their lifetime. That is incredibly low in the realm of the underworld. This binding spell is also fairly weak in general, but mine is a high level because I get to capture losers like you for coin. Anyways, the point of the story is that you are weak and useless right now. You will be given an opportunity to level up and hopefully, in time, you will be able to break this spell in mere moments. For now, you go where I want."

I tried to speak, but the binding spell had also covered my mouth. *Note to self. Next time you see an imp, punch it in the face.* Who was he calling fat and lazy? I played soccer and ran track, but it was summer so it was the offseason. Besides I still worked out… sometimes. Fine, I'd gained fifteen pounds. I did plan on getting in shape for my senior year in high school. My mom kept reminding me that she wasn't going to cook for me forever.

With a mix of panic and focus, I forced myself to examine my situation. When the imp said another command and I was suddenly floating, I gave him another round of walrus aerobics. The next thing I knew the imp whispered something and blew in my face.

My eyes began to blur and I felt woozy. I was about to lose consciousness and I hadn't even gotten my snack!

Chapter 2 – Goodbye Ranch

Dressing

I awoke leaning back against a cold stone wall. The first thing I noticed was how hungry I was. Hadn't I been getting up to get a snack?

The room was one of shadows. To either side of me were other people, both guys and girls, about twenty of us all together. Everyone was starting to come to. They wore simple, uniform gray pants and long-sleeved shirts. Their shoes were leather that reminded me of moccasins, except they were laced up the middle. Wait...

Looking down I saw I had identical clothing on. Remembering the shelless turtle with wings, I turned my head, frantically searching the shallow room for my kidnapper. I really needed to punch an imp in the face right now. He must have violated me by stripping me and changing my clothes.

I heard someone enter the room before I saw them. Movement came from the darkest area on the far side, which I assumed was an open doorway. To its side, I could barely make out ranks of equipment on tables with an inclining face that was nearly the length of the wall. Was this a torture chamber as well?

"Welcome to my labyrinth!" came the most seductive of voices. "You have been handpicked from the human race to be energy sources for your beloved Head Mistress Lilith."

The voice belonged to an extremely beautiful and extravagantly dressed woman. To her side was a hunched over man in a butler's suit.

Energy sources? You've watched too many sci-fi movies, lady. Where's the food?

With the raising of his hand and the whisper of his lips, the hunched man produced a large glowing globe that shone softly but somehow filled the room.

"You see, I brought you here so that you can make something of yourselves. Each and every one of you spends the majority of their time trying to escape their current existence through video games. Here in my labyrinth, the games you spend so much time playing will become your reality. You will get to level up in real life as you fight monsters, find items, and most of all, try to survive."

The solemn moment was quickly broken by a chorus of outrage from my fellow captives. The only thing that anyone had heard was 'energy sources'. Now everyone was on their feet demanding to go back home.

I stayed sitting, taken aback by what was said, processing each word. My interest was piqued even if it made me feel dirty for even considering it.

Stepping forward, Mr. Ten-Thousand-Wrinkles-for-a-Face, the butler, responded. His voice didn't match his appearance. He sounded like a young man in his prime. "Your outrage is not unexpected, but let me help persuade you. Head Mistress, if you please."

"This is a magic that has taken half a century to develop," she said. Swirling masses of darkness the size of small ropes came from her palm and wrapped themselves together into a ball. "Branding."

At her word, the dark magic shot out toward all of the captives in the room including myself. It was too difficult to see with the limited light in the room, so when it strung itself around my neck there was little I could do to stop it. The dark rope tightened and turned into a black hot coal. The sudden searing of skin sent electricity up and down my spine; my fists clenched.

Thankfully I had still been sitting so when I fell, it didn't knock me out.

"The pain is necessary to bind you to the Head Mistress for the collecting of the energy that naturally escapes your body through normal activity. This will not take your energy directly from you. It is an energy catch of sorts. Even low-level creatures like yourselves are constantly leaking energy. As you level up the amount will only grow. It doesn't matter where you are in the Underworld; just like your internet, this excess energy is already being sent to us through a network of magic.

"Furthermore, you are now marked by her Grace. If she wishes to locate you it is as simple as a thought."

I joined the sighs and complaints of my fellow captives with clenched teeth.

"Escape is not possible unless you want to flee to your death. Here—" He motioned with his hands to the surrounding room. "—is your only place of safety. Monsters await if you leave this new home that I have prepared for you."

Suddenly the wrinkly man clapped his hands together before him and a pop-up window the size of a normal sheet of paper shot up in front of me. From the immediate silence, everyone else had the same window that came up in front of them as well.

"This is your status screen. Your branding does not come without gifts. The ability to access your leveling system is something that few humans have had access to for nearly a thousand years. Anything under level 100 is considered what you would call newbies in the underworld. Most humans don't reach level 100 in a single lifetime. I know you are used to starting a game at level 1, but that wouldn't be realistic. It doesn't take into context the different stages of a human's life. All of you are around level 25-35."

CHARACTER SHEET

Name: Elorion Edwards

Characteristics: Gamer, Athletic, Lives with Parents, Waiter at Cheap Restaurant, Meat Lover, Connoisseur of Ranch Dressing, Unknown Future.

Race: Human

Age: 17

Level: 31

Health Points: 590

Mana Points: 190

Endurance: 400

Attributes:

Strength: 47

Dexterity: 58

Constitution: 59

Intelligence: 38

Wisdom: 30

I was blown away. The screen looked like old worn parchment. My level really was 31. As an ex-soccer player my stats reflected my athletic career with a higher Constitution and Dexterity, but how did I compare to others?

"This is you. You have all played games, so you know what each of these categories means. Your stats and levels will vary. Normally, humans have a base of 10 attribute points for each category and get about 5 attribute points to spend per level, but if you train, you can gain attribute points without leveling up.

"Look closely at your levels and stats. You are all rather pathetic, but each of you was chosen because of your love of Role Playing Games and surprisingly high potential. To help with this, our beloved Mistress here is going to grant you a few gifts. You will now receive a rush of insight, or experience as you call it. Even with this help, it is likely some of you will die today."

With a nod of her head, the lady with deep red hair and purple dress lifted her hand and blue strands of light shot out like a spider's web, striking each of us in the head.

A chime went off in my head and the words *Level Up* in see-through yellow floated up quickly from the floor and disappeared just above my head. It was nothing compared to the rush of clarity that seemed to flood my mind.

Without hesitation, I looked to my status screen and my level read 38! I now had 35 attribute points to spend however I so desired. 7 levels! Not bad!

Just moments ago, the people I was sitting next to were contemplating a rebellion. Now they were all carefully examining their screens, completely oblivious to how easily they had been distracted from their anger.

There were a few exceptions. One girl still sat against the wall hugging her knees, a guy was obviously distracted by the Mistress's womanly qualities and a couple of girls were huddled in the back holding each other. Oh, and a redheaded guy still had his head propped against the wall and was sleeping.

"Now I would highly recommend that you allow me to finish before you spend your points…"

A maniacal laugh interrupted. "Too late!"

An already large guy with a crew cut who reminded me of your typical football lineman started pumping his finger against his screen that was ethereal to me, but very clear to him. Before my eyes, he began to grow. Not only did he get slightly taller, but his muscle mass increased almost 50% before our eyes.

My chin dropped to the floor.

Everyone went nuts. At least two other guys started pumping away at their screens. Talk about a newbie move. How can you min-max without knowing how the game system worked?

Wrinkle man waited until the noise died down before he spoke again. "As I was saying, next we will unlock your natural talents. Some people are naturally stronger, others faster, others smarter, and some have special abilities or proficiencies with magic. Although a number of you could probably do with an extra 50 points in intelligence and wisdom."

The murmur of my fellow captives was silenced at the mention of magic.

"Depending on your talent, it might be wise to spend your points on attributes that will benefit what you are naturally good at. It is my turn for this trick."

He held up his hands palm out and closed his eyes in concentration. A yellow light was emitted, almost like he had a light bulb in either hand.

"Take your time to examine the windows before you."

Warmth entrapped me. That was when I saw another pop-up window about half the size on top of my status window.

The first pane was titled *Skills*.

A number of mini windows popped up within this main window. There were dozens of these. Many of them were just acknowledging things I already know. Intermediate Logic. Intermediate Sprinting. Intermediate Distance Running. Intermediate High Jump. Intermediate Cooking. Novice Persuasion. Expert Procrastinator. Etc.

I closed each mini window, making sure to check each one, but there were no surprises. When I closed the skill window I found a delightful surprise under it. Spells.

A few mini windows had popped up here too. Light Magic Proficiency. Lesser Heal. Talent: Natural Healer.

The talent window, which was the only window that mentioned the talent the old man mentioned, read as follows.

Light Magic Affinity

Due to a natural affinity with light magic, the user's healing spells will heal health, endurance, and exhaustion. As individual spells level, this can grow to heal status effects as well. Healing spells will level faster than normal.

Noooooo! This was terrible! I didn't want to be a support character! Give me lightning or fire… give me a big gnarly club for all I cared to bash stuff, but why did my talent have to be healing?!

Blue Magic

You now have access to Blue Magic.

As I closed the window, I leaned closer to a second window under it in hope.

Lesser Heal

This is the novice level healing spell for those who have unlocked the Light Magic Alignment.

Base healing of 100 HP

Base cost of 50 MP

Creature Observation

This is the basic skill that all blue magic is based upon. It allows you to steal the natural skills of other creatures and mimic their abilities through magic.

That was all it said. Unlocked? What did that mean? Blue Magic could be better than healing though, right?

"Very good. Very good indeed!" The hunched over wrinkled man was using some kind of examination skill on each of us in turn. "Talent in Constitution. Talent in Persuasion plus Speed. Talent with Traps. Talent with Wind Magic. Talent with Strength. Fire Magic. Green Magic spell tangling roots. Talent with Dexterity."

He went on and on, not missing a single one of us. One in every three people had a talent in some kind of magic, but no one else had healing or blue.

Stopping when he came to me, he sighed.

When the lady joined him in examining me, she whispered just loud enough for me to hear, "He has old blood."

"You there!" Mr. Wrinkle man called me to attention.

"Yeah?" I replied, more than a little startled considering he was standing directly in front of me.

"You stink. Healing Magic gives off a scent to those sensitive to it."

"I assure you that being a healer wasn't my first choice."

"Mistress?" Old Man Wrinkles asked.

Under her gaze, I immediately felt my heart beat faster. She was incredibly beautiful. I didn't deserve such attention, but I certainly wanted it.

"You will probably be dead soon." She tapped a few times on her chin with a long slender finger. "Here's a consolation prize."

A ball of yellow light shot from her hand and ended in my chest. A new mini pop-up window came up under Spells.

Blue Magic: Explosive End

The moment before death you will have the option of directing your remaining mana into a finale of fireworks, injuring the targets you set your sights upon.

Note: After you have used this spell you are dead. There is no way to cheat death and watch the cool effects of Explosive End; dead is dead. If you just so happen to know someone with a resurrection spell, then perhaps, but you will still probably miss the show because of the long cast time of such spells.

The Mistress smiled. "You have a chance to survive longer if you master blue magic. It will allow you to learn skills and spells from the monsters you face. The problem is it is not a quick magic to master."

Turning from me to the group, she continued, "Now for some novice spells to help all of you survive."

In quick succession, light shot from her hand and hit each of us in the head in turn. Three different colors of light, white, brown and green, all hit home.

Looking to my new pop-up windows there were three new ones just like the three different beams of light that hit me.

Light Orb

This orb will obey your will and light up the path before you. The higher the level the further and brighter the light can extend. This spell can be essential for survival or a power outage.

Mage's Deodorant

When unable to use deodorant because of unavailability, poverty, or strange religious alignment, this spell will keep you from adding smelly funk to your social engagements. The smell is neutral. As this spell levels up you can add special scents for any special occasion.

You got to be kidding me! Why bother? Give me a damage spell already! With my fingers crossed I exited the screen and viewed the last one. Horror!

Mage's Toilet Paper

Never run out of this household essential again! For anywhere you find yourself you will never be without! As the spell levels up lotion can be added to the effects of the spell!

Are you serious? I guess I could light Mage's Toilet Paper on fire and throw it at something, but where was the good stuff?

"These are spells that I demand you use. Light orb will save your life, but the other two will keep you from totally disgusting me. You will find even my slave imps use these spells often or find themselves purified to death with fire. Do not neglect them," she warned.

"Now for equipment." Mr. Wrinkle threw a second ball of light to hover over the far side of the room. The wall was lined with an odd assortment of weapons.

"You can choose more than one weapon, but be careful not to overburden yourself. Humans are weak so two weapons at the most will benefit you," the lady instructed.

Without hesitation, the group of kidnapees headed to the other side of the room but gave the two instructors a wide berth.

I examined my spell screen one last time. Besides Blue Magic Proficiency I didn't get a blue spell other than Explosive End. There was an additional skill called Creature Observation.

Turning to the Mistress, I tried to activate Creature Observation.

Due to an unseen force, you are unable to use this skill at this location.

Blah. That's no fun.

There were a few things missing that I normally expected every MMORPG to have. There was no mini-map or menu where I could find features like an inventory, the party system, etc.

Before I joined everyone I studied the rest of Light Orb's description.

All that is necessary to cast this spell once it is learned is to will it. Saying the name out loud often helps newbie spellcasters to focus the mind correctly.

"Light Orb," I said.

Immediately a much dimmer version of the orb the old man had cast appeared a meter above my head and in front of me. It was only a matter of thought to move it further back and have it hover over my head.

I had just cast my first spell. It was like eating a new food that was no doubt going to be another favorite.

Being a blue mage definitely excited me more than being a healer. If I found the right creature I could wield lightning, fire, or whatever other abilities it might possess. Well, that was common among games, and as the Mistress seemed to imply, having gaming experience would help.

There was hope!

Even though I was among the last to pick out a weapon, I certainly hadn't missed anything. Whether it was a sword, club or spear, they were all worn, crude and would probably break after moderate use. You'd think they would give us some decent equipment if they really wanted us to level up.

At least the belt I found seemed decent. I sheathed a short sword on either hip and grabbed a spear that would make a better walking stick than a weapon. Just because healers always use bashing weapons, I grabbed a one-handed mace that I strapped across my back. 1 to 2 weapons max? I was a gamer. It was time to take advantage of free loot while there was an opportunity! Besides, until I knew what I was up against I would rather keep my options open. I could always rest between fights.

Sadly, there was no armor to speak of. I wasn't exactly a fan of paladin type class, but if I had to be a healing tank, that would be better than a full-time healer. Eyeing the majority of the men in the group, with the exception of three or four of them I seemed to be among those in the best shape. Gamers aren't always the most active people in the world, as the most common attribute in the room, chub, confirmed.

Only half of the girls in the room had this same problem. Most of them were in much leaner shape. No one in the room was what I would call chunky. The only one close was the now massive lineman-looking guy. His muscle mass made up for his gut.

Mr. Wrinkle and the Mistress were looking at me as I realized I had spaced out. Was I an idiot for not taking their advice with regard to taking 1 to 2 weapons? Glancing around, I saw the players were all staring at me as well. I was the last one to gather a weapon, or in my case, four.

"This room will now belong to all of you as a group. You can add and take items from these racks as you want in the future," the old man said with one last look at me to see if I would put any equipment back.

I just grinned like I was oblivious to his and everyone else's objections.

"There is also a kitchen with a bathroom and barracks. To move out of the barracks to your own personal quarters you will have to earn enough coin or favor to pay for it. The same goes for food. To earn more than two meals a day, or anything besides gruel and bread, you will have to do more than survive.

"To earn coin, you know the drill. The monsters you kill can drop items that have value. The stronger you get the stronger the monster you can fight and the better the items and coin you will earn. There will also be more than one merchant to allow for competitive pricing.

"One last thing before you proceed. As you leave this room you will pass the dining hall and merchants on the left and the barracks on the right. If you keep heading straight you will head into the labyrinth. This labyrinth is an area of the Underworld under the control of the Head Mistress. Anything in this area has been summoned for you to fight. The monsters get progressively harder as you go deeper in. In order to leave the Head Mistress's realm, you will have to become strong enough and complete a few obstacles.

"The first area you enter into has decaying skeletons that I have personally summoned. They are the weakest of all undead and will prove useful to begin your training. Don't count on making much money from them. Most of them are barely level 50. Any questions?"

One girl, with short brown hair, an elf-like nose and large eyes, gritted her teeth and asked, "Can we go home?"

With the sweetest of smiles the Mistress stepped toward her and cocked her head with empathy, or so it seemed. "No. You are mine," she said with mock sweetness.

"For a thousand years I have hunted and devoured your kind. This is the largest group of humans I have been in the same room with that has actually survived in centuries.

"Don't be mistaken. You are still alive because you have the potential to provide me power. Currently, you are indebted to me not just for your lives, but that I am giving you a chance to live and live in a way that each and every one of you has only dreamed of. Welcome to the ultimate roleplaying game! Don't dwell on what you don't have but the opportunity that you do. Otherwise, you will do something stupid and I will suck the life out of you. Any more questions?"

Half a dozen of us, including me, stepped forward and placed ourselves between the wicked chick and the girl.

The Mistress giggled and shook her head. "At least you show the will to fight. We will take our leave. Bread and water will be available in abundance at all times in the dining hall during the first two weeks. After that, you will have to purchase anything beyond breakfast and dinner. And don't forget. If you die here you are really dead. No game overs to start again. Sweet dreams!"

Sweet dreams? Was it night time? In the top right of my status screen, it gave me the time. 4:00pm. What time zone, it didn't say. Not exactly the time to go to sleep. Or was she meaning the final slumber of death?

I closed the status screen pop-up window.

Before the old man and the Mistress left, four imps flew into the room each holding a lamp-stand in one hand and the lamp in the other. They placed them in the four corners of the room. With that, our kidnappers left. The stone wall was made up of massive, misshapen, dull gray stones stacked upon each other. The floor and ceiling were large slabs of rough cut stones. High traffic areas of the floor were worn smooth from years of use.

Above the imp's heads was floating red text.

Servant Imp

#*$%

There was gibberish under the creature's description that I assumed was where its level would appear. Because our levels were so much lower than theirs were, the text was red and it wouldn't even show us their levels.

I wondered why the old man and Mistress didn't show anything above their heads. Nor did the other humans…

Chapter 3 – Home Base, Bread, and Some Pain

With a now well-lit room, everyone could see each other much better, but no one said anything or even moved at first. The real freak out moment happened half a minute later when the reality of what was going on started to really sink in for everyone.

I stood back against the weapon rack as everyone unleashed their feelings on the matter with complaints, anger, and tears. Anger was the closest thing to my own response, but I didn't let myself dwell on it. We had just started a new RPG, or role playing game; a deadly one. More accurately a MMORPG, or massive multiplayer online role playing game. It was time to decide which strategy would keep me alive the longest.

Stepping up next to the large-eyed girl, I asked her and all those around her, "Do you guys know what time it is?"

I received a few shrugs, and a single "no" from the girl that had had the courage to ask what we had all been thinking. Directing them to the status screen I brought the time to their attention.

"It might be a good idea to get some food," I said to no one in particular.

A girl that had been standing close with rich caramel skin and shoulder length extensions rebuked me. "How can you think of food at a time like this?!"

"Because I don't know when I last ate." I shrugged. "The imp that kidnapped me knocked me out with some spell."

"I'd worry more about if the food is even edible," a chubby guy with glasses added.

"Might as well find out."

When the elf girl, who wasn't really an elf but cute like one, nodded, about three other people followed us to find this dining hall.

Just as the butler had said, we passed a dark room with cots that must have been the barracks. The merchants were back and off to the side, so I didn't see them or what was for sale as I passed by.

Smells of freshly baked bread assaulted our senses and we were more pulled by the smell to enter the large stone square of a room with about eight stone tables lined with benches. On the far side of the room was a long table with enough bread for a hundred people. They were long loaves the size of my arm. The water was in normal plastic water bottles. I had expected them to be in animal skins or something.

So I downed a whole loaf in a few minutes, sitting with five other people I had just met. Eating is always good when you have something on your mind…

"My name is Aeris from New York," the elf-looking girl said, breaking the silence. "My talent is wind magic and dexterity."

The rest of the group followed her lead. Everyone was suddenly weighing one another. A hunting group was starting to form.

"I'm Travis from Cali. My talent is tracking and piercing weapons." He was on the shorter side but thickly muscled if you didn't count his gamer's gut.

"Olivia. I'm from Denver," introduced the girl who had rebuked me about the food. "Nature magic and traps."

"Russ. Constitution and blacksmithing. Texas," said the pudgy guy who would probably make a good tank once he slimmed down.

"Elorion. Florida. Healing and blue magic. I played sports all my life so I was hoping to fight up front though."

"Of course you were," Olivia mocked, eyeing my many weapons. Since the Mistress and old man had given me a hard time, she seemed to think it was appropriate to continue the practice.

Before I could think of anything witty to throw back at her, the guy who had pumped his status screen with strength burst in with about ten people at his heels.

"I don't know about you, but the sooner I can make some money, the sooner I can get out of those barracks. The cots are miniature."

The rest of the group seemed to be in agreement.

Ignoring our group entirely, he marched over and grabbed a loaf and a water bottle, then led his congregation out the way they had come.

There was suddenly a stir among my group. The competitive gamer in each of them didn't like the idea of a large group getting a head start on them. I was pleased that the group I had fallen into seemed motivated.

Staying at the back of my group, I followed as I planned my course of action. I needed first to figure out how to use my Creature Observation skill and Healing spell. Once I got those down I needed to try and learn as many blue magic spells as possible, but I was afraid it would take quite some time. Not to forget, I needed to pitch in on the front lines as much as I could to make sure I was getting experience.

It was a 100 meter walk down the hall to reach the hunting area. At the end of the hall, there was an opening to a room that seemed to have a natural light hanging in the air. Though I couldn't see any door, I guessed there was some kind of magic barrier here keeping monsters out.

As we entered the large room, I saw that the ceiling was at least two stories up, even if it was hard to see because of the lack of light up there. There were numerous side passages, some well-lit and others pitch black. Random light orbs were placed on the walls in seemingly no logical pattern.

The larger group was already ahead of us preparing to fight. Three pathetic looking, vertically challenged skeletons were roaming on the other side of the room next to them.

After overhearing the other group who had figured out how to open the party system, our smaller group all joined up together. The trick to opening up the party window or any window for that matter was to just say 'party' with the intention of opening the window. It seemed to work just like magic. At your will, it would open and close.

And then we were joined by an unexpected visitor.

"Elorion," called a throaty, familiar voice that summoned an intense anger inside of me. A sudden urge to hit an imp in the face returned.

My party turned to see my kidnapper flying toward us. Or, more specifically, me.

The imp didn't seem happy to be joining us, at least from what I could tell from his ugly turtle face.

"Yes?" I acknowledged him.

"The Head Mistress wanted me to teach you some blue magic that might be helpful." He eyed me suspiciously.

Something was off. He had mocked me in every way possible, then kidnapped me. If the Mistress had really wanted him to teach me, then why didn't she do it herself? "What's the catch?"

"Only that the quickest way for you to learn blue magic is if you experience the spell yourself. The one I will teach you is a stun of sorts, so I will have to cast it upon you for you to learn it."

I doubted he would dare kill me after all the work that went into kidnapping us and bringing us here. My excitement overrode my concern. "Okay…"

He seemed to hesitate when I agreed so easily. The creature smirked before uttering the word, "Pain."

A magic cord shot from his finger and struck my chest before I realized what he had just said.

Suddenly every muscle in my body flexed tight at the same time as if an electric jolt had shot through me. It was a moment before the pain began. When it did it overwhelmed all of my senses. All that existed was an intense burning sensation like all of my muscles were extremely sore and someone was stabbing me in each muscle over and over again.

Time no longer had meaning to me. There was nothing but pain.

Eventually, as if waking from a deep sleep, all that remained was a searing memory. Opening my eyes, I looked up from my back and saw my torturer and four other humans looking down at me in horror.

The pop-up window that indicated I had comprehended the blue magic *Pain* was like rubbing salt in my wounds. A new spell had been born from my troubles, but the gamer in me that would have normally been thrilled was enraged. *Pain hurts!*

Standing up, my adrenaline pumped through me.

Everyone gave me a wide berth, except the imp who stood his ground.

I ignored him initially, looking down at my hands as they trembled. It was time.

Without so much as looking at him, except through my peripheral vision, I relaxed as much as I could manage and relaxed my arms to my side.

Stepping forward, I twisted my torso.

My father had taught me the key to throwing a punch was to be as loose as possible because muscle tension will slow you down. I brought my hand up, only making a fist milliseconds before contact. My left hook came in from a deceitful angle. It caught the imp square on the chin. He was caught completely unaware.

Finally! His neck snapped to the side, knocking him woozy enough that he fell to the floor.

There was a popping noise during the impact, but it didn't come from the imp. Hitting the imp's face had been like hitting nothing but solid bone. My fist had connected low on my knuckles breaking my ring and pinky fingers.

I was an idiot. My adventures with pain had just begun.

Cheers came from my immediate group as they saw what had just happened.

The larger group had moved on and were facing their second set of skeletons already.

If I hadn't hesitated and had just started stabbing the monster before it got back up it would have been dead and I would have saved myself from what happened next.

"You dare challenge a level 200 imp?!"

Everyone around me, including myself, was suddenly filled with terror. I suspected some form of fear spell had been cast.

When the imp attacked me again with *Pain*, they ran.

I screamed, unable to run, frozen in place like an electrified cat.

Before the pain overtook me, I heard the imp say, "I don't have permission to kill you, but there is still a lot of fun we can have before you reach that point."

CHAPTER 4 – TO HIT AN IMP IN THE FACE

Over and over again the imp cast Pain. There was no rest. Death sounded like a welcome vacation from the state I was in. Slowly, something started to happen.

One way or another, the constant pain started to lessen. Not that the imp had stopped his attack, but it seemed I was getting used to it to a point.

Though it was a small step, I was able to open my eyes from my place on the floor. Notification window after notification window were stacked on top of each other. Each of them seemed to say the same thing.

Your understanding of the Blue Magic: Pain has increased

The spell was leveling as the imp was using it on me?!

Speaking of spells, my Lesser Heal spell was at my disposal and I needed to use it. Now!

How exactly I pulled it off I didn't know, for saying any word out loud was difficult. Somehow what I said had been interpreted correctly because immediately relief filled me all over my body.

A scream came from nearby from the same direction as my torturer. The imp had jumped back.

"Light!" he spat as if it gave him pain.

The spell literally caused a blanket of light to fall on me.

With the relief from the spell, I was able to track my attacker hovering a few meters away and there was no doubt. Somehow my healing spell had hurt him.

It did make sense really. It was common in games for healing magic to damage creatures of evil or dark alignments. Normally though humanoids weren't harmed by it unless they were undead. Was this a part of my talent?

Immediately I healed myself again. I almost dared to direct it at the imp, but now that my mind was clear, I knew if he was really level 200, then my spell might hurt him, but he would likely retaliate by attacking me with something much more dangerous.

When I healed myself a third time, the imp spat and left me while mumbling nastily under his breath.

I sat up and caught my breath. Pulling up my status screen I only had 40 magic points (MP) left. It seemed my healing spell cost 50 MP for each cast.

Moments ago, I was in the middle of the worst pain in my life. Now I suddenly felt refreshed and energized. I took back what I was thinking earlier. Healing was amazing. Then it hit me. It was especially amazing if it could nuke evil and undead monsters for massive amounts of damage.

Wait. Did someone with healing magic really stink? The old man had said as much. It wasn't until the guy had looked at my screen that he had noticed though. And the imp hadn't noticed until I had cast it on myself. I would probably be safe, for now. Perhaps as I leveled up healing magic might become an issue then.

A mischievous smile spread across my face. Danger or not, healing magic had just become my main priority.

Then I realized I was in the labyrinth all alone. Neither of the human groups was in this room anymore, whether they had finished off all the skeletons or they had fled because of the fear spell. It seemed the imp's aura must have done its job well. Sadly, I didn't learn that spell as well. Perhaps it wasn't magic at all.

I quickly cleared away my pop-up windows but stopped on one that caught my attention.

You have advanced to an intermediate understanding of Blue Magic: Pain. The spell's stun time has increased from 5 seconds to 10.

Due to the direct means by which you learned this spell, you have also learned to resist it. Lesser Pain Resist.

Did the spiteful imp realize he had just leveled up my Pain spell from novice to intermediate? He must have used it a lot. I wondered how high of a level his Pain spell was for it to level me up this much. Maybe mine was even powerful enough for me to cast it on him now. With the stun, I might be able to really hurt him.

Looking at my status screen, my health points (HP) were now completely full. It was time for some number crunching.

By touching different aspects on the status screen I was able to get a good description of what each attribute did and how they worked. Most importantly, I only had 40 MP left after healing myself. How long would it take to recover?

When I clicked my blue mana bar it indicated that I recovered 18 mana per minute (MPM) while resting and 6 mana per minute while standing. In other words, if I stayed sitting I would recover 1 mana every 3 seconds and if I stood 1 mana every 10 seconds. It was pretty pathetic really, but it could be worse. In approximately 8 minutes I would be able to regain my full mana if I was relaxing.

If what I had in mind worked, I was going to need a lot more MPM. I had a feeling that skeletons would take damage if healed just like my favorite punching bag Mr. Imp. Perhaps all undead and evil alignment monsters would. Not to mention after healing myself and seeing how powerful healing really was I was much more excited about a possible healer-tank combination.

There was still more to consider. I had 35 attribute points to spend. I clicked Intelligence and Wisdom; they worked as I suspected they might. Intelligence generally increased spell strength and how much mana I had. Wisdom increased my mana regen rate and also affected the power of spells to a lesser extent.

I could also spam strength, which might just make things simpler. Grabbing my spear that was lying beside me, I checked my status screen again. Just like I thought, a new category *Weapon Damage* was added. Approximately 27 to 227 damage with the spear. Why such a span? Setting the spear down, I unsheathed a short sword with a new damage of 11 to 74. Hmmm. My mace was 3 damage to 91.

On the other hand, my healing spell healed 112 points of health. Did that mean it would also do damage for 112 points on the right creature? Before spending my points, I needed to find out. It was essential I figured out as much as I could so I didn't waste anything.

It had been about 5 minutes so I had recovered 90 mana to give me 130 in total. That was enough for two castings of *Heal.*

Welp. I better get busy. Standing, I grabbed my pointy walking stick and headed for the closest side door to the left of the entrance. The door hung slightly open, hardly staying on its hinges from so much use.

With help from my spear, the door creaked open to reveal three decrepit skeletons. These were also on the shorter side like the ones I had seen earlier. Their bones were also far from white, with dark brown and sickly yellow patches.

A notification popped up before me that was easy to ignore due to its transparency. Since the skeletons didn't seem to be aggressive or close enough to cause me any serious threat in the immediate future, I studied it.

You have noticed the discoloration of these summoned skeletons' bones. You are closer to understanding their nature.

It seemed I wouldn't have to activate *Creature Observation*. Could I learn blue magic just from watching creatures from afar instead of having the spell cast on me? It needed more testing.

Heal cost 50 mana per cast, so it was time to try it out. The closest skeleton to me had a short description above its head.

Decrepit Skeleton

Level 48

Well, its level was higher than mine. If killing creatures of higher level gave the experience bonus like in most games, it was probably a good idea to camp skeletons until I was at least level 50. Since I was 38 now, that was an additional 60 attribute points.

Whispering under my breath I cast *Heal*. Warm light extended quickly from my fingers and enveloped the skeleton. It crumbled to dust without so much as looking my way.

One Level Up after another floated up from below. A window came up following it.

You have killed your first skeleton species of the undead variety. Bonus experience!

Just like that, I reached level 40.

More impressive was my healing spell. I didn't wait and cast it again on the next skeleton. Again it fell to dust. This time I didn't level up, but my experience bar filled up about a fifth of the way. Too easy.

Without enough mana to finish the last one, I dared to sneak up from behind it while two-handing my spear. My victories had made me bold. It was time to see how weak or strong these creatures really were.

My weapon was a spear which didn't seem like a great tool to use against skeletons, but I wasn't planning on using the pointy end.

Winding up, I swung the spear like a baseball bat, sweeping low, just below the knee. A jarring vibration found my hands and the sweeping blow was not nearly as effective as I had hoped.

The skeleton stumbled but didn't fall. A fracture was now visible on its shin bone.

When I had used my healing spell the skeletons never even had time to react, but now I had a four foot animated pile of bones stumbling toward me.

Every part of me had thought this would end just as easily as casting a spell had. Surprised, I foolishly thrust my spear at the monster's chest. The rusty iron spear point chipped a rib then slipped between the rest of them while leaving me off balance.

An open-handed skeletal blow flew at my head. It was easy enough to raise my arm up to fend it off, but the pain that followed from bone on flesh left a deep bruise.

Jumping back to get to a safe distance was easy enough. At the speed it was moving there was no way I should have been hit. My VR gaming skills weren't translating over to real life very well. I was allowing the situation to get to me way too much.

With a nerve alleviating laugh, I clumsily grabbed my mace.

I let the skeleton close the distance and frantically swung my mace onto the top of the skeleton's skull when it got in range.

Instead of turning to dust, the bones simply lost life and fell into a crumbling pile. No loot yet, but I was already halfway to the next level.

My mana had replenished enough that I was able to heal my bruised arm. Only 15 damage had been done, but there was an annoying ache. *Sweetness!*

All considering, it had gone fairly well. Once I got into a rhythm I could probably make it to level 50 quickly and there was always the added benefit of leveling my Lesser Healing spells.

Seeing how beneficial healing magic really was and its dual use of healing and damaging undead, I had pretty much made up my mind. Since it was my talent would that mean it would level up faster than it would for someone else as well?

Bringing up the spell I looked at its description more closely. There was a leveling and a rank system for the spell itself. Already it had leveled to level 3. With just that it healed 120 health, where before it had only been 112. It now also only cost 49 MP instead of 50.

The gamer inside of me was doing a funky Japanese dance. Dancing didn't go over well for me in real life, so if you can imagine a drunken turkey doing the YMCA then you might have a worthy comparison. That didn't stop my celebration though.

I sat against the wall to let my MP recover. Before my MP bar was full, the first skeleton I had killed respawned. To be more accurate, its pile of dust started to glow then reconstructed as a skeleton. The power the old man possessed was scary if these skeletons would just consistently respawn like this.

Instead of attacking right away I remembered the pop-up I had gotten about the coloration of the skeletons' bones. Once again, I examined it. When it first spawned the color wasn't as prominent.

The second skeleton spawned soon after, but I continued to watch. They didn't seem aggressive unless I attacked first.

When the third one spawned only a minute had passed, but I noticed a difference in their color already. It deepened the longer they were animated.

Blue Magic: Decay

Through careful observation, you have understood Blue Magic: Decay. This spell stacks with itself and other corrosives.

Against non-living objects or creatures, this weakens and even destroys the target with enough time.

Against the living, this spell weakens and can cause harm. In time, because of a living creature's ability to self-repair, the spell will be overcome.

So easy! Not only that, but it only cost 20 MP to cast! Stacking debuff! Amazing!

A debuff is a spell that weakens a creature instead of harming them.

Time to test it. First, I quickly finished two skeletons with Lesser Heal. With the third, I cast Decay. Immediately the coloring of the skeleton darkened. Additionally, it was moving visibly slower than before.

Standing without haste, I leaned my spear against the wall and readied my mace.

I circled around the monster. My fear of it had passed. Letting it swing at me, I examined its speed. There was no doubt it had gotten slower.

To further my experiment, I cast Decay again. With sheer joy, I watched as the Decay stacked with the Decay already present and the skeleton slowed even more.

It might be considered cruel, but I cast the spell three more times until the skeleton could barely stand on its own two feet. Decay leveled up!

The skeleton was finished with no effort at all.

Too bad Lesser Heal wasn't leveling as fast.

I added two points to intelligence to bring my MP to 200. With the cost of the spells I cast, this would give me an additional cast for very little cost. The rest of my points I would save until I was sure how I wanted to spend them.

Within an hour I had reached level 48 and the experience I gained started to slow. I now had 83 points total to spend! These skeletons had treated me well.

I was also able to confirm Mage's Toilet Paper was little better than the cheap stuff you find in gas stations. With a little leveling though...

My blue magic spell Pain I found was worthless against skeletons. They experienced no pain, so it didn't affect them in any way. It bummed me because I couldn't wait to see it in action. The suffering the imp had put me through had leveled the spell up through all 99 levels of Novice to level 4 of Intermediate. I couldn't wait to test it. The description promised a 10 second stun for a single cast. It was basically overpowered.

From everything I had experienced I was now convinced it was worth focusing on becoming a mage character. I would no doubt be a hybrid of sorts because my magic was blue and light. This also meant Intelligence (Int) and Wisdom (Wis) would be my main attributes.

There were three ways I could proceed to spend my attribute points. First, if I added all my attribute points into Intelligence then it would increase my maximum mana and spell power. If I focused only on Wisdom that would increase my MP regeneration rate. Or I could also mix the two. Normally I was more of a regen fan, but this was just like a game. If I just did the math I would find my answer.

If I pumped all my points into Intelligence I would end up with 121 and a mana pool of 605. The drawback is that this would leave me with my current regeneration rate of about 1080 MP an hour. Altogether, I could kill about 33 skeletons with just my Healing spell in that time frame.

On the other hand, if I loaded up on Wisdom, I would only have 200 base MP, but I would regen 4248 MP in an hour. That's approximately 132 skeletons I could kill with my heal spell.

After seeing the math there was no choice left to make. It was time to grow in awesomeness!

As I added all my points into Wisdom, something happened that didn't surprise me, but I hadn't really anticipated. My mind was more and more enlightened. Though my literal vision wasn't better than before, I suddenly saw more than I ever had before. Everything had an equation behind it. Everything was logic.

When I hit 100 Wisdom a few pop-up windows appeared under my status window. Exhilaration filled me from head to toe.

I exited my status window as quickly as I could finish pumping my stats and what I found took my breath away. Though I really shouldn't have been enjoying myself, I couldn't deny that I was. New skills were given when I reached 100 Wisdom.

Novice Mana Flow Understanding

Sitting is no longer required for quick mana regeneration.

Total mana multiplied by 2. Your 200 mana has now increased to 400.

All spells cost 20% less mana to cast.

All spells are 20% more powerful when cast.

New skill: Meditation

Mana regeneration rate slowly ramps up the longer you meditate reaching a maximum of 5 times your current regeneration rate reached after 10 minutes of meditation.

Warning. Meditation can be dangerous because it requires your complete focus.

Note: The first minute of meditation is the normal regeneration rate.

Though I was thrilled, it also concerned me that I was progressing so quickly. This was just day one and it seemed I was already overpowered. Either that or the little bit of power I had now was only that of a newbie. How powerful were the old man and Mistress really? It was a frightening thought.

Now that I had completely outgrown the skeletons, I decided to move on and find my group. It was odd that they hadn't come back to find me.

Chapter 5 - Regrouping

My group hadn't gone far. I found them three rooms deep in the labyrinth from the room we first entered if you continued straight from our base. Basically, they had moved on from skeletons to the second enemy in the dungeon. Decrepit Zombies.

As I neared, I got about a twentieth of my experience bar filled thanks to a zombie they finished killing. It had been level 55. Slightly higher than the skeletons, but it was still far less experience than I had been getting by myself.

It was the stench, not their decomposing mugs, that mostly repelled me from wanting to get close to the zombies in the area.

Olivia screamed as if I was a zombie when she saw me.

"He's alive!" big boy Russ yelled out.

"You thought I was dead?"

Aeris turned to Olivia. "I thought you said you saw him dead?"

"I did! He was just lying there not moving!" she insisted.

"Why is he moving now?" Aeris demanded. "And I assume the imp isn't guarding his body."

"He's a zombie!" Travis jeered, stepping up and grabbing my shoulder. "Sorry we left you, man. It's true what Aeris says. We thought you were dead and didn't want to face an imp yet so we took off. You missed a lot. We have all gained at least 6 levels."

Though my initial feelings were to hold it against them, I genuinely had no idea what they would have been able to do if they had tried to fight the imp and save me. Logically it would have been a waste. They would have been attacked with Pain or worse. There also seemed to be more to their reaction than just running away. Why had they sent Olivia of all people to check if I was okay though? She obviously didn't like me.

"I don't blame you," I replied.

Now to the present. How had they only raised 6 levels? What had they been doing all this time? Not that I said that out loud or anything. Perhaps joining them wasn't a good idea after all. We couldn't see each other's levels so I'd keep my speed of leveling up to myself.

"Elorion. You can heal, right?" Russ asked.

Seeing he was favoring his shoulder, I didn't wait for him to explain the details.

"Heal," I commanded and the warm light engulfed him.

His eyes went wide. "You guys got to try that! Thanks, man!"

I gave in to the request and healed each of them in turn. It would benefit them even if they hadn't lost any HP because it had the added benefit of healing fatigue. How much though I wasn't sure. It's not like there was a fatigue bar like mana and health that went down when you were tired.

It was no problem thanks to my increase in mana and Heal only cost 48 mana to cast now. It seems novice spells leveled pretty fast.

"That really is amazing," Olivia said—the first time she had said something nice to me. "It's like downing an energy drink without heart palpitations."

Everyone else was just as surprised.

"You guys ready to get back to it?" Travis said enthusiastically, just like a true gamer.

With a grin, I joined the others as we pulled one zombie at a time.

It was a slow beginning.

Aeris had a spell called Gust that slowed the enemy down by blowing from the opposite direction they were coming from. The problem was that the zombies weren't fast in the first place and it wasn't strong enough yet to knock them off balance or to the ground. In time I was sure it would be a powerful spell, but right now it needed to be leveled.

Olivia had the same problem. Her spell Under Growth was designed to slow a target down by growing a large patch of tall dense weeds in the monster's path. It was mostly ineffective.

Russ and Travis were doing most of the work. Russ had a wood chopping ax and Travis a long sword he was trying to fence with.

I stayed back during the first zombie fight to watch. At level 55 it was much stronger than the skeletons from before. Their only real weak spot was their head or spine.

Before the next fight, I stopped everyone. There was nothing to be done about the girls. They needed to power level their spells and now was as good a time as any. To Travis, I offered the spear. He was talented in piercing weapons so that should translate to two-handed weapons as well. It took a little persuasion, but he finally agreed.

The next round I began to help. I first tested Pain. Though the result wasn't as powerful as it would have been with a living creature, the zombie was still affected because it forced muscles to tense violently. I knew from first hand experience of the spell's power that it forced all your muscles to tense up; even a zombie that didn't feel the pain couldn't move if he was stiff as a board. Even as a 3-second stun it was overpowered.

Russ stood there and stared at the effectiveness of the spell in awe. Travis didn't hesitate and finished the zombie with a single thrust from the spear. *Now, this is what I'm talking about!*

"What was that?" Russ shouted overly excited.

"Pain. The blue magic that… the imp taught me."

"Amazing! Do it again!"

"Okay, but I can't cast it often." There was no reason for them to know how often I could cast it. With my 400 mana I reserved 100 MP just for Pain, 200 MP for Heal to cast on players only, and 100 MP for casting Decay. This was all so I could power level my spells.

My heal spell wasn't really needed often, but because it healed fatigue I kept casting it on Travis and Russ to keep them at peak performance. It worked wonders.

As things became repetitive and easy, I realized that up until that point I had been ignoring the severity of the situation we were all in. I allowed myself to be fully engrossed in the gaming aspects of this place. In truth, I was terrified.

Some crazy thousand-year-old chick that was terribly powerful and an old dude just as frightening made an imp kidnap me. Not to mention the flying shell-less turtle had tortured me with magic. I shouldn't be okay. I wasn't okay, yet I was here in a real-life dungeon casting magic like a real mage. This was the same thing I had always done to escape from my problems before, except back then they were really just games I escaped into.

I had to admit, this Mistress had really chosen wisely when we were picked for this evil magic. Just look at us. We were doing exactly what she wanted. Should I give in and play this dangerous game for the rest of my life? There was no way I could just ignore what happened.

First, I needed to become strong enough to survive. After that, I would look for a way to escape and take everyone else with me.

The monsters here were not what I was worried about. The imp said he was level 200. The way I was leveling so quickly when it was only the first day put the level of the imp within my grasp. I was sure leveling would start to slow eventually, perhaps after level 100. Right now we were still within the realm of what humans were normally capable of.

But what of the Mistress and old man? What were their levels? Was it possible that they would have put us in a position where we could become as powerful as they were? In time, could we defeat them? Or was that simply too much to ask? Would I die long before I could ever level up that much to defeat such long-lived monsters?

Either way, my only move forward was to fight. Mission Power Level initiated!

As we fought the zombies I only got 1 Blue Magic pop up during our entire time there. It was after the first 30 minutes of fighting.

You have begun to understand the Essence of the Undead

Once I reached Level 55, the experience gained here became a third of what it was. Ultimately, I reached level 57 in the two hours we hunted before heading back to base.

As we headed back, we split the fairly depressing monster drops. Zombie eyes, skin, ears, toes… There were only enough for each of us to have two drops apiece.

Stupendous! Torn flesh the size of my hand and a zombie's eye! Just what I always wanted! I moped.

"Dude. You don't have to hold it. Use your inventory," Travis said.

Looking around, everyone but me was already stashing their items. Seriously? If there was an inventory then why had it been a problem for me to grab four weapons earlier?

"Inventory," I said while willing it to appear.

A window with something similar to a checkerboard came up. Holding the gross items up to it they magically disappeared from my hand and were added to two different slots out of the available thirty.

"Anyone have some sanitizer?" I teased.

A chorus of chuckles followed.

***

Three merchant stalls were set up in a tight room. Behind each was a long, deep room stocked with goods. The three wooden tables before each room had a strange assortment of goods on display and even stranger looking merchants behind them.

The first starting on the left was what I suspected was a dark elf due to the dark, dull silver skin and pointy ears.

Elves existed? Aeris had elegant elf-like features, but this was something else entirely. Why was the existence of an elf more shocking to me than the undead?

Stranger still, the first dark elf I had ever met just happened to have a potbelly. So Elves weren't automatically good looking?

Next was a dwarf with dark eyes and black hair. Minus the skin, he was dressed much darker than even the dark elf. Since when did dwarves go goth?

Finally, there was a Halfling? He didn't have a portly belly, curly hair or carefree personality. His hair was slicked back, his eyes were sharp and he had well-toned muscles. Eh? What kind of world had I stepped into?

Of course, the first thing I did was activate Creature Observation.

Due to an unseen force, you are unable to use this skill at this location.

Bummer. The Mistress must have had some kind of magic use aura protecting this place. *Oh well. Whatever.*

"Anyone buy a zombie eye and flesh?" I asked aloud after taking in the room from the back of the group. My boldness surprised everyone, which let me step past them.

I had jumped in front of the others for two reasons. The merchants didn't know what all we had, so I could take advantage of them not having a bulk of something they had already bought from us which might lower the price. Also, by asking aloud for all to hear, now the merchants would have to bid if they were in the market for what I had.

"How about I give you the flat end of my blade on your rear?" the dwarf grumbled.

Not exactly the bid I had desired.

"3 copper a piece," the dark elf replied, his arms across his chest.

"I only pay 2 for the skin, but I'll give 10 for the eye!" the Halfling hollered.

After a moment of waiting to see if there were any new bidders, I called cheerfully, "Done!"

Even though I could have gotten an extra coin if I had split my items between merchants, they now knew I'd act kindly to any merchant that treated me fairly.

At least it was easy to understand how money worked. 100 copper equaled 1 silver, and 20 silver equaled 1 gold. Pretty standard setup in a gaming world as well.

As I walked out past my group Aeris met my eyes and smiled broadly in thanks. Olivia, on the other hand, was glaring at me. They had two vastly different interpretations of what I had just done.

I'm not sure I helped the matter when I winked at Olivia in spite. Oh, bother.

Being the first one done with the merchants made me the first one in line for food. The only reason I knew it was dinner time was that there was a big sign above the serving area that said, *Serving Supper.*

A blonde girl wearing glasses was sitting all alone at the stone table staring at one of the free loaves of bread and a water bottle. She hadn't taken a bite. It seemed she was taking all of this really hard. If I could afford anything extra I would get her something.

There was really no more than a long open window through which we could watch a few imps floating while preparing food in the kitchen.

When I asked what was available for 12 copper the imp said, "Bread."

"What about all the bread there. That's free!" I said, pointing to the table still fully stocked with bread from earlier.

"Fresh bread," the imp replied, annoyed.

"What about butter or cheese?"

"A wedge of the cheapest cheese is 40 copper and a tub of butter is 25."

Not happy at where this was going, I wondered, "How much is ranch dressing?"

"It depends on the brand, but 80 to 220 coins."

"I'm going to die!"

"If you do, we could sell you for approximately 200 coins a helping. Human meat is a specialty dish."

I looked at him blank faced.

"Give me the gruel. What is in it? Or wait! Don't tell me!"

At least the bowl I got contained a good portion. Honestly, I wasn't afraid of being poisoned or anything. The Mistress had already proven that she thought we were more useful to her alive. The grossness aspect to whatever was in the gruel did frighten me though. I'd be sure to heal myself a few times after I ate for good measure.

The others in my group didn't fare better with their trip to the merchant. When the others started to trickle in, Aeris and Olivia came together, stopping to talk to the girl that sat alone in silence.

I don't know what was said, but she joined them as they got their food.

We all sat down to eat our gruel gruelingly. There were now conversations going on as opposed the uncomfortable silence from before. The main topic wasn't hunting, but what to do to escape.

"If we get strong enough we could probably escape somewhere else from inside the labyrinth," Travis plotted.

"I say we just wait until it's dark and sneak out from here," Russ whispered.

"Have you guys seen any exits?" Olivia rolled her eyes.

A commotion came from the hall just outside the dining hall interrupting the conversation. Numerous feet echoed through the stone complex. It first headed toward the merchants' quarter just as we had at first. Minutes passed before the large group joined us. The group of 10 or so people following the guy who had pumped his strength entered the dining hall like they were conquering heroes.

I admit that the two pretty girls following as groupies caused me a tickle of jealousy. It grew when it became obvious they had a surprisingly successful hunt. I shook the absurdity of the thought away and nodded a greeting as they passed.

A cheerful fellow with curly blond hair walked up to us. "Hey, guys! How'd everything go? We found a zombie boss and defeated it. Everyone got like three levels with one kill!"

"Congratz!" Aeris was the first to reply. "We mostly just focused on leveling our skills in the first zombie area so we only got about fifteen levels each."

My respect for her grew. She didn't boast or sugarcoat anything.

"Hey, that's not bad. We got about 20 a piece, but we were also looking for harder mobs."

Others wished him well, but before he left I needed some information.

"What was the zombie boss like?" A smile reached my eyes.

"Oh. He was like seven feet tall, and other zombies seemed to follow him around. He was level 75 and was named. His name was Boris."

It was probably more likely an elite named mob, not a true boss, but still, the first any of us had run into. You could call it a lesser boss if you liked. Named monsters in games usually have a special history and are more powerful. That doesn't make them full on bosses though. Those are usually on an entirely other level.

"Nice!" I encouraged without correcting him. "Did he drop anything good?"

An excited nod toward the big guy in their group pointed out what had dropped. He wore a dull skull cap atop his head.

"The helmet also has the magical property of adding +20 to HP. Awesome, huh?"

It was indeed awesome. 20 HP wasn't really much, but just knowing what was possible was extremely important info.

"One last thing, did you guys see any other mobs besides skeletons and zombies?"

"Only stronger skeletons."

So it seemed stronger skeletons came after the zombies. I thanked him for the information.

Chapter 6 – Going Solo

That night, after everyone was asleep, or at least trying to sleep through the many sobs, I cast heal on myself, which seemed to recover my mental and physical endurance just as well as sleep would. How long it would last, I didn't know. I needed to test its effects and whether it really was a substitute for sleep or not. My inventory had a good stock of water and bread, so I headed into the labyrinth.

Currently, I was saving the attribute points I earned earlier. I was torn between upping Intelligence to 100 for the likely bonus or just stacking everything into Wisdom. No telling if there would be additional bonuses at 200, 300 and so on.

I began my hunting with zombies. Since I hadn't used Heal against them I needed to test it before I moved on. Thankfully they were just as slow as the skeletons had been and weren't grouped together. I knew from earlier they were aggressive when they saw me though, so I had to be careful. If I got too close they would attack.

The first one that noticed me I cast Heal on. It didn't kill it. Sadly, monsters didn't have health bars so I didn't know how well I was doing. Casting Heal again killed it.

On the next one, I cast Decay first, which cost only 10 MP now. Much cheaper than Heal, even though that only cost 39 MP now. This time the zombie died in one shot. This would save me quite a bit of mana.

So at least I knew that worked, but I didn't yet understand why.

An experiment commenced where I started to issue any command I could think of that was related to observation. If you ever get stuck in a dungeon and see a strange guy making circles around his eyes like he has pretend binoculars, he's not crazy but trying to find his examine skill. A more interesting question. How stupid do you think he feels when he exhausts every idea he has and concludes he doesn't have one?

Out of desperation, I tried activating Creature Observation.

A window populated and my mouth dropped open. Seriously? *So it's not just passive, eh?*

Lesser Zombie

Level 56

600 HP

0 MP

Str: 70

Dex: 10

Con: 50

Int: 2

Wis: 2

Description:

Dead human risen to life. Mindless devourer of raw flesh.

This made Blue Magic much more valuable than just stealing creatures' abilities. I was the only person that had such in-depth info on the monsters I faced. It could be life-saving.

More importantly, I found out basically how Decay worked. It put an attribute penalty of 20% on all physical stats like Strength, Dexterity, and Constitution, lowering the HP of a monster by 20%. In addition, it added a 20% bonus to damage from light magic. This was stackable but only went up 5% for each additional cast. It also increased 1% every minute on its own. With my current level of heal, I could just kill one with all my buffs.

Also, my heal spell did double damage against the undead. It was like a super critical attack!

It was then that my hunt truly began. I started by casting Decay on five of the closest zombies. The closest of all I cast Pain on. As it squirmed, I healed each one, in turn, trying to finish the other four off before the fifth was done with the 3-second stun Pain gave it. I could do this twice before I needed to rest.

To fully regenerate all of my MP it took about 7 minutes. As you can imagine, I left myself a little bit of extra mana in case something went wrong. Approximately two hours later I moved to the next room and continued my strategy. My spells slowly leveled as did I.

That was when I heard a quick patter of feet. Zombies only gave off the random moan and didn't really move fast enough to make much noise. When I heard the sound it gave away the cause of the noise's position immediately.

It was no taller than five foot, the shortest zombie I had seen yet, but with its small size came a huge jump in speed. There was little time to think up a strategy because it was coming right at me.

My first reaction was to cast Pain. The spell did its job, but I feared it wouldn't last as long as normal. It was a named monster. Immediately after, I used Creature Observation.

Boris the Runner

Level 75

HP 1400

MP 0

Str: 100

Dex: 40

Con: 180

Int: 5

Wis: 2

Description:

Dead human raised to life. Mindless devourer of raw flesh.

Special bonus due to his past. Runner in life. Runner in death.

1400 HP? I only had half my mana to fight it. So I spammed Decay on it, half panicked. I have no idea how many times I cast it, but Pain had worn off. Not sure I had enough MP left I cast Heal as it ran at me.

The first cast didn't kill it! I turned, readying to run.

Only a meter away I cast it again and leaped to the side. Struggling to place my mace between it and me, I turned and saw there was no need. It was dead.

The Level Up notification was a relief to see.

I cheered up when I saw that there was a pair of boots that had been dropped by the monster. They were much better than mine just by looking at them, but the size wasn't quite right and I found no way to identify if they were magic or not. I would ask the merchants, if any of them were still open. It was time to head back anyway. That was too close of a call. I would be stingier with my mana in the future when soloing just to be safe.

Before leaving, I was close to a far wall, so I sat down to relax and healed myself. I'd wait for my mana to fully recharge before going back.

Movement from the entrance of the room caused me to stiffen where I sat. Suddenly my kidnapper was walking past, looking over his shoulder multiple times as he went. The imp's eyes never found me on the far side of the room.

What would one of the Mistress's evil creatures have to hide? What was he up to?

As foolish as it might sound, I followed him. Not closely by any means, for I already knew he was suspecting someone. Just that day my entire world had been turned upside down. If there was some information I could learn that might help me I would take the chance.

The zombies were surprisingly easy to weave through. He had also already left this room, so killing one or two was safe.

When I spied into the next room, I saw him meet with a hooded figure. They both headed to a side room.

Just my luck there was another room just beside them that would keep me out of view. I could perhaps hear their conversation if there weren't too many zombies.

The two I found I finished quickly. The light of my spells wouldn't be seen by those I spied upon since there was a stone wall between us. I was suddenly extra thankful for the leather shoes. They made me nearly silent.

Hearing them was no trouble. The room they were in acted as a magnifier for the sound they were making. It carried their voices right to me.

"She is allowing humans to grow in power to feed off of their excess auras?"

"Yes. I am sure of it."

"And this just began?"

"Today."

"Very well. The old hag has broken the covenant. Here is your reward. I'll take care of the rest. It would be wise for you to disappear in a day or two. I can't promise you will live when I return."

There was a clank of what I was sure were coins. The imp was betraying the Mistress? Why?

This didn't bode well for me or any of the humans. Whatever enemy she had would most likely kill us or worse if anything happened to her.

The hooded figure left the room first. I was able to steal a glance, and I saw it was a hooded, hunched over figure that floated more than walked.

Unknown Title

Lich

Level ?

HP ?

MP ?

Str: ?

Dex: ?

Con: ?

Int: ?

Wis: ?

Description: ?

That was all the information there though. I at least knew it was a lich, but its level was just too high. There was no way I could defeat him or the imp. The only thought that made any sense was to tell the Mistress, but even that had its dangers. I had little choice. It seemed the way to give us the best opportunity of survival was to rely on her.

I let the imp leave next and I waited before he was out of the large room before I followed. It was as I was heading toward the entrance that another scuffle of feet made a commotion. About 50 meters away there was a Lesser Skeleton, a stronger variety than the first ones I faced, and he was heading my way.

There was no time to think up a strategy. I cast Decay, and then Heal immediatcly after. It took two heals to finish it.

As it died, it gave bonus experience, but the timing was terrible. I turned and saw the imp had returned and was scanning the room to see what the commotion was.

I was stuck. There was no way I wouldn't be seen. I ran.

Quickly I found myself in the same room I had hidden in just moments ago. The zombies had yet to respawn.

I had only a handful of seconds to think up a plan. A gamble was a better way to describe what I intended.

When the imp entered the room, outrage skewed its face. There were no questions. He greeted me by casting Pain.

The imp probably had more deadly spells to attack me with, but I was hoping this was how things would go.

I could have easily cast a spell before he did, but I knew if he cast Pain my resistance to it might catch him by surprise. Why let him win the first round? I hoped he would let his guard down if he thought he had already won.

Just as before, my muscles tightened before the pain came. My mind kept a semblance of focus and I cast Heal like last time. The only difference was that this time I cast it on him.

His surprise gave me the opening I needed.

While I was still under the effects of Pain, I cast Decay before he could recover. I was praying it would magnify the effect of Pain just like it did Heal. It was one thing I hadn't had a chance to test.

I cast Pain just as he started to recover.

He screeched, "How?!"

Seeing the spell take hold, I spammed Decay over and over as his back arched away from the cold floor. Before he could recover again, I cast Pain again. With so many casts of Decay, it was plain that it magnified its effects.

Finally released from Pain myself, with little mana left, I unsheathed my sword and jumped on the imp as I threw a heal spell in its face. This would be my only chance.

Driving my sword repeatedly into its gut I bashed down with my mace against its skull like a starving orc. All the while I cast Heal until my MP was drained. Whether it was my physical attacks or my healing spells that did him in I didn't know, but I didn't stop attacking until there was a multitude of pop-up windows and a steady stream of Level Ups; so many that I wasn't able to count.

With a heaving chest, I pulled myself off the dead creature. My kidnapper was dead!

Chapter 7 – The Head Mistress

I laid my head on the stone floor and closed my eyes. It was foolish, but I was exhausted. With a heavy sigh, I sat back up and quickly examined my surroundings. No zombies as of yet, so I began studying my windows.

Bonus experience for defeating your first Imp!

Bonus experience for defeating a creature 100 levels higher than you!

A maniacal laugh would have slipped from my lips but I was too exhausted.

Before I could bring up my status screen the zombies that I had killed before reappeared. I only had enough mana to kill one of them, so instead, I cast it on myself. The rejuvenation I felt was amazing.

Standing up to face them, I took the zombies to task with nothing but my mace. It was like a cast iron victory dance, but much more graceful than my normal showing.

Afterward, I checked my status screen. I was now level 83. I stood there stunned. In a single kill, I had just gained 18 levels. Suddenly I had 175 attribute points to spend.

The possibilities now were as good as having bacon with your bacon. Extra, please! I could now put all my points into Wisdom and have over 300. I wondered if I would get any bonuses if I reached 200. I would regen 2.38 MP a second or 8,568 an hour. That's a lot of dead zombies.

There was also the option of getting my Intelligence to 100 which would likely give me a bonus. I'd also have over 1200 MP. There would probably be an extra increase in my maximum mana and in the damage I did.

If I faced another imp it would be nice to be able to keep casting Pain without running out of mana so quickly. Perhaps even lifesaving.

It wasn't the time to make the decision. I had to warn the Mistress regardless of my fear of doing so.

Only one thing left to do. The loot!

Unlike the skeletons and zombies, the imp didn't disappear when it died. Its entire body still remained.

Not that the imp wore much in the first place, but I searched the few pockets I could find on his knee-high pants. His belt held multiple little pouches. Inside were vials of red and blue liquid. I suspected they were health and mana potions, but they were far smaller than I expected. Lying to either side of his body on the ground was a money purse and a long dagger with an obsidian-like handle. There was a ring on both of his middle fingers.

His personal money pouch contained about 200 copper coins worth 2 silver. The other pouch the Lich had given him was filled with 30 silver, not copper coins. I had a feeling this was a small fortune.

I had no way yet of identifying the knife or two rings which I believed to be magic. They would have to wait.

As insane as it sounds, I put the entire beat up body of the imp into my inventory. His items I put in separate slots in hope the Mistress didn't ask for them.

The imp only weighed about 60 lbs. all together so even though an invisible burden was on my shoulders it was manageable.

My trip back to base was a quick one where I only killed what got in my way. Because of the filth the dead body had left on my hands and shirt I stopped by the empty dining hall and washed with a water bottle. Afterward, I downed a few big swigs from another.

I found one of the serving imps asleep on a chair on the other side of the food window. It was tempting to kill him for the experience, but instead, I woke him.

"What do you want?" he complained.

"The Mistress has been betrayed. I need to see her immediately."

He choked out a laugh.

Opening my inventory just enough, I pulled out the head of the battered imp to show him how serious I was. Not only was it to make my point, but it was also a threat.

It jarred him enough that he fell off his seat.

Moments later he was hovering and nearly begging me to follow him.

That was when I learned why we hadn't seen any other passageways in the base that might be an exit. The doors were concealed by magic.

He spoke a word in an unknown language, which I began to mouth to myself under my breath. HidaGrach, or something like that. If it worked with a passcode then this might come in handy later.

We ascended stars that were identical to the stone the base was made from. The stone remained when we reached the top, but the room was laden with reds, purples, and gold. There was an endless supply of fabric.

Out of the room, past a tough, well-polished steel door, we entered a hall with matching décor. Past many side rooms, some open and some closed, we finally came to the Mistress's living quarters.

The imp knocked on the door, more gently than I think he intended. He was shaking in fear. Perhaps this really wasn't the best idea.

"Come!" commanded the familiar voice.

The imp tugged open one of the two golden doors. A cushioned couch stretched along the length of every wall of the room. In the rear was a pearl throne. The Mistress sipped from a large golden goblet. Two other women dressed in skimpy silk sipped from their own goblets. At the feet of the three was a slain dark elf. His shirt was torn down the middle showing a wound that led to his heart. He was dead. There was no divergence from the lean muscular build you would expect from the race.

As the Mistress laid eyes upon us, her finger flicked toward the imp, who fell to the ground entwined in something similar to the Bind spell the imp had captured me with before.

"Fool!" she said with deadly grace.

Before acknowledging me, she stood and addressed the ladies perched to either side of her.

"Sisters. I beg your forgiveness, but I must ask that you leave me to settle some business."

"Oh, dearest," answered one of the girls, "do share." She licked her lips while eyeing me like a piece of meat.

"Alas, I have parted with our traditions as you will recall. Besides, I regret that this matter will not be one of pleasure."

"Oh well. Do call us if you change your mind."

The ladies left through a side entrance, all the time teasing me with their eyes.

Was I missing something? There was a male dark elf in the middle of the room dead. What exactly had the Head Mistress parted with exactly?

I forced my eyes away from looking at anything inappropriate since the two ladies' garments didn't leave much to the imagination. Danger was at hand. It would not be wise to get distracted.

The Mistress, her attention now on me, struck me as much more alluring even with her more modest purple silk gown.

"You. Answer very carefully. If what you say doesn't please me I will invite my sisters back to do to you as they like. I guarantee you will not survive."

My throat was dry, stomach in a knot, but this wasn't the time to shy away.

Bowing my head, I swallowed where she couldn't see to hopefully hide my fear as much as possible.

"I caught someone in the act of betraying you."

She stared at me when I didn't continue with my explanation. On the bright side, she hadn't killed me yet.

"An imp was leaving the base tonight when I was coming back from the hunt. He was looking over his shoulder so I followed him. In the room where lesser skeletons begin to appear, a Lich met him."

I gave her their conversation as close to word for word as possible.

The mention of the silver earned me a moment out from under her heavy gaze. She didn't look worried but calculating.

"Can I see this silver?"

"Yes, Mistress. I have also brought the traitor."

Taken off guard, she looked at me like she was seeing me for the first time. "You killed an imp? How?"

Here I had to be careful. My natural snarkiness wanted to rub it in that the smelly Light Mage had put the smackdown on one of her minions who was nearly three times his level. Instead, I controlled myself.

"When he left to head back to the base, I followed only after he left the room. When a skeleton came after me I ran to a side room. The imp must have heard and followed me. When he came in I let him cast Pain on me since I had built up a resistance from the time you had him teach it to me."

"Wait." She stopped me. "He said I asked him to teach you and then he taught you by casting it on you? He lied to you. A bit of a cruel joke, I'm afraid. There is a much easier way to teach someone blue magic and it doesn't involve pain."

"Good to know." I exhaled, wanting to hit the dead imp in the face again even if I did break my hand.

With the rise of her brow, I knew she wished me to proceed.

"I then cast Pain on him—he seemed surprised that it worked. Next, I used a blue magic I learned called Decay. When I used Pain again it worked even better."

She nodded me on.

"Then I snapped. I started to spam Heal while stabbing him with my short sword and bashing him with my mace until he died."

Taking it all in she hesitated a moment before asking, "Show me the silver and the imp."

The silver I took out first.

She reached toward it with some kind of telekinesis. The money floated out of my grasp to her.

The imp I grabbed by the wrist and lugged out of the magic window that was my inventory.

She examined the coin and only glanced at the imp.

A giggle leaped from her lips. "You are quite fortunate. This imp could have used numerous spells that would have immediately killed you."

Pulling out a clear ball that fit in the palm of her hand, she spoke into it.

"Our secret is out. A lich was informed of our plans by an imp in our employ. The lich was last seen in the realm of the lesser skeletons."

"Very well. I will go after the lich. What of the imp?" responded the same voice of the wrinkly old man.

"Dead already. Go! I'll catch you up on everything later."

"I'm on my way."

After depositing the glass ball, the Mistress smiled at me sweetly. "Well, aren't you a pleasant surprise."

With the wave of her hand the imp she had bound made it to his feet.

"You have done well." She tossed the bag of 30 silver and he greedily caught it.

I mourned the loss of so much coin.

"Thank you, Head Mistress."

"Leave us now."

The imp was quick to fly away, leaving me alone.

"Come in."

With a tug from her telekinesis, the door shut behind me.

"You also must be rewarded, but first..."

With a word, energy fell upon me which set my skin tingling.

"You stink, so I will take the liberty of cleaning you. Put the imp back in your inventory. They are disgusting."

I did as she said and the tingle reached my hands after the task was finished. Even my clothing was good as new.

Suddenly, I found myself in a room alone with the most attractive woman I had ever known.

The stern dangerous face that had been there moments before was gone, replaced with a soft and inviting one.

"What would you have for your reward? Money? Power? Pleasure?"

Before my imagination could take over, I spoke my request. It almost surprised me. "Your wisdom."

The answer seemed to please her for she sat down and looked at me with a raised brow.

"I would ask for you to reward me in the way you think would be the wisest for me to grow as strong as possible, as fast as possible."

"Interesting. That was not something I expected to hear." After a moment's thought, she agreed. "Very well. Come here and show me your status screen."

I made my way around the dead dark elf and boldly got closer to her than I felt comfortable with. Everything about her was enticing. The closer I stood the worse her magnetism grew.

The allure was suddenly gone as if she had dismissed a spell that had been causing an unnatural pull.

"Thank you," I said, acknowledging she had done something to lessen the attraction.

She winked in response.

"Status," I commanded.

My high wisdom and 175 points to spend became visible to her.

"Oh, my. You have chosen well. Wisdom is the best choice over Intelligence at your level. Next, you should get your intelligence to 100 for the bonus. It's worth the points. These bonuses only come in multiples of 10, as in 100, 1000, 10000. After getting intelligence to 100, stick to wisdom. The path of wisdom far exceeds the path of intelligence in the long run. Now show me your spells and skills."

This time she didn't mock me when seeing my Heal spell. Many of my blue magic spells were fairly high. With Pain at Intermediate level 11 and Decay 83, it must have looked to her like I was indeed focusing mainly on blue magic.

"Hrmm. So you want to get stronger as quickly as possible. Since our goals align this will be my reward to you. May I ask why you have chosen to ask my opinion instead of something more tangible?"

Shrugging, I decided to tell her the truth. "I am too weak now to guarantee my survival. Also, if other forces attack you, all of the others will likely become casualties as well. We are too low of a level to help you right now. I need to get stronger as quickly as possible to protect myself, and them, and to help you."

She acknowledged this with a nod. "All of what you say is true."

She started shaking her head, mostly to herself but smirking at the same time. "I have a spell in mind that is nearly perfect for a blue mage. There is a creature that is not powerful in strength or martial prowess but instead possesses one of the most powerful forms of invisibility that exists. This skill is incredibly rare. The Slithe is unknown to most because of its unique ability to stay hidden even to those with the magic to see through invisibility.

"You see, the creature's ability is not even considered magical in nature, so except for the most powerful invisibility seeing spells and items, almost nothing will work. Only blue mages can learn it because of this. It will make studying creatures to learn blue magic much easier, even those of the highest level. Killing something when it's not expecting you also becomes much easier. You will still need to take care. It will not mask the sound you make or smell. Some predators are sensitive enough to these senses that invisibility is nearly worthless. Here."

With a finger to my forehead, she muttered something in an ancient tongue. The knowledge of the spell filled my mind in an instant.

"There is one last thing you will need to become a mage assassin. Few spells are element neutral even in the realm of blue magic. That means few creatures have any resistance to them if you happen to learn one. Most elemental spells will be more powerful than this one, but it is nearly the perfect backup spell if you find yourself unable to harm your opponent."

Again, my mind was filled with knowledge. A damage spell called Alpha Bolt.

"You have benefitted me, so I have repaid my debt. Use these gifts wisely and we will both grow more powerful. If you please me I will reward you again. Now, leave me to my snack." She smiled wickedly while licking her lips.

"Of course." I bowed, my lowered head once again hiding a gulp. "A final question, if I may?"

"Yes?" she said as if I might be starting to get on her nerves.

"Should I warn the others that we might be attacked?"

For a moment she didn't follow my meaning. When understanding registered she replied with a considering frown. "Do tell them your tale if you so desire. Perhaps warning them of coming danger will produce better results with their training."

With a final bow of my head, I turned to leave without another word.

The door opened before me at her command and shut behind me when I left. The stairs were easy enough to find.

As I headed down, I was overcome with fright. Minutes later I shook off the terror that held me huddling against the wall.

The spells the Mistress gave me were powerful in their own right, but it was obvious that they were just a few out of a multitude she possessed. She was more than a monster.

I healed myself, which made me feel a bit better.

As I entered the dining room I determined it was necessary to become powerful as quickly as possible with the gifts she gave me, but that wasn't enough. Even though I preferred hunting with the others I couldn't let them hold me back. First, I would tell them what I learned, but time was against me. That meant sleep was also my enemy.

***

Leaving the merchants I was feeling much better. The elite zombie I had fought earlier had dropped 20% increased speed boots. I sold them and instead purchased a sturdier pair of shoes similar to mine that increased sound concealment by 30%.

The imp's rings had been +50 to strength and +400 to HP. They seemed extremely powerful, but when examining everything else on the market, they were little more than average. I was only impressed because I was a newbie. At least they sold well. I got a full set of magic smokey gray leather armor that added +25 to cold and fire resistance in total. A matching leather cap added +200 to HP and leather gloves +20 to Dexterity. Not to mention the armor rating it added, or the fact it was cold in the labyrinth and this would help me stay warm.

I was able to get so much for the two rings simply because rings were on the rarer side.

Finally, the dagger was actually the most costly item the imp had owned. It was a perfect assassin's weapon with Lesser Frostbite cast when thrust into an opponent. This caused a rapid freeze to the area around the wound making it harder for the target to move. As you could expect, I kept this.

The last thing I purchased was a large bundle of identity scrolls and a few pounds of beef jerky! The scrolls allowed me to identify items myself without having to come back to town. They would come in handy. The beef jerky would help me stay sane. This left me with 1 silver and 33 copper.

If I had my way, I wouldn't be back in town except to sell and buy a good meal or two for the next couple of days. That of course mostly depended on how powerful my heal spell really was when it came to relieving my exhaustion. If it really could replace sleep, then I might have a chance to become much more powerful before the Mistress's enemies attacked. So far it seemed to be working. It was already 3:00 AM and still my exhaustion hadn't caught up with me.

As I set off, I pulled up my status screen. Without hesitation, I raised my intelligence up to 100 and got my Wisdom to 233. The bonus she promised was proven true with the pop-up of a trigger window.

Novice Mana Manipulation Understood

You can now charge a spell to cause greater damage.

The amount of mana per point of Intelligence has doubled.

All spells cost 20% less mana to cast.

All spells are 20% more powerful when cast.

Intermediate Meditation

Mana regeneration rate slowly ramps up the longer you meditate reaching a maximum of 10 times current regeneration rate after 5 minutes of meditation.

If you continue meditating after you have reached maximum mana, you will be able to store mana through meditation of up to double your current maximum mana.

Warning. Meditation can be dangerous because it requires your complete concentration.

Note: The first minute of meditation is the normal regeneration rate.

So I left the base with my newly acquired gear, a new MP of 2k and the ability to put more mana into a spell to make it more powerful. With just my increased Wisdom I was now able to regenerate 2.33 MP a second or 8,388 MP in an hour. Now that I could cast invisibility I would be able to take advantage of Meditation. Instead of 2.33 MP a second I'd be regenerating 23.3, or approximately 83,880 MP an hour minus the ramp up time. I could also double my maximum mana to 4k.

I cast Invisibility for the first time and walked right past the skeletons, an invisible blur.

CHAPTER 8 – STRESS RELIEF

As I neared the exit of the first room filled with Decaying Skeletons, I stopped short. After being kidnapped, tortured, and face to face with an immeasurably powerful succubus queen who would likely eat me if the mood ever took her, my nerves had reached their limit.

Pulling out my mace, I didn't bother trying to soften my footsteps as I marched up behind the closest Decaying Skeleton. I could have uncast Invisibility, but I thought I might as well leave it running until my movement caused it to fail. I wasn't a fan of overly micromanaging spells in games and I wouldn't start here.

Choking the worn leather grip of the mace with both hands, I teed off on the undead creature. There was a loud pop as its lower spine separated from its frame and scattered against the floor.

Clenching my jaw, I leveled the steel ball upon its skull now lying against the stone floor. Bone dust and fragments exploded out as it crumbled from the blow.

I noticed my arms had become almost entirely visible the faster I moved. The rest of my body had done the same, but, to my surprise, my Invisibility spell didn't fail. As I slowed, my ethereal state slowly returned over a few seconds. My jaw dropped. This spell was far more powerful than I could have hoped for. There were no countdown timers or having to hide before casting invisibility again.

There were few situations I could imagine where this spell wouldn't come in handy. As a basher, fading in and out of invisibility was an amazing advantage. As a spell caster, I could throw a spell and become invisible a few seconds later. As a rogue... Muahahahaha!

After a deep breath, I stomped toward the next skeleton, catching it on the side of the skull. The bone cracked, but without being braced against the floor the bone's natural durability won out. It took another swing to the head before it burst like a dust-filled firework.

One after another I pounded on the weak creatures. My nerves worked themselves out through the physical exertion. In less than five minutes the room was clear. Without the imp to hit in the face, these decaying-bones-of-stress-relief were a welcome substitute. They didn't cast nasty spells either.

I allowed the room to fill two more times. After I had finished clearing it the last time I was drenched with sweat and leaning against the cold stone wall to catch my breath.

Normally, I would have rebuked myself for wasting time in a gaming situation. This was something I had needed though and this wasn't a game. With a clear mind, I cast Heal on myself, fully recovering from my exhaustion. *Such an amazing spell.*

Before I began my serious power leveling, it was time to test my new spells. If this had been a game, then I would have just figured it out as I went. I couldn't afford to do that here. If I misjudged things just once it would mean a gruesome, painful and lonely death. There was no one to impress, so I would take no chances.

A few rooms deeper I was second-guessing sneaking up on the lowbie zombie right in front of me. The worst part of its rotten smell was that it reminded me of fast food. Since I would probably never have a magnificent, grease-dripping, I-don't-know-what's-in-the-meat burger again, I wanted to remember them fondly.

It was easy enough to come up behind the zombie without making too much noise. My new Boots of Concealment literally made my footfalls sound lighter. I was creeping myself out.

Slipping my Dagger of Frostbite into the middle of the zombie's back, I saw dozens of blue magic fingers seep into its flesh and muscle around the blade. It chilled everything within six inches of the puncture wound. Stepping back, I gave it some room to see how powerful the Frostbite effect really was.

As it turned to face me, it tried to look back in my direction. Noticing something was wrong, it reached back and tried to scratch at the wound in its back. Besides the distraction, it didn't seem to really affect its movements.

I had been still long enough to have gone invisible again. Circling, I came around behind it and considered what might be the best place to stab it. The neck might do more damage, but if it didn't kill it then it would only limit its neck movement. In its lower back or glutes…

Thrusting low, I punctured the zombie's right rear cheek. Part of me wanted to apologize immediately, but instead, I jumped back to see the effects of the spell. The zombie was struggling to twist at the middle. It was able to turn its head but was unable to lift its leg to fully face me. With a sudden jerk, it tried to turn the other way and dragged its leg as it did. I had successfully given it a frozen tush.

It wouldn't work on skeletons, but this was exactly what I was hoping for. The zombie's HP was already low, so I finished it with a swing from my mace. Before I moved on, I tried stabbing a zombie in the lower back to compare the effects of stabbing one in the glutes. Thankfully the lower back worked just as well.

Alpha Bolt cost a lot of mana. 500 for a single cast. Now it was time to see if it was worth it, or if it would take some leveling before it was of much use. I knew its damage output was about 500, so it should be overkill on the Decrepit Zombies. I didn't know what to expect from the spell or the form it would take.

Ready or not. I held up my hand toward the closest zombie. As I willed it to life, gray smoke the size of a golf ball seeped out of my palm and quickly solidified with an added purple hue and grew until it was about the size of a bowling ball. Once it reached that size, I already knew that Alpha Bolt and I were going to be great friends. About a second after casting, the dull purple energy shot toward the zombie knocking it firmly off its feet and collapsing its chest. One hit kill!

It needed leveling up, but I couldn't deny the Mistress had kept her end of the bargain.

***

With that out of my system, I moved on. I was careful not to move on too early. If I hadn't killed the imp it would have been wise for me to face these zombies a bit longer, but after reaching level 83 I was through here.

I doubted there were any creatures I would run into for quite some time that would be able to see past my invisibility spell, but that didn't mean I would take any chances. There was no manual or tutorial here. This was my new life.

Trying not to snack too hard, I gobbled down some mouth-watering dried cow. Nothing like some beef jerky to help me forget the rotten zombie smell.

The next creature I ran across was a Lesser Skeleton. My knife wouldn't be much use here so I sheathed it. Directing spells was easier empty handed anyways. Sneaking up on the first skeleton, I tested Invisibility, finding I could stand directly in front of its line of sight. It was level 61 and didn't have any discoloration to its bones, but was almost identical to the Decaying Skeletons I had faced before. When I was within arm's reach, I was convinced it was completely oblivious to my invisible state.

Backing up, this skeleton was slightly taller than its Decaying brother. When I was at a comfortable distance, I cast Decay.

It noticed me right away but was confused, perhaps not seeing me clearly or at all. I let Invisibility shroud me fully to see its reaction. For about ten seconds it looked toward me, but then seemed to forget me entirely.

Decay had started to take effect. The same discoloration I'd seen on the Decaying Skeletons now appeared on the Lesser Skeleton. With my new 2k MP, I didn't waste the opportunity to power level my spells. I spammed the room with Decay, casting it on every Skeleton I could see.

Next, it was time to come up with my mana usage strategy. I needed to level both Heal and Alpha Bolt without neglecting Decay and Pain. Not that Pain would do any good against Skeletons, but that didn't mean I couldn't level it by casting it on them.

So I segmented my MP usage. 500 for Alpha Bolt, 500 for Heal, 500 for Pain and Decay. The Extra 500 I kept as a buffer in the case I needed to use an Alpha Bolt or Heal in an emergency. Since I had 142 Mana Regen a minute it wouldn't take me long to regain my pool. Less than fifteen minutes to be precise.

Lesser Skeletons crumbled in heaps of bone dust. I saved my Alpha Bolt for the last skeleton, scattering its bones across the floor. There were two drops that remained after the skeletons disappeared. A femur and bone meal. The drop rate here was pretty low, but higher than the lower level Skeletons.

After killing the first, the level up notification streamed from the floor. Thanks to the bonus for killing a Lesser Skeleton for the first time, I reached the next level and upped my Wisdom. The experience other than that could only be described as awful. I would be in this same area all day to level just once if I didn't move on.

As I headed to the next room, I continued killing every Skeleton I came across. Leveling spells would likely be as useful as leveling up itself. If there were only a few enemies, I would first cast Decay, Pain, then Heal, unless it was time for Alpha Bolt. I decided to make Alpha my primary focus since it cost so much MP and would take that much longer to level. Heal cost so much less that I could cast it at least five times more often.

I considered going room to room looking for new creatures to kill. It would certainly gain me new levels quickly, but eventually, I would run into a creature that was too strong for me and end up dead or mangled. I had a feeling leveling up my spells would be just as important as levels themselves. I had played too many games where that was the case.

After five rooms filled with Lesser Skeletons, I reached a higher level creature, the Skeleton Scout. These actually used a variety of weapons, although most of them were of lesser quality. They ranged from knives to clubs to the rare bow. Their levels ranged as widely as their weapons anywhere from 70 to 85. I had found a satisfactory hunting grounds—for now.

The room I entered had started to change. The gray stone was smoother and looked less weathered. It was almost as if the room was a living thing and leveled up with the creatures inside it. There were also about fifty skeletons total, about twice as many as the lower level rooms. This still left many side rooms and gave them plenty of space to spread out in the football field-sized area. The rooms did vary in length and width, some half this size and others larger. It seemed the first room was commonly one of the largest rooms, if not the largest.

For the first time, I really had to consider the best strategy for survival. The archer scouts were of the highest level, between 80 and 85, but also had the lowest HP at around 400. It was still beyond the reach of a single cast of my Healing spell, even with double damage. Alpha Bolt could one-hit an archer I was confident, but the sword-wielding Scouts had close to 600 HP. If they were aggro'ed, then I'd end up having to run as they tried to attack.

I knew what I had to do.

Finding an archer by itself wasn't easy. I was afraid every other creature around it would go aggro and start attacking me if I wasn't careful, so I waited and watched their patrol patterns.

If I was honest, the unknown damage a bow could do scared me. I found an empty side room without a door that I could snipe out of. As I watched, it became clear they really didn't have a specific pattern. At least, not one that they shared between themselves. Instead, each individual seemed to roam around at random, according to a nature I didn't understand. As I acknowledged I didn't understand them, or their motivation, a notification popped up.

You now better understand the essence of the Undead.

I was being rewarded for realizing I didn't understand?

I finally saw one wander far enough away from its companions that I felt comfortable taking a shot. If I was wrong I could just jump out of the doorway behind the stone wall, and go invisible until they got bored of looking for me.

I led with Decay and Pain, before casting Alpha Bolt. As soon as the first spell was cast, the Scout became aware of where I was and drew back his bow. I was able to cast Pain quickly enough to stay arrow free, but I jumped to the side before I was able to cast Alpha Bolt.

The arrow soared through the now empty doorway where I had been. I stared at the projectile as it hit the far wall and dropped to the floor. That could have killed me.

Unsure how aggressive the Scout was, I began casting Alpha before I peeked around the corner. It only took about a second to cast; a second that could prove life-threatening.

Only daring to reveal the smallest amount of flesh to my enemy, I peeked around the corner with caution, seeing the archer had moved to get a better angle on the direction I had fled. His arrow was drawn back, but Alpha was already cast. My spell released faster.

Throwing my hand forward, the purple cannonball of energy shot straight at it. Aiming was easier than I would have guessed considering it was done by a matter of will.

I leaned back in a panic.

When no arrow flew past me, I took a deep breath and looked out again. The archer's bow was snapped at the middle, as was its body. There were dozens of pieces scattered across the floor.

Two level ups shot up from the ground, reminding me this was the first Skeletal Scout I had faced.

Next, I picked a Scout with a sword. Decay and Pain went off without a problem. This one also proved to be quite alert and was running at me a moment later. Spamming Heal, it took three casts to bring the monster down. The experience was pretty good. I estimated twenty more for the next level.

After putting down a knife wielder, I got my first drop. It was a pretty terrible quality knife but gave +4 to Dex. It was worth keeping to sell. I had already learned that the addition of the magical properties this dagger possessed was garbage, but it was better than selling zombie flesh and the like.

As I began to get into a rhythm, I found my mind wandering. The loot was good and the experience was better, but even these higher level skeletons were very limited in their ability. I was capable of facing something with a lot more difficulty.

Leaving the shelter of the room, I continued to pick them off one at a time. If a second one was close to catching aggro, I skipped casting Decay and Pain, instead fully laying into it with my offensive power.

My spells continued to level and my confidence grew. Soon I was purposely taking on two, then three, being most careful of the archers.

When I felt I was ready, I stepped forward, taking on groups of skeletons one after another. My mana regen was good enough that if I limited my use of Pain, I could leave piles of dust in my wake.

As I entered the next room of Scouts, I carved out a corner to myself and went to work. Strolling past the side rooms on my right I challenged myself by continuing to fight without slowing my pace. It wasn't a fast pace but forced me to put all of my focus on what was in front of me.

Two groups of three, one directly in front of me and another to my left out in the middle of the room turned their attention to me as I sent an Alpha Bolt barreling into the chest cavity of one of the two archers.

Before they could take their first step, my Heal spell was already blanketing the other archer. A second one ended him before he could notch his first arrow.

A sword and a club wielder ran at me. They were the two remaining from the group in front of me and were much closer than the others.

I prepared an Alpha Bolt. Taking a large step closer to the wall, I let it go as they lined up in my sights.

The soccer ball-sized ball of energy plowed through one and continued on to leave the other crumbling to the floor.

Laughter escaped as I turned to the last two. There was no denying the power I felt. I was actually using magic.

My laughter was stopped short when I felt a stinging sensation in the back of my arm.

Looking down, an arrow was embedded in the back of my arm. The arrowhead had stopped just before it had broken the skin and exited out the other side. I turned a ghastly white.

Spinning, I saw an archer with a second nocked arrow was pivoting its bow to me. It stood in the center of the doorway of one of the side rooms. I had completely forgotten to check. It had been able to see me because of all my movement and casting despite Invisibility.

My predicament dawned on me in that moment. Knife- and sword-wielding skeletons were approaching from behind and I was about to be shot with a second arrow.

Instinct took over. I lunged to the side while throwing up my arms.

The second arrow jabbed into my leather armor, just nicking the skin of my lower ribs. The arrow cartwheeled to the floor. I retreated into a room. The two melee skeletons were already at the door when I turned around to meet them.

My hand cocked back like I was about to throw a punch, but with an open palm, I summoned Heal, but unlike any time I had ever cast it before.

Adrenal necessity drove me as I let mana drain into the spell before I let it go, blanketing the both of them in liquefied light.

Not only did they die, but they burst apart, sending the archer behind them onto its rear.

Looking to my mana, I had very little left. I must have subconsciously charged the Healing spell. It just wasn't enough to finish the skeleton where he sat.

My wits had recovered enough that I cast Heal on it once and then stepped to the side, putting the wall between us.

I let Invisibility take me.

Listening to it get up made my already pounding heart beat like a drumline. Still, I stayed where I was, trusting Invisibility.

It entered the room, with an arrow nocked pointing right at me.

The muscles in my calves and quads tightened. I was about to jump to dodge when it turned with a jerk to the other side of the room suspecting I was behind it.

With a deep breath, I let a few seconds pass as my mana built up. Normally I would get a kick out of watching the skeleton struggle to find me, but the pain in my arm demanded I respect it.

I gritted through raising my injured arm and turned it to dust.

Immediately I cast Heal on myself, which took care of the cut on my ribs but did nothing to my arrow wound. *Archers are worse than brussels sprouts on pizza.* The arrow needed to be removed.

Sitting against the wall, I examined the wound, finding no easy way to take it out. If I pulled from the end it entered, it was likely the arrowhead would get stuck inside my arm. The other option was to force it to exit out of my arm from the other side. Pushing it through the skin was not what I considered a good time. It had to be done though.

Since I was already against the wall, I lined up the arrow and found it was the right angle. This was going to hurt.

Stretching my arm forward, I made sure I had the room to build up enough momentum.

I needed a distraction. *Think of food. Homemade meatballs and pasta. Large rump roast that has been cooking in a hot tub of gravy and meat juice!*

With clenched teeth, I pulled my arm back, like I was trying to elbow someone behind me. The tail of the arrow struck the wall solidly, forcing the arrowhead to jut out of the other end of my arm about ten inches.

I would have made most banshees cringe at the screech that erupted from me. Grabbing the bloody shaft of the arrow, I took advantage of my adrenaline and tore the arrow the rest of the way through.

There wasn't a millisecond before Heal bathed me. Within a second I was already feeling better. That didn't stop me from casting Heal another two times.

I had been so stupid. A mix of arrogance and neglect had nearly gotten me killed. What if that arrow had hit me in the back of the head?

You might think I second-guessed staying out here and hunting alone. Not so. There was no way my adrenaline would allow me to relax after what had just happened. I was alive and in the mood for a massacre.

My cry of pain brought a few skeletons to me to see what was going on. I started with them.

I ended up hunting Skeletal Scouts for another two hours, before reaching level 92. It wasn't the experience that kept me going, but they deserved all the death they could get. I decided it was a wonderful idea to try a few experiments.

Casting Decay on a high HP club-wielding Scout caused the bow wielder about thirty feet away to turn its head. This seemed to be the aggro range of this specific monster unless I screamed at them or made a lot of noise. Anything within thirty feet would be noticed if one of their fellow skeletons was being attacked. The distance between it and its companion determined how quickly it would find me.

At a range of about twenty feet, I cast Alpha Bolt, hitting the bow user as the basher ran at me. Two heal spells later and it was dead. My novice Heal spell had been leveling up extremely fast. It was already level 23 and doing over 300 damage more than it had at level 1.

From now on I would have to give the archers some extra loving care anytime I passed through here.

CHAPTER 9 – GETTING STARTED

With the Scouts behind me, it was time to move on. My breathing grew heavy and my nerves were on edge. I hadn't had any close calls since getting shot, so it couldn't be that, but I felt as if I was drowning in an ocean of stone. Never before had I felt claustrophobic. Although, that might not have been what I was experiencing then. One thing was sure, the reality that I was in an underground dungeon surrounded by an endless supply of monsters had become very real. I was alone.

Was I afraid of the dark? Perhaps. Real monsters lurked in the deep recesses of the underworld, which I was now a part of. Who knew how many meters or miles of stone and earth sat over my head between here and the world of men? Once you reach a certain age it is considered childish to fear the dark in the world above. Was it childish to fear the dark here? If any of us lived long enough to have children and see them grown, what would we teach our children about the dark? How different would their lives be in a world like this?

Finding an empty side room with a mostly intact wooden door before I left the Scout's area wasn't difficult. Entering inside, I cast Light Orb in each corner, lighting up the room enough to make it feel like it was in the middle of the day.

I was trying to limit my use of Light Orb because it obviously gave away that someone was in the area, even if they still couldn't see me if I was using Invisibility. There was enough unnatural light in these tunnels that it wasn't really necessary anyway. I knew if I forced myself, I would eventually grow accustomed and it wouldn't bother me anymore.

After a few minutes break and a couple of healing spells, I was able to breathe much easier. Casting Heal on myself helped to keep exhaustion at bay, supplying me with a great advantage in fighting off what might be considered mental status effects. It was not something I would have been able to handle if I had been overly tired. I would have ended up going back to the base and waiting for the others.

There was one thing that would make things even better. I grabbed a foot long strip of jerky from my inventory and tore a generous sized bite off and went to town. I could almost imagine sitting in the back seat of the car on a road trip when I was young, eating jerky and playing road sign games. The only thing that would make things even better was having half a dozen chip flavors and every sugary drink you can imagine at my beck and call. Ewww, and dip. Can't forget ranch dressing, spinach dip, onion dip, french onion dip, bean dip, buffalo chicken dip, roasted garlic, artichoke, guacamole, picante sauce, guacamole tummy buster, liquid cheese, salsa, and butter...

I only allowed myself a few more minutes rest, not to forget the time sensitivity of my mission. Maybe I shouldn't admit this, but in that time an idea had developed. Getting to my feet, I continued on. The first solo scout I ran across I cast Light Orb into its eye socket to see how it would react.

It didn't hesitate but jabbed its dagger into its own eye finding nothing to pierce. The force it used was enough that the tip of its dagger exploded from the back of its skull leaving a quarter-sized hole and relieving it of 30 HP.

My mouth dropped open, as disbelief hit me like trying cheese steak for the first time. The snort that escaped from my gut shook me and had me doubling over to the point I could hardly control it. Never before had I needed to laugh so much.

Though it was a tactic that would never work on a more intelligent creature, I spammed Light Orb into the eye sockets of a group of three skeletons close by. A club, sword, and bow slammed into their bony faces nearly simultaneously. It was the sword that did the most damage, as the scout took the same approach as the knife wielder, stabbing itself in the eyeless socket.

As they moved from the place they had been standing when I first cast the spell, the Light Orb stayed in the same place and their heads moved right through it. The distraction it caused didn't end when the light had left the inside of their heads. An arrow pierced one of the orbs and a knife slashed through another.

I happily cast Decay on each of them, then Pain, and took my time finishing them off with Heal.

***

Standing a few inches taller than me, much thicker boned than all the skeletons before them, Skeleton Warriors filled a room of blue-gray brick. It was wider than it was long, with arched doorways to its many side rooms and a much larger arched doorway exiting to the next room.

It wasn't just the size of these skeletons that was different. Not only were the warriors armed, but the swords and shields they wielded were unlike anything I had seen. They were made of bone.

I wandered off to the side and found a safe room to view the monsters. Almost immediately my Creature Observation skill went to work. As I examined a level 102 Warrior's sword, a pop-up appeared.

You have begun to understand Skeleton Warrior's Sword.

It didn't surprise me when I saw what it said, but it would have been nice if there was more information.

The Warriors held their swords in a relaxed position resting against their shoulders like a practiced swordsman that respected its weight. Another pop-up.

You better understand Skeleton Warrior's Sword.

I was all teeth as I grinned. This was easy. Or at least, so I thought.

Ten minutes passed as I tried to study the Skeleton Warrior and his sword. Nothing. I used Creature Observation and the monster's stats popped up, but my understanding didn't improve. Then I turned my attention to the Warrior's shield and soon got my first pop-up for the Skeleton Warrior's Shield. Another ten minutes and nothing.

The time wasn't a total waste. I learned their basic movements, or lack of movement, at least in comparison to the skeletons I had seen before. These mobs patrolled with a precise pace as a trained soldier might, but still seemed oblivious to the other Warriors in the area. So much so that more than once two warriors bumped into each other.

Understanding the mob itself didn't help me understand their swords or shields. I knew what I had to do.

The lowest level Warrior had 2000 HP, meaning even with the leveling up of Pain and Heal, it would take multiple casts. Assuming the 30 feet radius for aggro would apply to Warriors as well as Scouts I attacked my first Skeleton Warrior.

I aimed Decay at the monster's shield, easily hitting the round bone structure about the size of half a car door.

You better understand Skeleton Warrior's Shield.

The Warrior's head jerked in my direction. It bore into me with its empty eye sockets before it started to jog right for me.

Saving Pain until I had figured out how to best face this new enemy, I next cast Alpha Bolt.

Swallowing back the dryness in my throat, I launched a magic bowling ball through the air at high speed.

I forced myself to watch as it barreled into the creature's shield, the structure holding firm, but the force so intense that the shield caught the Warrior and dragged it off its feet a couple of meters and back onto its rear.

You better understand Skeleton Warrior's Shield.

Even with the shield blocking the attack, the Warrior lost over 300 HP.

Before it was able to get to its feet I had already engulfed it in Heal twice, driving its HP into the red.

When it did reach its feet, its controlled demeanor had fled in face of the first emotion I had seen on any of the summoned monsters I had faced. Rage.

There were no facial features to give away such emotion. Its shield sagged to the side and its sword hung loosely in its hand as it puffed out its chest and jutted its jaw forward. It leaned forward and moved to lunge forward, but a third Heal spell seeped into its frame and drove the life from its restless bones.

Level Up!

Level Up!

Level Up!

I allowed my mana to regen before I attacked the next one. Decay to its shield, followed by Heal, which I was able to aim directly at its shield. It barely harmed the mob, but it accomplished what I was waiting for.

You have learned Skeleton Warrior's Shield!

I ignored it as the monster headed my way. Two Heals later, followed by an Alpha Bolt to the head and it was over.

What I had just learned about Creature Observation would certainly come in handy. The passive version of the skill allowed me to learn Blue Magic just by watching. If I activated it, then it worked like an observation skill.

After knowing that I needed to target the Warrior's Sword to see it in action, I acquired that after defeating the next warrior.

Casting Skeleton Warrior's Shield for the first time, a bone as thick as a knife handle formed in my empty hand, the bone growing before my eyes, expanding into a large oval about the size of a kite shield and weighing maybe five pounds. The face of the shield was made up of rows of rib-like bone, one on top of the other in neat rows. At the edge all around was a seamless mass of bone with a rough, almost ragged edge. It cost 50 Mana Per Minute to use. With my mana pool, I didn't think twice of leaving it active.

I unsheathed my knife from my belt. The Skeleton Warrior's Sword cost the same amount of mana, but when cast, the bone engulfed the dagger I was using, its bone blade extending beyond the steel tip another six inches. The blade took the shape of the dagger, making a great piercing weapon, and surprised me further by producing a skin parting edge I found as I tested its sharpness.

Healing myself, the parted skin of my finger knit itself back together.

Seeing I had just leveled, I said, "Leaderboard," out of habit. When nothing happened I started looking around as if something was broken. When I remembered this wasn't a game I facepalmed. Well, it was worth a shot.

It was time to get serious. Each of these creatures was at a higher level than me. They also ranged from levels 100-115.

Chapter 10 – Lydia

Light Orb appeared between two Skeleton Warriors. There was little hesitation before they were both slashing through the immaterial light.

I sighed.

At first, I had feared these creatures, but despite their superiority to lower level skeletons, they were still little more than a pile of bones pretending to be alive.

Directing Light Orb to move away from an incoming attack, one of the skeletons whiffed, missing entirely.

Casting a Decay spell didn't even grab its attention. Pain was noticed even less if that was possible.

Instead of immediately finishing them off with my fairly high-level Healing spell, I redirected Light Orb to begin moving, encircling the Skeleton Warriors as they chased after it.

If I was honest, I was living in a horror movie. It felt like a hidden DJ would start to play suspenseful music as if something was going to jump out and get me if I wasn't paying attention. What was a man to do? Change the music.

I began singing under my breath, "Let the bodies hit the floor. Let the bodies hit the floor," as the Skeleton Warriors bumped into each other and did a terrible job of coordinating their attacks.

The rear skeleton shifted his head from side to side to try to get a better view around its frontline friend.

Swing after swing of the front skeleton's sword cut through the ball of light, as it chased it in its orbit, then swung again.

After a few seconds of frustration, the rear skeleton gave up trying to find its way around the other skeleton and raised its sword to intercept the Light Orb. As its sword flashed forward, the other creature's skull ran interference, a lopsided skull cap was parted from its head.

The severely wounded skeleton turned around to meet its attacker. Instead of attacking, it looked right through the other skeleton, looking for an enemy that didn't seem to exist.

Taking its place in the rear, it waited a few seconds as the other skeleton danced and slashed at the orb. Seeing no way around, it ignored the other skeleton and lopped off its arm.

They were low enough on HP that I hit them both with a Heal spell, not willing to lose their experience for the sake of entertainment.

More and more I had found myself needing a change from the repetition.

Get back to work, Elorion.

Remembering the imp's conversation, I rolled my shoulders, cast a healing spell on myself and determined to refocus on spell and personal leveling.

To make up for it I spammed the room with six or seven Light Orbs and drenched the Skeleton Warriors with Healing spells. At level 68, my Healing spell was two hitting even the 2k HP Warriors. It was by far my fastest leveling spell, other than Decay that was at level 94.

Leveling up my personal level had become much harder once I reached level 100. I calculated I needed at least three times the experience I had needed before. That's why I had been here for the last six hours straight and only reached level 109. Still, my mana per minute was growing more and more with every point of Wisdom.

The bonus for reaching level 100 was a worthless one for me.

Power Nap

When you sleep, you recover your HP and exhaustion twice as fast. Passive.

***

I remained invisible as I returned to base to sell loot and fill my belly with something hot and juicy.

My reason for remaining invisible was to keep from having the other humans see me. This wasn't because of any antisocial inclination of mine, but just the opposite. I knew if I allowed myself to stop and chat it would take very little to convince me to join them.

The first group I saw was the strength guy's group. It had shrunk a little since last time I had seen them stroll into the cafeteria boasting about their first hunt. Before there had been at least ten of them, and now it was seven.

I stopped momentarily to see how they had progressed while staying on the other side of the room so that none of them could unintentionally attack or bump into me. They had confiscated one of the corners of the room near the entrance where they were just starting to take on the Skeleton Scouts. Their level was really too low to do more than take a couple at a time. I knew firsthand how dangerous these scouts could be. They would have leveled quicker if they wouldn't have moved up this quickly.

Their leader had grown even more in size since the last time I had seen him. Checking his level, I saw he was level 67 and his name was Skyler. I hadn't quite doubled his level yet, but it was nice to see staying up all night had been worthwhile. If you considered the jump in experience needed to progress after level 100, then it was safe to say I had actually accomplished more than the number seemed to indicate.

Besides just getting larger, which I assumed was from increasing his strength, he still wore the skull cap but had also gained a red fur vest with black feathers flaring out over his shoulders. Odd, but it looked thick enough to probably make for decent armor at this level. His weapon was basically a granite rock in the shape of a shoe fastened to the end of a three-foot shaft. In other words, a stone sledgehammer.

Two of his followers looked to be following his character build, likely pumping strength and even wielding the same weapon, but minus the helm and armor. I just hoped they were taking advantage of their own talents. As tempting as it was to make a hybrid character, if I hadn't gone with what would work best for my own talents, then I would be nowhere near as far along as I was now.

There was another melee guy with them dual-wielding knives. He was doing his thing, which would probably be better in the long run anyways.

The other three were casters.

A black guy with cornrows wore a baggy shirt tucked in, to his too-baggy pants and his pant legs tucked into a pair of brown leather boots. It made him look like a monk of sorts. Since he wielded no weapon, I thought that might be what he was going for until he held up both hands and called, "Pulling!"

A crystal blue mass floated from his hands like a large snowflake. It wasn't a fast spell, but when it hit the nearest sword-wielding Skeletal Scout from behind there was an obvious movement debuff even though there was no obvious frost or freezing effect.

It was only when it turned that the other casters attacked. Fire no larger than a golf ball sizzled into the skeleton's chest cavity, quickly followed by a rock?

I almost forgot to stay silent, choking back a laugh when I saw the rock magically pop out of nowhere in the female caster's palm and shoot forward instead of being thrown. She could have just as easily bent over, grabbed a rock, and thrown it.

With a sigh, I had to remember it would probably become a much more impressive spell as it leveled.

As soon as the skeleton was in range, the sledge brothers went to work sending a nonstop barrage of stone crashing down on the skeleton.

The skeleton didn't bother fending them off with his sword, instead it held up its other arm and blocked the blows while trying to thrust. Even with their impressive strength, it took about a dozen blows to its arm before it collapsed. That was the difference between levels. The skeleton was 76.

After the arm collapsed, a few strikes to the skull and rib cage sent it crumbling to the ground.

I stayed long enough to see them take on an archer. These were at least level 80, so I feared I would have to step in.

It started the same way. The ice monk sent a snowflake at the archer, striking it in the pelvis. The fire and earth mages' attacks weren't as delayed this time, hitting moments later.

Instead of waiting, Skyler and the sledge boys ran at it.

Even after getting hit, the archer's bow was bent. Seeing the three guys running at it, the archer aimed at the more imminent threat and released.

Skyler didn't even try to dodge, instead, he let the arrow hit him high on the chest. It stuck there. It didn't look like it sunk too deep, but I saw him squint away the pain. It didn't slow him.

When they reached the archer who was about to release another arrow, Skyler grabbed the bow with one hand and jabbed his giant hammer into the archer's face.

With the bow in one hand and the sledge in the other, he wound his arms up over his head and drove them down, one after the other.

The other sledges joined him and they beat the crazy tough skeleton into submission.

Even though there weren't professions like in some RPGs, he seemed to have the perfect personality for a real tank.

I left them, finding my old group fighting zombies.

It was immediately obvious without even using Creature Observation that they had already caught up to Skyler's group. Instead of moving on to Scouts before they were ready, Aeris and the others were systematically mass killing the rotten meat-bags. The experience they were taking in, even if it was less per kill than the other group, was at least twice as much if you considered how many more kills they were getting in the long run.

Aeris also had a new Wind spell allowing her to knock a group of them off their feet if they were close enough.

Swallowing back a knot in my throat, I didn't stay any longer. The lure to say hi was too strong.

There was one last group that I passed who were fighting zombies. If you can call two people a group. They both seemed to be stealth users, but one used a short sword and the other was a water mage. I didn't think the water bubble surrounding the zombie's head would do any good, but at least the guy was leveling his spells.

Their invisibility spell seemed to work differently than mine. They weren't completely invisible but seemed to be cloaked in shadow. It was pretty obvious to the naked eye, but the zombies didn't seem to notice them at all.

Maybe the water bubble engulfing its head was to further help their stealth?

***

As I entered the cafeteria, I stopped short. I was still invisible, but I had been stomping around loud enough that an old deaf goat would have noticed my presence. Instead, she didn't even seem to notice as she sat at one of the stone lunch tables staring off into the distance.

It was the same blond girl with black rimmed glasses that Aeris and Olivia had convinced to join us for food after our first hunt. To my shame, I hadn't even noticed she hadn't been with them. This time her loaf of bread was nibbled on.

Stepping back to leave her alone, I hesitated. It was one thing to not join the others because I thought they'd convince me to join them, but just ignoring her was cruel.

Sighing, I moved to uncast invisibility, when I heard footsteps scurrying toward us from the direction of the merchants.

Stepping out of the doorway, I was just in time as a familiar guy rushed by. It was the guy with curly blond hair that had originally been following Skyler's group. Using Creature Observation I saw his name was Chris.

"Lydia! I got good news. The halfling said he would sell me the *Basic Alchemy For Newbies* book for only 5,000 copper. That's half price!"

Alchemy? I guessed that was her talent. 5k was still a pretty extreme amount. Maybe in a couple of weeks or as much as a month, but it wouldn't be a quick road to that much coin.

She didn't say anything, but she did turn ever so slightly and feigned a grin.

It really didn't surprise me seeing him here trying to help her. I remembered how friendly he was when we first met. It was foolish for him not to be trying to get stronger, but generous all the same.

Well, there wasn't really much I could do for her that he wasn't already. Instead of escaping, I removed invisibility and walked toward the other end of the room to order my food. I nonchalantly threw them both a heal as I walked by. It would do little more than heal their exhaustion, but it was the least I could do. I nodded when they looked up.

"Hey!"

I almost fell on my face. The mostly mute girl had just called out as if I had bashed her over the head with a ten-pound pretzel.

Standing just past them on the other side of their table I turned to face her.

She wasn't looking at me but was holding her glasses six inches from her nose, examining them like they were a foreign object.

Chris was just as shocked as I was, standing still as a crippled ghost. It was just as obvious to him as it was to me that something impossible just happened.

"What did you do?!" she asked. Peering up at me with her mouth hanging open.

"Uh. I healed you."

"I can see," she said under her breath. "My prescription wasn't bad, but now..."

"Oh," was all that I could think to say. I was as surprised as she was.

"Thank you!" she said, before jumping up and running at me. She hugged me and continued to say, "Thank you! Thank you! Thank you!"

"Heh. You're welcome. How about some food. You guys hungry?" I said, smiling and trying to keep myself from turning red.

Without really waiting for their permission, I wiggled away from her and went to get us all a meal.

CHAPTER 11 – POWER LEVELING

A potent aroma of mouthwatering goodness had soaked my plate with meat juice. *Beloved steak!* I had eaten a t-bone so big it could mask a zombie and make him attractive. After some food and the selling my goods, it was time to get back to work.

Healing myself helped fight off any dreariness I felt coming on from a full stomach. It felt wrong not to sleep even though I knew in body and mind my Healing spell had succeeded. I might never need to sleep again.

Skeleton Archers came after the Warriors. Just like the first time I had met the bow-wielding Scouts, I feared ranged attackers more than the melee fighters. If I wasn't paying attention, I could end up with an arrow in the back.

The bows these archers possessed varied. There was both a recurve and longbow. The Scout's bows had been short children's bows in comparison. Remembering the arrows I dodged before, I scoffed at the idea that they were children's bows. There was no doubt, this would be dangerous.

The first archer I killed gave me the customary bonus experience and two levels. They were more aware with a wider radius of sensitivity. There still wasn't any teamwork, but for the first time, they seemed aware of one another. They were also level 120 to 140. The good news was that they had 1800 HP, 200 less than the Warriors. In a few levels, I could one hit them with my Healing spell and Alpha was already powerful enough to do just that.

Foregoing any Decay or Pain leveling, I focused on killing them quickly to limit the number of arrows flying at my head. My Skeleton Warrior's Shield would likely save my life, but there was no way I was going to test it.

The slow process of finding one, or at the most two, mobs alone began.

I had hoped that the skeletons' bows would be a Blue Magic spell I could learn, but instead, they were just higher quality weapons. It made sense really. What body part would make a good bowstring? Hair? Sinew? I cringed at the thought.

An hour later Heal reached level 90 and the experience needed to reach the next level doubled. I had a feeling hitting level 100 would be as good of a surprise as reaching 100 in a stat. More importantly, I was suddenly able to one hit the Archers.

The real power leveling had begun!

I saved 300 MP for an emergency cast of Alpha Bolt, that now cost 246 MP and a few Heals that now cost 10 MP each to cast. With the rest of my mana, I unleashed my full arsenal of Heal and Alpha Bolts. Entire rooms of archers were wiped out in a few minutes. I began to ignore whether they could see through my invisibility because of all my casting and strolled from room to room. The danger of their arrows had nearly disappeared after I was able to finish them with a single cast. I went from level 122 to 132 in less than two hours.

Decay maxed out at level 100 after I had continued using it, giving me no bonuses except that it now cost 1 MP. I completely removed it from my spell leveling strategy. I hadn't really had the opportunity to take advantage of it fully. I killed these too quickly to use the cast Decay and wait method to get the full use out of the spell. Eventually, I was sure I would run into something where it would become necessary.

You'd think my boredom would return now that I was quickly slaughtering the things, but they had gone from the most dangerous monster to an easy one with the simple advancement of a spell. I was getting stronger.

I allowed myself to bask in the joy of progression. It felt like I'd had just discovered energy drinks for the first time.

An archer's bowstring drew back. It took little aim to get me in its sights.

My empty casting hand was relaxed at my side. The bone enhanced dagger was looped in my belt and my shield was sitting lazily low. I dared the creature to release its string. In anticipation, I held myself back as long as possible.

I saw the bow snap into action before I heard the twang of the bow.

My hand shot up, a partially developed Alpha Bolt already forming in my hand as it rose to meet the arrow.

Leaning to the side, I positioned myself in case I had taken my dare too far.

The arrow was a blur that screamed into the developing ball of purple energy. It splintered into oblivion where it met Alpha Bolt, shearing off in all directions. My shield and leather vest caught most of the splinters, but one pierced me in the muscle between my shoulder and my neck, and another in the meat of my palm. Alpha Bolt continued to grow.

Heat rose up in my chest and my jaw flexed. I nearly screamed at the bloodless thing, but instead, I let Alpha Bolt fly; redirecting it at the last moment toward the archer's head.

The skull of the archer was pummeled into powder before it even hit the floor. Its vertebrae tumbled like dominoes followed by the rest of its corpse.

If the splinter in my neck was any closer to center mass it could have really been dangerous. Removing the splinter half as thick as a pencil, and a thinner but much longer one from my palm, I left them on the floor as I healed myself. I had only lost about 92 HP in total, but real pain was... just painful.

As I started to rebuke myself, I forced myself to remember I wasn't a bot or machine. I feared a monster that was strong enough to think it could challenge the Head Mistress. It would be here at any time. I needed to level up as quickly as possible, but the repetition was getting to me. Even with my ability to heal away my exhaustion, I didn't have the discipline for this.

Remembering the pain I felt when the imp taught me the blue spell Pain, I shook my head. I better learn the needed discipline quickly.

***

Once I had hit level 140 in the early evening, I found a side tunnel to sit back and have a snack in. The stone bricks were the same color and size in this long hall I found myself in. Four people could fit shoulder to shoulder, but the length of the room was at least forty meters to its end. A door faced me, unlike any door I had seen in all my time in the underworld.

The frame wasn't arched, but square. It was a single door, but large enough that even someone ten feet tall would be comfortable using it. The door itself was white stone, with charred soot around the edges of the door and frame. Had there been a fire?

I stuffed some jerky into my mouth as I approached it and started to examine it closer. Besides the soot, stone seemed like an odd material to make a door out of. The door hinges were solid brass and much thicker than I remember seeing in my old life in the world above.

Sitting down at a comfortable distance, I considered seeing what was behind it instead of moving on from the Skeleton Archers. This was the first room I had entered with a hall and door to another room. Since I usually ignored rooms with doors and used those that were mostly doorless to limit the noise I made, I knew there were probably others like this.

It might be wise to find a side tunnel anyways to kill the repetition. I suspected that the creatures I had been facing in the main rooms of the labyrinth were nothing more than training wheels created by the Mistress so that we would have an easy time leveling up. The more we grew in strength the more energy she would leech from us. It only made sense she would try to make leveling easy as well. My fear was that once the opposing Lich arrived to attack the Mistress, and us, even if I was stronger, how would I fair against intelligent creatures that had likely lived in this world their entire lives? My strength didn't mean anything if a monster that I should easily be able to defeat killed me because of my lack of knowledge.

There was also the very real threat that the Lich and whatever army it brought with it would have to pass through the main passage I was used to hunting in. I didn't want to test my Invisibility spell against whatever was coming. If it thought it could take on the High Mistress than it was likely it would be able to see me.

The door handle wasn't round, but an iron bar jutting out and bent to accommodate a much bigger hand than mine. Despite that and the door's weight, I was able to pull open the door without much difficulty. The world that opened up to me was nothing like the stone halls of my hunting grounds. Red and brown stone mixed with gray in a cavern of uneven walls and a ceiling that peaked so high I couldn't see its top. Rock and worn stone met my foot as I stepped into the new room or cave.

There was still a dim light that filled the lower twenty feet or so of the cavern here. It was pale with an unknown source. In the distance a warmer light mixed with it, this seemed to have a source, but there was only one way to find out for sure.

Placing a plastic bag that held a quarter of the two pounds of beef jerky that was originally its contents into my inventory, I moved forward as silently as I could manage.

I expected more undead, so my nerves kept steady. As I got closer to the light, its source was clear. Multiple small fires were lit. What was their fuel, the rock itself? In the orange light, the walls became clearer and my eyes relaxed a bit. I hadn't realized I was squinting.

Soot covered the walls and floor in patches where other fires had been. *What is that all about? I could go for some BBQ!*

Fire suddenly sprayed across the room directly toward me, billowing into a ball of flame against the wall at my side.

I froze where I stood. It had just missed me.

The little devil that blew it out of his mouth was three feet tall with crimson skin and ears that rounded up into points like little horns. It was humanoid in appearance with a black skinned mug that reminded me of a flat nosed dog. Its eyes were more feline than canine.

Even after its flame filled the room with light, it didn't notice me. So it hadn't been aiming for me.

Creature Observation told me it was a Fire Imp and about level 100 with 1200 HP. An easy one hit for Alpha Bolt. I considered testing Heal on it. This would be a good test for Light Magic. I suspected a lot of creatures in the Underworld were weak against it, but that didn't mean all of them were. I knew the normal imp I had killed had been, but this was a Fire Imp. Shouldn't it have a nature of fire?

Then it came to me. Pain! Pain should actually work against this creature since it wasn't undead and actually had a body. That should give me the time to test Heal on it, and if that didn't work then Alpha Bolt.

Still oblivious to me, the Fire Imp had gotten closer as it studied the wall it had just scorched.

I took a look around to make sure the two of us were alone. Somehow I had missed the little hot tamale and it was lucky I hadn't stepped into its spray of fire.

When I was sure I was alone, I cast Pain.

Not only did the stun work, but I almost felt sorry for it as it fell to the ground wide-eyed.

Heal followed right after Pain, but its effects shocked me almost as much as Pain had the Fire Imp. Not only had Heal not killed him, but it seemed to lessen the effects of Pain.

The muscles in my back clenched in panic as I began casting Alpha.

It was then that it saw me. Its wide eyes turned down into a snarl. When it opened its mouth I knew what was coming.

Alpha flew after reaching its full size, a ball of power twice as large as the Fire Imp's head.

If any flame escaped its mouth its head was crushed before it could harm me.

I got another level thanks to the first kill bonus experience.

For being such a low level it had certainly given me a surprise.

Well, that answered my question about the light element. I wouldn't be all-powerful down here just because of gaining the ultimate element. Man, was I thankful for Alpha Bolt! If it wasn't for that I would have had to try to kill the imp melee-style. That would not have been a fun experience.

Another idea came to me. I was very interested in finding out if the flames it blew out of its mouth was a creature skill I could learn with Creature Observation. Since I hadn't gotten a pop-up yet, and the first Fire Imp surprised me, I didn't think I had really concluded one way or the other yet.

Letting myself settle for a moment, I soon moved on to find another Fire Imp to observe.

The room seemed to end after another hundred feet or so but that was because it split off in two directions. I considered stopping there because of the danger of getting lost in a cave. Because there were only two large tunnels that continued and no small ones to confuse things, I took the tunnel on the left. Almost immediately I ran into another Fire Imp.

Did I say another? Make that three. They were actively scorching one part of the wall after another.

I stood there at a momentarily safe distance and watched as thin streams of flame spewed from their mouths. They seemed to have control of how wide the flame spread, but at the end, it always engulfed its target in a ball of fire.

It was not much time before I got the first pop-up.

You better understand Flamethrower!

I wasn't sure what I was looking for. Watching the creature itself, it breathed in through its nostrils, its chest expanded, and then it bent forward to blow its fire. There was no way to better observe it unless I let Flamethrower be cast on me and that wasn't happening. I couldn't use the same tactics I used on the Skeleton Warrior either. How could you attack fire to see how it reacted?

The temperature this close to the Fire Imps wasn't exactly comfortable. I spent at least five minutes watching them before my sweat was starting to annoy me. Was there another way?

I looked at Creature Observation closer. What was strange was that it didn't describe itself as an active or passive skill, yet I was about to use it as both. I had an idea.

My mouth dropped open and elation rose up in my chest. Thankfully magic was controlled by the will, otherwise I probably never would have figured this out. My idea had been to cast Creature Observation as a spell instead of a skill. As a skill, it always just gave me basic information about the creature. I went to activate Creature Observation, while trying to push mana into it.

You have unlocked Force Learn!

With a thought, I was able to execute Creature Observation as a spell for the first time. I felt energy, or a pressure, gather around my eyes. As a Fire Imp leaned forward to vomit up its flame, the mana around my eyes surged into my eyes themselves, crystallizing my vision for a split second. It was as if the creature was suddenly in front of me frozen. I had a front row seat to examine the creature and that moment in time as well. Not only did it work, but only cost 10 MP. I immediately I got the pop-up I had been hoping for.

You have learned the Blue Magic Flamethrower!

To celebrate I gave everyone a shot of Pain and Alpha Bolted them one after another.

Sadly, there was no other blue magic I discovered while fighting them. Their cave just kept going. I made it a mile in before I turned back.

Why they kept frying the walls was a mystery to me. Maybe there was something more to it, but I didn't have the time to do the research.

If I wasn't in a hurry, it might be fun to explore while looking for other creatures in this area of the dungeon. They were too low of a level to hunt for experience, but I had certainly enjoyed meeting them.

Back to skeletons for now, but next time I got bored, I would start peeking my head into the side rooms to see if there was anything interesting I could find. Getting extra blue magic was worth an extra fifteen-minute detour here and there.

***

Fighting the Skeleton Archers allowed me to level up a lot faster than all the other mobs that came before them. It was because I was able to one hit them, which nerfed the danger they possessed. After I made it to level 145, I moved on.

The stone of the next area was of a deep turquoise and very reflective, filling the room with more light than I was used to. That wasn't the only way that it was unique. The number of skeletons that filled the room was three times more than the most populous room before it. Not only was there more of the enemy, but there was also a variety of them.

Both Skeleton Warriors and Archers filled the room. They were broken up into groups of three to five and actually walked in loose formations, promising to be more difficult than anything I had faced yet.

It's about time!

Checking them with Creature Observation, I confirmed that they were higher in level than the Warriors and Archers from before. The Warriors were now as high as level 130 and the Archers 150. The biggest difference was going to be their HP. The Archers now possessed 2200 which was close to my range of one hitting them. The Warriors were pushing 2500 and since some of the groups had more than one, their shields would be a problem if they worked well together.

Besides the added challenge of finally fighting something that might be semi intelligent, I was also a level away from reaching level 100 in my Lesser Heal spell. There was a possibility that, unlike Decay that simply maxed out in progression, that Lesser Heal would evolve into a better version of itself. I was almost sure of it.

The desire to see what happened when Lesser Heal reached 100 determined my strategy against my new enemies.

I snuck into the first room that was longer than it was wide like a gothic ballroom. It reached at least 100 meters to the other end of the room and had an estimated 150 skeletons packing it tight. My old strategy of getting one skeleton by itself wouldn't work here. There was no way I could attack without having other groups of skeletons joining them. The best I could hope for was keeping the adds down to one to two groups.

Still, a strategy presented itself. I entered one of the side rooms that had an arched doorway without any doors. I was in a wide room, but not very deep. The stone walls were thick here, so it would do the job. I readied my shield as I turned to face the enemy just outside my improvised kill-box from the back of the room.

The closest group was made up of two Warriors and an Archer. My first target was obvious enough.

After taking a deep breath to make sure my nerves were as ready as they could be, I cast Lesser Heal on the Archer.

As I feared it had depleted all except the last 5% of his HP. He didn't look in good shape, but I now had three Skeletons turning to face me.

The cast time on Lesser Heal was pretty minimal. I could pull off about two casts a second, although there was another half second delay before the spell reached the enemy at this distance. My second Lesser Heal reached the Skeleton Archer before the Warriors really got moving.

I didn't delay and started to spam Lesser Heal as quickly as I could. The first Warrior was dead before he reached the room. If the other Warrior hadn't been out of view from behind the wall it would have died much quicker.

It came in view when it rounded the corner to join me in the room.

Another Lesser Heal was already on its way and rammed into its shield. The damage was reduced significantly.

I aimed low for the next one. Lesser Heal nearly finished it and I followed it up with another.

The three Skeletons were defeated before any of them really got close, but the fight had just begun.

Already another Skeleton Warrior was entering the room.

I began by blasting low. There was no time to mess with their shields.

Even with a direct hit, it took another cast to finish it.

Two more Skeleton Warriors filled the entrance, struggling to fit through at the same time.

I smirked.

As their bodies hit the floor, the beginning of a bone barricade started to form. It wouldn't last long. Their bodies would dissolve in a few seconds, but there was more where that had come from.

Level Up!

I'll take it!

An archer stood behind the fallen Warriors, arrow nocked and drawn. Its arrow released before Lesser Heal countered.

Raising my shield as I ducked, the arrow struck solid, high on my shield, but spun off to the ground. I hadn't wanted to ever have to test my shield, but that was pretty impressive.

Even as the Archer fell, more Warriors reached the room's entrance.

At first, their numbers worked to my advantage. They tried to pile in and instead ended up bones and dust helping to block their group members from getting to me.

There was really no danger of running out of mana even if the entire room of Skeletons came at me. It was my rate of fire that would ultimately hold me back. I defeated four or five groups, or about twenty skeletons, before one Skeleton Warrior pushed past the others and the small barricade of ankle high bones.

It fell before it got too close to me, but another Skeleton had already come in behind. A second was behind him and there seemed to be no end to them. Perhaps I had really pulled the entire room.

After finishing the closest Warrior, I sent an Alpha Bolt into the shield of one at the entrance, knocking him back into the incoming horde.

It bought me a few seconds.

I shifted my position heading to one of the side walls, all the while continuing to fire off Lesser Heal. Since the room was wider than it was deep, this gave me more distance between me and the skeletons. In addition, I hoped that they may lose aggro if I was less visible.

That didn't seem to be the case. They kept coming. The only benefit was that once the Skeletons entered the room, I was finishing them off fast enough that they couldn't look to the others to know where I was but had to take the second or two to search for my action location.

Seeing that this was the case, I place myself in the corner closest to the entrance and ducked low with my shield up, making myself as hard to see as possible. Invisibility was doing me no good because I was casting too quickly, but the angle gave me a slight advantage.

With most of the Warrior's gone, the Archers started to enter the room.

Even as I killed the first one, an arrow grated against my shield.

I received a pop-ups but there wasn't even time to glance at it.

My breathing quickened. The Archers found me much quicker than the Warriors.

With a clenched jaw, I ducked lower to make myself even smaller.

Another arrow rapped on my shield, but I never stopped casting Lesser Heal.

Soon enough, arrow after arrow was pelting me in my corner while four Skeleton Archers bombarded me.

An Alpha Bolt found one, knocking him out of the picture for a time as I finished another with Lesser Heal. If a Skeleton Warrior joined I had no idea what I was going to do, but I was seriously in a tight spot.

When an arrow hit the ground between my feet, I decided it was better not to just stay here.

Rolling to the side, I threw a Lesser Heal, finishing the Archer I had hit with Alpha Bolt. With two Archers left, I had an idea.

With my shield in front of me, braced with both arms, I bull-rushed the closest Archer and plowed into it.

The collision was more than I had expected, jarring my shoulder, and only knocking it back. *Operation Skeleton Baked Oven!*

I threw my arm forward, and willed Flamethrower to activate for the first time. When the energy didn't shoot down my arm but up into my throat, I looked at the Skeleton Archer like I was about to be sick.

I dropped my shield as much as moved it out of the way as my stomach muscles tensed and something felt like it was going to erupt out of me. A red light flicked on under my nose and energy spewed out. A long stream of flame shot forward, hitting both skeletons. Remembering my entire point of casting the spell, I shifted my head to redirect the flame at their bows. Both bowstrings were rendered useless! The whole experience had felt like vomiting except without the disgusting taste.

In the confusion of losing their weapons, I finished them off with Lesser Heal.

Before I tested my luck that I had finished the last of them, I took a seat out of sight.

When I was breathing easier I check my pop-ups. The one about leveling up I had already seen, but the next one brought me back to my feet and I started bounding around the room like a bunny in a straitjacket!

Lesser Heal had reached level 100!

Heal has been unlocked!

This is the intermediate rank for Light Magic: Heal.

Heal

Base Heal of 1000 at level 1.

Cost 100 MP per cast.

If I was going to get a surprise like this from almost dying I would do it more often! Even though it cost twenty times the MP to cast Heal in place of Lesser Heal, with the double damage to undead and my damage bonuses I could now one hit these bums. Not to mention, I couldn't even imagine how powerful it was going to become as I leveled it.

I was still in for a long night, but it felt like I was finally getting somewhere.

Boney feet scurried in my direction. I stopped my celebration and let Invisibility take me.

I really needed to learn not to celebrate when there were hordes of undead within hearing distance. Regardless, I was still grinning from ear to ear and ready to try out my next level Heal spell.

CHAPTER 12- RETURNING FROM A

SLEEPLESS HUNT

Hours and hours had past. It was about time to return to my home base to sell a full inventory of goods and get some food. I had started my solo hunt 48 hours ago and besides a few other trips to town, I hadn't stopped since. So much had changed. I had reached level 192 in that time and was much more powerful. Still, there was one last thing I had to do before I headed back home.

Three blue slimes as tall as a large dog were communicating through the vibrations their bodies gave off. At level 120 they weren't even close to the highest level monster I had faced, but I was sure there was blue magic to learn from them. The green slimes that were level 100 gave me Fluid Body, which gave me physical resistance. Currently, it lessened 26% of all damage at spell level 87. I was hoping the blue slime would give me magic resistance in a similar fashion. So I watched.

Invisibility had started out costing 200 mana per minute. Thanks to constantly keeping it activated it had leveled a lot and now cost 44 mana a minute. It was level 78. I couldn't imagine there being multiple spell levels, like novice, intermediate and advanced. Once it reached level 100 I suspected it would be maxed out.

This cost over time didn't bother my hunting speed anymore. I had over 463 mana regenerating every minute. I had room to spare.

My biggest accomplishment was the Lesser Heal had reached level 100! Already Heal was doing well over 1680 points of base healing at level 17 with spell cost reducing skills. Maxed Lesser Heal only cost 3MP with close to 800 healing without bonuses; with bonuses it was just over 2000. Last night had only required half the number of self-casts to stay awake after Heal had progressed to intermediate.

Then came my Alpha Bolt. It had started out costing a whopping 500 MP. As you can expect it was taking longer to level up. Now it was only level 61, but even then it had lowered the MP usage to 156 with level and bonuses. The damage had begun at 500. Now it was close to 2300. Not as good as Intermediate Heal, but if it was against anything that wasn't undead or evil alignment it was the way to go. These slimes were a perfect example. If it wasn't for this spell it would have been impossible for me to kill these magic resistant goo-blobs. It slipped by their defenses because it was element neutral.

So I waited and watched. Out of all the blue slimes, this was the highest level I had found at 121. Its two companions were 114 and 118. Then I saw what I was looking for. A single strand of blue electricity jumped from the highest level slime to its neighbor, and then to the last one. The blue electricity returned back to the initiator of the energy. I immediately cast *Force Learn*. A pop-up appeared!

Through observation, you have learned Fluid Mentality

Fluid Mentality

5% resistance to magic

Your resistance will grow as the spell levels

Finally! This was my first magic resistance blue spell. The cost of 100 MP was greatly lessened with my 40% reduced cost to cast bonuses. 60 Mana Per Minute at level 1!

Here's a quick list of the blue magic I had learned in the last two days.

Alpha

Decay

Invisibility

Skeletal Breast Plate

Skeleton Warrior's Sword

Skeleton Warrior's Shield

Flamethrower

Fluid Body

Fluid Mentality

It was a small list, but a great start!

Even after speaking with the Head Mistress about how I should level up, it wasn't as easy as just following her directions. She had confirmed that at 100 all of my stats would give a bonus. The bonus that Constitution and Dexterity would give could literally save my life later on. Increased speed or health; either of these seemed worth the points, but she hadn't even mentioned bothering with anything except putting 100 in intelligence. Perhaps she assumed I would add some to Constitution or Dexterity because it was the obvious thing to do. I was spamming Wisdom, so perhaps I should actually use the wisdom I had.

Thankfully I had not gotten these spells all at once because I would not have been able to level them up at the same time if that was the case. Here's a list of their base cost without leveling as an example. Invisibility costing 200 mana per minute at level 1, Skeletal Breast Plate 100 MPM, Skeleton Warrior's Sword and Shield 50 MPM a piece, and Fluid Body and Fluid Mentality 100 MPM each, so with my regeneration rate of just over 463 mana per minute it just wouldn't have cut it against the 600 MPM cost. After leveling everything up though and my 40% reduction in spell cost they now cost me approximately 200 MPM and that was with a new level 1 Fluid Mentality that still cost 100. Soon I would be able to have all of my MPM spells active with an excess 300 MPM.

Another theory presented itself. Perhaps the reason the Mistress directed me to max Wisdom was because of all the Mana Per Minute blue magic spells available. I didn't have too many spells yet myself, so I just wasn't sure, but it was a good possibility. I held off spending points in Constitution and Dexterity; at least for now. Currently, it would cost me 16 levels to reach 100 in both stats.

There was always the option of training outside of leveling up. Constitution and Dexterity were the type of stats I could also gain points in just by working out.

I had run into these slimes in one of my few mental breaks. The cavern here was much like the Fire Imp cavern except it was wet and the rock was smooth with stalagmites and stalactites in abundance. My only complaint was that they were more complex than the undead I had been fighting, but because of their lower level, the experience wasn't as good. It felt wrong, like they deserved more credit or something.

I was decked out in Skeletal Breast Plate that literally formed a magic breastplate over my leather armor made of solid bone. It looked amazing, as if I had thirty ribs on each side all sitting one upon another. I hadn't yet had the guts to test it out though. My shield, on the other hand, had caught a number of arrows, and I happily carried it everywhere I went. My bone-covered dagger I kept looped in my belt so that I could switch shield and casting hands.

With all of my MPM spells cast, I begin casting Pain. The Blue Slimes were only stunned a fifth of the 10-second timer, but it was still worth casting.

My Invisibility spell casting downtime had decreased. As an example, when I cast Alpha Bolt it only took about one and a half seconds to go completely invisible again. If you asked me what was better, bacon or invisibility, I'd say eating bacon while invisible of course! It was possible to chew slow enough that you didn't become visible. I know, because I tried it. You don't have to choose between the two, but it's easier to come by bacon if you have invisibility, so it's bacon's best friend.

The lowest level Slime was killed immediately after my first Alpha Bolt fired. I was able to cast Alpha one more time before the other two were able to respond. With one left alive, the 120 level Blue Slime threw its customary blue bullet which was easily blocked by my skeletal shield. My last cast brought his health down to dangerously low levels, but it wasn't finished yet. Another bullet flew at me as it started to slime its way toward me. There was really no hope for it. Alpha went off a final time and ended its life.

Eyeing my inventory I had two slots left for monster drops. I had forgone picking up ingredient type drops like zombie eyes and bones, instead sticking to the rare potion, weapons, armor and the odd ring or gemstone.

Heading back out of the slime area, I killed the odd mob. Not that it was necessary in my invisible state. Nonstop hunting made spell usage natural and I didn't have to think about what I wanted to cast anymore. I just reacted.

Back into the skeletons' domain, I decided to wipe the room quickly, since it was only filled with Skeleton Warriors. Not only were the undead weak against life magic, but also fire.

While standing in the very middle of the room, I clapped my hands together as loudly as I could. This would bring skeletons from the side rooms as well which was my intention.

A few that were too close to reaching me I cast Lesser Heal on killing them instantly.

When a group was within the required five meters I grinned from ear to ear. This never got old. With a deep breath, I exhaled, casting Flamethrower at the same time. Fire spewed from my mouth engulfing everything within five meter before me. Roasted bones dropped like toothpicks in a bonfire.

I had to spin to make sure none of them got the better of me, but even though the warrior's speed was quicker than a human's average walking pace, I still considered them slow. The room was cleared in less than two minutes.

The experience was almost better than terrible. Doing this another 75 or 76 times would net me another level. That was because these skeletons were only around level 100 and I had just leveled. It definitely wasn't the best place to level up at this stage in the game.

Drops scattered the floor and two caught my eye. A rare healing potion that healed 30% of my health over a minute and the short sword I grabbed. Even with my healing ability, potions were still back up for the occasion I ran out of MP. The sword was magic but on the cheaper side. I identified it as adding +10 to strength. Since my 3 healing potions stacked in my inventory I still had a single slot left.

Sure that I would get a drop on the way, I headed back to base. I wasn't terribly deep in the labyrinth. Only the Skeleton Scouts and Lesser Skeleton areas came before I would reach the Decrepit Zombies, newb Skeletons and then home base, so it would be twenty minutes or so to get back.

As I entered each room, I took the time to clear it with Flame, Alpha and Heal.

An elite Skeleton Scout with a speed aura was waiting for me in the scout area. It caught me in its sights as my Invisibility lessened due to my constant casting. Its name was Jimmy Quickshot. A single cast of Heal owned him, but his drop was nice. It was a pair of greaves that added an entire +30 Dex. The drop was a little above average for this part of the dungeon.

This was typical. Most mobs dropped something similar to their characteristics. It followed a logical pattern like so. Only skeletons with swords dropped swords. Elite mobs with high health dropped Con items. Slimes dropped crystals or slime. Well, you get the picture.

***

When I reached the base, I deactivated Invisibility and headed into the dining hall. The imp that had escorted me to the Mistress was there waiting for me. His respect for me had skyrocketed after that night, and my skeleton armor had improved it even further.

"Good evening, sir. Will it be a steak and taters again?"

"Thank you, yes. That sounds perfect."

I grabbed the plate from him after handing over the 220 coins I owed him, plus an extra 10 coins for remembering what I had eaten the night before.

He was surprisingly warm toward me as he nodded his goodbyes. I guessed after killing another imp and earning him 30 silver I had won a friend for life.

Having second thoughts, I turned back. "Tomorrow I would like steak as well, but could you make it with pasta in red sauce instead of roasted potatoes?"

"Of course, sir."

I flipped him a full silver coin to show him it pleased me. His face lit up.

Money had become much easier for me as of late. My steak and potatoes, yes with Ranch Dressing drenching them both, cost approximately 220 coins. Currently, I had over 14,000 coins. There were a few items I was saving up for specifically in the 20k range.

I healed myself with Heal, not Lesser Heal, since its effects refreshed me more and I had the mana to spare. Doing this before and after I ate had become my habit. It was so I wouldn't get tired from a full belly. I didn't want to have the Thanksgiving effect if I was going to go back to hunting as soon as I sold all my item drops.

Because of my constant hunting, I made sure I ate at least two full meals a day, not including the free bread and some jerky on the side that I had bought to tide me over while I was gone. I saw no reason to think nutrition deficiencies wouldn't hurt me as much here as they would before I learned magic. Besides that, I was 100% human and loved food.

After the steak, I loaded up my bread slot. My inventory allowed 10 bread to stack and 10 water bottles as well. Not that I used this much between hunting trips, but it was still better to be safe.

Next, I headed to the merchants. Only the dwarf was up this late, but he paid the best for weapons and armor anyway. The halfling and I did business every couple of trips, but there were only rare ingredients that he paid well for. He was happy to tell me what to look out for though.

The dark elf was the oddball out of the group. He would make an offer on everything but was always the lowest bidder. Every once in a while though he would pay much higher than the others.

My take this time around was nothing special, so the dwarf happily relieved me of my items and I was 2075 copper coins richer, or 20 silver and 75 copper.

I had only upgraded my armor once. It was another dark leather armor set that helped with Conceal and Fire, Ice and Nature Resist. It looked similar enough that all that was important was that 50% of Fire, Ice and Nature magic damage was cut. The set cost me the first 10,000 coins I had made.

With two rings on each hand, I had an additional 600 HP and 10% increase in HP regeneration. One added +25 to spot traps. It was the only one of its kind I had seen. In the two days I had been hunting I had yet to see a trap. The labyrinth had been designed by the Mistress and the old man so this was probably abnormal for the Underworld.

Other than that, everything was the same.

That didn't mean I wasn't in the market for something. There was a cloak of shadows for 20k that concealed 50% of noise that I might make. If I bought it I would have had nearly 80% noise concealment.

There was also a scepter that caught my eye and would give 50% bonus healing or damage to any healing spell. That was 26k, but I didn't think was as essential as the cloak yet. I was powerful enough that safety came before damage output. About two more trips before I would buy the cloak, I figured. That would be me some extra coin and not leave me broke.

As I turned to leave, I was startled to see Aeris standing there watching me. She wore a gray cloak with padded green leather underneath. It was a fairly average armor, but good protection for the price.

It couldn't be helped. I couldn't exactly insist the merchants deal with me when I was invisible.

Seeing my reaction, she placed her hands on her hips readying a rebuke. "So you are still alive!" she cheered sarcastically. "You know, if you are going to continue to insist on hunting alone you should at least check in with us instead of sneaking around. We won't know if you get in trouble, or worse, dead!"

This was the very reason I was sneaking around. To not be dissuaded. She didn't understand how dangerous things really were for us. No one was safe.

"I'm sorry. Time is of the essence."

"I know that. That doesn't mean you have to be a jerk. If only there was some kind of messaging system you could at least send me group or private messages, but there isn't."

"We should ask the Mistress if we can get cell phones. Do you think they would have reception down here?"

My bad joke worked. She struggled to hold back a chuckle.

"Very funny. But, more importantly, Elorion, are you doing okay?"

Her question hit me hard. I didn't answer right away. Did I even know the answer to her question? I'd been awake going at full speed for 48 hours and I wasn't tired. That wasn't exactly normal, or natural. "Considering everything, I am doing well. That doesn't make us safe."

"You keep saying that. Whatever. Are you sure you couldn't just hunt with us to level up? We are all close to level 100 already. Is the danger you are putting yourself in really worth it?"

Not sure how to explain it without saying that they were slowing me down I decided to show her.

"Here." I waved her over and brought up my status page.

CHARACTER SHEET

Name: Elorion Edwards

Race: Human

Age: 17

Level: 192

Health Points: 590+(800 items)=1390

Mana Points: 3460

Endurance: 400

Stats

Strength: 47

Dexterity: 58+(20 item)=78

Constitution: 59

Intelligence: 100

Wisdom: 705

"No way!" Her eyes widened. "192? How is that possible?"

"To be honest, with my healing spells I haven't had to sleep since I got here."

Somehow her eyes got even wider if that was possible. "That's not good."

"I have tested it out. It rejuvenates my body just like sleep would, including my mind. Boredom is the only thing it doesn't help. I could cast it on you if you wanted to get some hunting in tonight."

She immediately shook her head.

"Hunting alone out there really isn't my thing. Thanks though."

I cringed. "I know what you mean. Well." Internally, I was rebuking myself as the words left my mouth. "You could come with me. I was planning mostly on going to Skeleton Champions to hunt for items to sell. I'm close to the coin I need for a cloak I have my eye on."

Though it didn't hurt, I felt pressure where she hit my arm. "You idiot. You seriously face those things alone?"

"Yeah... Here. Let me try something." I cast Invisible on her and to my amazement, it actually worked. The 36 mana per minute that it normally would have cost me to cast it on myself was now doubled. This was incredibly convenient.

"What! What happened?!"

"You are invisible now. You should look ethereal to yourself and only visible to others if you move quickly or cast a spell. This is why I don't fear Skeleton Champions. They are quite easy actually."

"Fine. I'm going with you. Try your Healing out on me too then."

"Sure."

To my surprise, I could see the outline of her features even though she wasn't moving. Even her facial features were clear.

When Intermediate Heal hit her she looked down at her hands and all around like the world itself had changed. "This is totally cheating! So you really have gone the last three days without sleep… Elorion."

I shrugged.

"When are we leaving?" she asked.

"Now, if you're ready."

We partied up for the first time in two days. She was obviously not fully convinced being invisible would be enough, but her fears were quenched enough that she joined me. As I had feared, all it had taken for me to give in to my loneliness was to face one of the others. No, that probably wasn't completely accurate. All it had taken was for me to run into Aeris.

CHAPTER 13 - WIND MAGIC

As we headed through the labyrinth, I let her fight as she normally did so I could see how she had progressed. There were really only three spells that she used. Unlike blue magic where I had to learn mine from the creatures I ran across, her spells she learned from a spell tree. With enough experience she got different spells to choose from.

We both basically ignored the decrepit skeletons. When we reached zombies, she used Gust, the original spell she started with to blow them out of the way. The word blow might be a bit of an understatement. Gust was an area of effect spell that spanned 10 meters wide and it blew out from the caster. The closer the enemy to the caster the more violent the wind they faced. At twenty feet she blew them back off their feet a few meters. At ten feet they nearly caught air. A few feet away and they were nearly launched twenty feet in the air. In that way, it could be used to damage enemies as well.

Once she reached lesser skeletons she showed me her spell Gale. It was similar to Gust, but it funneled air into a tighter area and could literally launch even a fairly aerodynamic skeleton with little air resistance against the wall if it was close enough. She seemed to enjoy blowing one skeleton into another.

Such a kind girl was getting a kick out of skeleton bowling?

When we got to the scouts, she got serious. We weren't in any danger because of Invisibility, but she was used to having to fight after this point. The last spell she was hiding was called Wind Slash, and then she started to shine!

Depending on which way she swung her hand while casting it, an intensely compressed torrent slashed out toward the skeletons like the slash of a giant blade. If she swung it up and down a single skeleton would receive most of the damage from skull to groin. She could easily one hit even the Skeleton Scouts. If she swung her arm from side to side while casting, a slash about three meters in width cut across anything in her path. In this way, she could slash multiple monsters if they were close enough.

"Do you have control over how wide the slash is?"

"To a point, yes. I can try just flicking my wrist and the slash is only about a foot long. The more concentrated the slash the higher the damage, but it doesn't work well for skeletons since it's harder to aim. I have a tendency to get them between the ribs."

"It really is amazing." *This is the power of elemental mages I guess.*

If I didn't know better I'd think I saw her blush.

"Let me show you a few tricks I have learned myself." I redirected the conversation. "Honestly I was only brave enough to try this because of invisibility. It's pretty easy once you get the hang of it even without it though. Stand behind me. You get the monsters that come from that direction."

"Wait. What are you going to do?"

I grinned like a maniac and started to clap for all the skeletons to hear. They were really only a little stronger than Lesser Skeletons and wielded knives.

"All you have to do if you run low on mana is stop casting for about two seconds and you will disappear. They will try to hit where you are, but can't see you. The trick is just to walk to a new location without running into an enemy on the way. Oh, and don't run or your invisibility will be hindered."

"I hate you."

"You won't in a moment. Now the real fun begins!"

Continuing to clap, I cast Decay on all the skeletons in my range. Only one had to be taken out by Alpha because it was closer than the others. I liked things even. It just felt better to take out the largest group possible.

Aeris was attacking her skeletons way too early, but I didn't correct her. She would get the timing down soon enough.

I waited like normal and let them come. When about six had gathered within range, I turned on the furnace by casting Flame Breath. It created a wide fan of flame catching all six skeletons in its radius.

My partner screamed, not because of the skeletons, but the sudden bright light and heat coming from behind her.

After that group was finished, I teased, "Sorry. Forget to tell you about that part."

She growled from behind me, cast another Gust, then I felt a sharp kick to my rear that sent me to my knees.

"Elorion! You need to work on your manners!" Even if I had obviously frightened her, there was also humor in her voice.

Getting back to my feet I had to poke at her a little more, for fun's sake of course. "Forgive me, my lady. Could you turn on the air conditioning? Things are about to heat up again."

"Why don't you turn on the AC yourself! Guys are so lazy!"

"Suit yourself!"

I had to admit, while cooking some more skeletons, I hadn't felt this light-hearted since I was kidnapped.

We continued on and I explained more to her about what spells I had as we progressed. She agreed that Skeletal Breastplate, plus Skeleton Warrior's Shield and Sword were cool looking; handy too. I explained Alpha's element neutrality, Decay, and what I had learned about Healing magic.

I cast Lesser Heal on us after the fight and as she regained mana.

"Is that why your wisdom is so high? So you don't have to rest as often while you hunt?"

"Basically. The Mistress also recommended it because the bonuses would be worth it in the long run. She told me to get intelligence to 100 though. The Attribute Bonuses only come at 100, 1000, 10000 and so on."

"Oh, that's good news! I got lucky I guess," she mentioned. "I started out staggering my points between Wisdom and Intelligence because I wasn't sure which way to go. I think I will follow that advice as well and focus on Wisdom. I haven't put any stats in them since I got 100 in each. Well, besides about 20 in Constitution. Do you think I should do Con before Wisdom?"

"I don't think it would be a bad idea. The only reason I haven't yet is that I have defensive spells. Do you have any?"

"Besides wind magic being great for crowd control, my only defensive magic is an increase in speed if I ever have to run. No armor like that." She gestured toward my skeletal armor.

"Then I'd definitely do it. Perhaps later you can learn another elemental magic that has more defense options."

"I was thinking the same thing. I heard the new element spell book costs over 50,000 coins."

I stopped short. That meant there were other options than just sticking with blue and healing magic. "That's not too bad."

"Well, there's a catch. You can't learn a new element from the book itself. It just directs you to the location in the Underworld where you can learn it. There's more to it, but it's probably like a high-level quest."

It struck me then that everyone here really was a gamer. She thought like a gamer. It seemed ironic that the Underworld worked on similar principles that had only recently been created in the gaming world. Our experience with games made it easier to understand this world.

"What game did you play before you were brought here?" I asked her.

"Greece."

"Really? That's the Virtual Reality Online Multiplayer Game where you fight other players in massive wars with Greek weapons and formations…"

"Yup. I liked the strategy the best. What about you?" She grinned.

"I played Juggernaut."

"Sci-Fi Player versus Player, huh?"

"Yup. Plasma swords, laser guns, and concussion grenades. I wonder if there is a pattern to the games everyone that was kidnapped has played."

"There is. Greece, Juggernaut and Elite Tournament Online are the three games everyone seems to be picked from."

I looked at her sideways.

"If you would spend more time among the living you would know. We figured that out yesterday."

"Right." I surrendered.

"I'm always right. Girl power and all." She stuck her tongue out at me.

This was getting silly. I'd take silly over hunting alone any day. Shaking my head, I rebuked myself.

Room by room we cleared in a similar fashion. A few elites came at us, but there was no serious danger. Drops were average. In no time she gained 2 levels and she admitted my methods were worthy of praise but not in so many words. I gained another level myself and pumped Wisdom.

When we got past Skeleton Warriors to Skeleton Archers we ceased the old strategy and attacked smaller groups, quickly and in an overpowering fashion. I always stood in front of her since I had a shield and was better armored. It wasn't necessary. Not a single arrow flew our way.

It was as simple as her casting Gust and knocking them off their feet and the both of us competing to see who could kill them off first. The competition was fierce. I did higher damage and could often one hit them, but Wind Slash could hit more than one if they were close enough.

As we got closer to the Skeleton Champions, the stone walls began to change from basic large rectangles to smaller and smaller bricks. There were also pillars in places as the area changed.

We both agreed caution was a priority. Each champion was equipped with the same Skeletal Armor I wore, so they weren't just naked skeletons. They also had a variety of weapons, and some wore shields. I liked to consider them the first really complex monsters in the dungeon. Their tactics were just as advanced. They could full out sprint at you at a vicious speed and were handy with their shields.

This room was much wider than the average room, at least as wide as a football field. The side rooms had twin pillars marking each entrance.

In this first room it was possible to find solo mobs, so we would stay here until she got comfortable.

Our jesting slowed to a stop and teamwork became our focus. More than a single spell was needed to take them out. An Alpha Bolt to the leg was my preferred method to slow the enemy down on this level 150 monster. Without a leg, you moved much slower. Aeris's Wind Slash did an even better job at it because it could fracture both legs.

Here the battles took longer but the experience was much better. Especially for Aeris who was leveling up every half an hour. Perhaps I needed to bring some of the others here and power level them a bit. All I would ask for was free meals for life!

Skeletons were interesting opponents. Their real weak spot wasn't their skull, but their spine. It was hard to hit with their armor, but a good shot to the head or neck at the right angle and I could one hit them with Alpha. Channeling extra mana into my spell charged up its impact and made it even easier. Intermediate Heal was even more powerful, but cost the most mana so I cast it normally.

These mobs were a good example of how armor worked as well. The skeletal armor didn't have any magic resistance itself, but since magic had to be propelled from the caster to hit the target if the armor was between the wearer and the caster it took the damage from the magic first. Even something without magic resistance could block a spell, making shields and armor very useful.

It wasn't long before I couldn't help myself and showed her how easy it was to sneak up on a mob with Invisibility. We practiced for a while from different angles to determine what was the best part of their body to attack. Though it might be a bit morbid, if Aeris's Wind Slash was cast just right with a condensed width that focused the power, the skeleton's head would pop right off like a bottle cap. Seeing her laugh when it happened made me scratch my head at her personality.

Within two hours we were both filled up on loot and started to head back to sell. Something unexpected slowed our progress. The largest skeleton, perhaps 15 feet tall, stood at the entrance not letting us leave. Its skeletal armor was equipped, but instead of just a breastplate, his armor extended down his legs and across his arms. A large two-handed sword at least ten feet long was stabbed into the stone floor between us and the exit. No sneaking out this time.

Chapter 14 – The First Boss Monster

Before us was not just an elite skeleton but a real boss. The first one I had seen. Instead of a name, there was only a title.

The Decapitator

Boss Monster

Level 150

HP 50,000

MP 0

Str: 220

Dex: 40

Con: 300

Int: 10

Wis: 5

Description: With talent and hard work a person can become a master at their profession. Here stands a man that mastered his; the executioner of an ancient kingdom.

What kind of crazy description was that? Well, at least we were safe for now. With the food and water I had, we could last for days.

Somehow we must have triggered some kind of event that caused the boss to come out.

Too bad Pain didn't work on skeletons or this fight would be easy. Without it, I just wasn't sure.

"One second. We need to find a place to sit," I whispered.

She just looked at me as if I was out of my mind.

For the third time in three days, I was scared witless. First I had fought the imp, then faced the Mistress and now this head hunting mega skeleton. This time there was also excitement though. To be honest, every enemy I had fought up until now had been fairly easy once I understood it. Here was the possibility of a real challenge.

When we made it all the way to the wall on its flank, I stepped into a small room that happened to be empty of skeletons.

Turning to Aeris I motioned for her to sit. "You have meditation, right?"

She nodded.

"Build up as much mana as you can. If you have any ideas, I'm all ears."

There was a twitch in her neck when I mentioned she should share her ideas. Not wasting the opportunity, I stuck out my tongue.

Did I have a plan? Sure, about 30 different ones floating through my head. Take out a leg first, or have Aeris fire from one side of the room while I fired from the other, perhaps walk out in the middle of the area and charge up an Alpha Bolt with 2k mana and see if it finished the boss off in one blow… Oh, I definitely had plans.

What I hated the most was the fact that I wasn't sure how overpowered this boss would really be. Don't let the level 150 fool you. Usually, a boss of the same level as a normal monster could take out a small army of other monsters the same level. For comparison, he'd likely be much more dangerous than the imp.

With my mana finally capping out at 4000 it was time to get serious.

"So this is what we are going to do…" I said with a wink.

***

The signal for her to start was when I started attacking the boss mob. "Let's do this!" I said to no one but myself under my breath.

Considering the armor the skeleton had, I was pretty sure it was something I could learn with blue magic. I cast *Force Learn* on the armor and the sword it wielded. When the sword identified as a sword and not a part of the creature I knew it wasn't something blue magic could steal, but a real magic sword.

The armor, on the other hand, registered as the skeleton. Perhaps an upgrade of Skeletal Breastplate… If I was correct, I needed to make sure to use *Force Learn* to pick up the blue magic spell.

Before my initial attack, I ventured to the far side of the room and started spamming Decay on each and every part of its body, but mostly its head. The Boss didn't even look my way since it wasn't doing any immediate damage.

I didn't wait to cast Force Learn on each major area of its armor. It only cost 10 MP for each cast. After about 10 casts, I allowed invisibility to take effect and walked back to take my place. I had received the pop-up I had been hoping for.

It would be up to me to attack first to keep it from attacking Aeris just in case.

I left the Creature Observation screen up so that I could watch its HP and see how damaging my spells really were. With the thick bone armor wrapped around the creature's legs and extending over the foot, I wasn't sure if trying to take out one of the legs would be worth the mana.

When it was time to begin, I cast my first Alpha Bolt. My bolt flew—though this one wasn't charged. It was to test its effectiveness. The bolt hit it on the side of the face.

Even with Decay it only did approximately 750 damage on impact. Oh great. 66 more casts of Alpha and we could call it a day.

Immediately after, I cast Heal on it, causing approximately 3k damage. Now that was more like it. About 16 more casts to go if we could survive that long.

There wasn't a lot of room for us to run around without other skeletons joining in on the fight, so a lot of how well our fight went would depend upon Aeris.

I shot off Heal after Heal making sure to hit each and every piece of armor. Slowly, I started whittling its life down as it picked up stride, heading right for us.

When it was about 30 meters out and that large sword was way too close for comfort, Aeris cast her first Gale right for its chest. Even with the skeleton at a run, the gale caused him to stagger back and to the side.

As soon as I had seen her cast, I had begun charging an Alpha Bolt. It had one ability that Heal didn't. It rammed into its target with a lot of force. Honestly, I hadn't used Charge much yet just because it wasn't an efficient use of mana most of the time.

With the boss off balance I let Alpha reach 500 mana; about 5 times what it now cost me. This took about four seconds total and the normally bowling ball-sized orb of smoky energy grew to the size of a hippo. The Skeleton Boss was already recovering. At this range, it was easy to aim, so I launched it towards his face.

The massive boss didn't even try to move. A direct hit scored 3200 damage.

The impact of charging a bolt was far more effective than I thought. 4 times the damage for 5 times the mana. Where I hit it also had something to do with it, I was sure. Still, at this rate, the math just didn't add up.

It still had about 66% of its health left and I had used over a thousand mana.

Another Gale came from Aeris. This one hit it low in the gut. She didn't wait for another round, but fired off Gale again, this time high to the back of the head. The skeleton lost its balance and landed head first on the stone floor.

It was time to test the full capability of my new Heal spell. If a hacksaw is taking forever, take out the chainsaw!

Charging Intermediate Heal for the first time, I let it grow. The yellow mist that normally blanketed my target began to build in a golden cloud.

The boss monster started to shift on the group, pulling its arms up to brace itself.

Still, my Healing spell grew. After two seconds I had only directed about 1000 mana into the spell.

It pushed off the floor, lifting itself with its arms.

1500 mana, but it still wasn't enough.

It had made it onto one knee. I needed just another second.

The sound of bone against stone echoed through the room, as it got it finally got its foot underneath itself.

Finally. My Healing spell reached 2000 mana.

It began to rise and turned to face me.

I released Heal. A yellow swarm completely engulfed its head, and a large cracking sound reverberated throughout the room. It was so loud I was afraid it would bring every champion in the area to see what was happening.

That was not where it stopped. As if an earthquake was going on inside the Skeleton's body, its skull began to crack and fracture in dozens of places and the frequency increased. Soon the skull itself was left in rubble and the rest of the skeleton's body was shaking violently. The internal combustion of the boss moved further down its frame. When the destruction was finished all that was left was a pelvic bone and some legs. Had my Healing spell just done over 20k damage?

Pop-up windows galore!

As amazing as it was, we were in trouble if we didn't hide immediately.

I hurried to Aeris and grabbed her hand, making sure to walk slowly enough for invisibility to take hold. When we entered the empty room we had used before I motioned for her to send her light orb to the far back corner of the room. I did the same. We sat and waited.

Technically we were safe-ish with invisibility. The main problem with being invisible was that you didn't really disappear. If there were dozens of creatures around it becomes difficult to manage not running into them. Hence our retreat.

Anticipating another fight to win the items the Boss dropped, I started meditating, ignoring my pop-up windows for a few minutes more. Aeris did the same.

Once recovered, I let myself browse the trigger windows. I was level 201! And for a bonus of reaching level 200, I got 50 extra attribute points to spend! Wisdom 880! 24 more levels for the 1000 Wisdom bonus!

But that wasn't all. Skeletal Breastplate had become Skeletal Armor. Force Learn had come through for me once again. It was time to look fabulously terrifying and strike fear into the hearts of stuffed animals and kittens everywhere!

My final pop-up was another odd Undead one.

Your understanding of the Undead has grown. Soon you will unlock their secrets.

Blah. Just give me a cool spell already!

"Elorion! I reached level 100 and then some!" Aeris exclaimed in hushed tones. She was dancing where she sat. "I got a skill that passively fills me with Air magic, making me lighter so that I can jump higher and run faster!"

"Seriously? How much lighter?!"

"It starts at 5% and then gets higher as it levels."

Looking over at her status screen, my smile turned to awe. I saw that she had leveled up 7 times from killing just one boss with only two of us in the party. She was now level 103. The way we were going she would reach level 115 before the night was over.

I had to admit I was a little jealous considering I had got a worthless skill at level 100. It seemed the skill you got was based on your talents. The way she was going she would become extremely mobile. I wondered if she would eventually be able to fly.

"What was that spell by the way?" she asked.

"I charged my new Healing spell with 2000 mana. I thought it would do less damage than that..."

"Oh. That's amazing. I really haven't used charge yet."

We spent time examining our attribute screens. I gave her extra time since she had just gained so many levels.

"Elorion," she said, with worry in her voice.

"Yeah?"

"This is amazing, but do you think we are going to make it? I mean, do you think we will be able to survive down here?"

It was the question I knew we were all thinking, but I had kept putting it off.

"I don't know, but I think it's possible. All that we can do is get as strong as possible and hope that it's enough."

She nodded her head as if confirming something.

"I'm worried about the others. Being here is like having our dreams come true. The ability to level, use magic… It's everything I ever dreamed of. But soon, and the timing might be different for each of us, the novelty of this place will wear off. We're in real danger."

"Do you think they might hurt themselves?"

"Well, probably not. I was thinking they might get angry and do something stupid, like attack the Mistress or run off into the Underworld and get killed."

I was silent for a moment as I considered her words. One of my reasons for going off solo was so that I could protect the others, but I really hadn't spent much time thinking of them. My focus was survival. I was determined to grow as powerful as possible as fast as possible.

"I'm not sure we have the luxury of worrying about our long-term problems. Not yet. Who knows when we will be attacked by the lich…"

"I see. Promise me though that when the time comes you will discuss it with me. We are going to need you."

"Of course. I know you think it's selfish that I'm out here alone. I admit that in part it is true. I want to survive. But, I also want to protect everyone. I was kidnapped just like everyone else. I know what that feels like."

She chuckled softly, remembering we were in stealth mode.

"What is it?" I asked.

"I don't think you're selfish. A little crazy maybe. Getting attacked by that imp had to be hard. I think you know how serious the situation is. That's why you're here. It takes a lot of strength to be able to go off into the labyrinth alone and you are in here day and night."

All red faced I replied, "It's the beef jerky."

"What?" she asked, surprised. "Does it give a buff?"

I shook my head. "Not really. I'm just embarrassed, so I said something ridiculous to change the subject."

A full belly laugh burst from her, even as she tried to choke it off. "You are the first blushing skeleton I've ever met."

I shushed her as the sound of multiple footsteps neared the door.

"Watch this," I said, casting Skeletal Armor for the first time. What had been just a breastplate, started to creep down my arms and legs. Its weight was almost nonexistent and the rest of my armor was still underneath it as a second layer of protection. How effective it was really wasn't something I was excited about testing though. Eventually, I would find out.

"That's pretty gross."

"After watching you enjoy popping the heads off skeletons I thought you would be into this sort of thing."

She looked at me in disgust and just shook her head.

"Oh, come on. Admit I at least look cool."

"Sure. Cool to the touch."

I chuckled at the terrible skeleton joke. "You ready to finish these loot campers?"

"My bones are crawling to get out there," she teased.

We looked at each other. Even after discussing a more serious topic, the adrenaline high and exhilaration from beating our first boss was making us slap happy. These kinds of moments were what made massive multiplayer roleplaying games so thrilling, but this was real. I almost hugged myself.

A lot of our caution had disappeared as we strolled out into the room and started blasting away with no care for how many spotted us. About 30 Skeletal Champions were slaughtered as we teased each other all the way.

If Aeris was willing, I could see that she wouldn't slow me down, but only be an asset as I tried to become powerful as quickly as possible. We could hunt together, but I knew she wouldn't agree to that arrangement before I asked.

Hunting alone had been lonely and this had been a great change of pace.

Her goal of tying me closer to the others had succeeded. Perhaps I was attracted to her. I was definitely attracted to her. What guy doesn't want to one day marry a beautiful girl with elf features and a great sense of humor? She had insulted her way into my chest cavity. In all seriousness, it was even clearer now why I needed to continue to get stronger. Protecting the others meant a lot more now that I had actually got to know her.

A small treasure trove of loot awaited us as we finished the last Champion.

After a knuckle bump, two ethereal humans plundered the large corpse. Not only was it worth a good sum of money, the items were useful. Cloth gloves that added 10% elemental damage to spells. Aeris got those. A necklace of trap detection. She insisted I take it because Travis and Olivia both had trap detection skills. It stacked with my ring. A bronze small shield of toughness. Basically, it had crazy durability. Aeris got that. A bracelet that added a huge 400 mana. Aeris insisted that I take it since I soloed so much.

The rest of the items we split. Since I got the bracelet she got an extra odd item to sell. The main item that we would split the profits on was the Boss's sword. It scaled down to human size when dropped, but had a few unique properties. For one it changed weight and balance depending on the user to make it the perfect weapon. It was an item property I hadn't seen before. Secondly, it added a full +100 to strength. I imagined keeping it just for the fun of whacking Skeletons apart.

Lastly, it was capable of causing Wind Concussions which stunned anyone in range if the swing was fast enough. We had been at a far enough distance that we never had to experience them. Perhaps we had been luckier with this boss than I knew.

With the intake of items from the boss, we had to stash some of our other drops in the empty room we had been able to rest in.

And at that, we headed back to the base. I threw us both a Heal to relieve our exhaustion.

In the middle of our walk back, Aeris looked to me seriously.

"Yeah?"

"You need to share that ability. You have hunted, what, 48 hours in the last two days? We have only been able to go about 6 to 8 hours before we are too exhausted to go any further. If there really is something dangerous coming then it's important we all use any advantage that we can get."

It was like a giant fist had knocked me atop the head, leaving some sense where it had been lacking. I replied, "I really am an idiot. You're right. I didn't even think about that."

"I know you might not join our group because you won't level as quickly. If you could meet us a few times a day and night to cast heal on us that would be enough, I think. You have to come back to sell stuff anyway. Right?"

The lingering fear that she would insist I join them was alleviated with her words. She'd just given me an out. "That wouldn't be a problem. We just need to come up with a schedule."

So we did. We didn't bother keeping our voices down and just killed anything that got in range as we spoke on our return.

***

"150,000 copper coins is my best offer!" insisted the Dark Elf who had just outbid the Dwarf by a whole 10,000 coins.

Our merchant friends weren't happy at first when we woke them up that night, but their rudeness quickly changed. I made sure we spread the wealth around when selling to make it worth their time.

"Make it 140,000 and throw in the Cloak of Concealment and we have a deal."

He eyed the cloak with 50% noise concealment that he knew I had been looking at for a while and smiled broadly. "Deal!"

The cloak was worth over 20k so it was an extra 10k on top of the price for us. Of course, the merchant had a certain amount of mark up on the item so he likely didn't lose much. Did I mention we were rich!

Aeris hopped up and down clapping her hands in quick succession.

He handed over the coin in large currency. 14 gold coins the size of my palm were counted out. 8 went to Aeris, since I had taken part of my share through the item, and then the rest to me. These were not your normal gold coins. They were called Gold Marks and were worth 10,000 copper coins each.

After selling everything else, I had just over 90,000 coins and this was all before the loot we had stashed in the labyrinth.

"Shopping spree!" my partner declared.

The first thing I bought was the scepter that gave 50% additional power to any light spell cast from the dwarf. That cost 26k. After that, I realized I could start looking at higher tier items than I thought would be possible for a while. The two main items I had been eyeing, the scepter and cloak, were now mine. With the remaining 66k coins, what should I focus on? Defense? I just got a high offensive weapon. Perhaps something designed specifically for Blue Magic?

It was no surprise to the merchants when I asked aloud for them all to answer, "Anyone have any Blue Magic specific items?"

There was no answer at first, but scanning each face, I knew they were considering my question.

The first voice was that of the Halfling. "Would you be interested in a magic book?"

Would I be interested? Come on, little bro, what gamer doesn't drool at the mention of magic books? Not that I let my drool escape from my mouth.

"I'll look over what you have." I smiled politely, keeping my excitement under wraps.

He laid out about twenty different books he had on various subjects and there was only one duplicate. Now only half of them were magic books, but some of them were on other subjects altogether. Some of the names included: *Creatures of the Underworld, How to Make a Trap for Dummies*, and *I Love You to Undeath.* These I scanned quickly, but nothing really stuck out.

As for the magic books, two of them seemed to jump out at me. *Healing Magic 101: Is Light Magic Really an Element?* and *The Blue Magician: Magic Theory and Where to Find Common Spells* were basically no-brainers. The rest of the books were on using the different elements and there were three on dark magic. Anything about learning a new element though went for...

"How much are they?

"50k for an Elemental Compass. 15000 each for the books on theory, except the dark magic books are 20k each."

"Oh…" *The books teaching you how to learn a new element were called Elemental Compasses?*

When he saw my reluctance, he shrugged. "Sorry. Supply and demand," he said, meaning the dark magic books.

It wasn't the dark magic books costing more than all the others that caught me off guard. It's just that that was a lot of meals.

"I'll take these two." I pointed toward the healing and blue magic books. Before I spent more I would see if they were even worth the coin.

"Very well."

After that transaction of 30k, I had my share of shopping. I'd save my leftover 34k for a rainy day. Not that I was likely to ever see rain again.

Aeris, on the other hand, quickly came over and grabbed the book on Wind Magic and kept going. Soon she was decked out in very good scale armor with a mix of physical and magical resistance. She grabbed a wand designed specifically for Wind Magic that was just as powerful as the scepter I bought. Not to mention, now she had a pair of earrings, about eight different rings, and two bracelets. These gave additional Constitution and Dexterity stats. She told me since they didn't match exactly the bracelets were both supposed to go on the same wrist.

I didn't get it but didn't say anything.

When she was finished, we went back out to hunt some more, not forgetting to grab the items we had stashed. After two more trips back to the base to sell items from our hidden stash and additional hunting, somehow, I felt human again. Loneliness was not something that I could just ignore anymore.

CHAPTER 15 – MAGIC BOOKS

Over the next two days, we mastered scheduling our meeting times so that I could cast Intermediate Heal on all the members of the party to keep them from exhaustion. It seemed a single cast would do them for an additional 3-4 hours of hunting before they started to struggle.

By Saturday, the fifth day after we had been kidnapped, I had reached level 235, only a level away from having 1000 Wisdom! Booyah! Leveling after level 100 had become much more difficult. After level 200 the amount of experience I need to advance had doubled again. I had also reached the last room and almost outgrown the Mistress's leveling tunnels as we started to call them.

I had gained some really good additional info from the other captives about the creatures I would have to hunt down to try Force Learn on. You can never have too many spells!

With my help, healing my old group's exhaustion, their leveling rate went up drastically. All of them were at least level 125, with the exception of Aeris who had reached 154. What can I say? Her company kept me sane.

I had started eating with them twice a day. More than once I was tempted to ask if I could join them, even if it was only for a few hours, but none of them pushed me. Aeris had taken me at my word that I would stick to solo.

Even spending the little time I did with them helped to keep my motivation high. It was mutually beneficial in that way. Also, Aeris kept my supply of ranch dressing stocked. They all seemed very thankful that I was willing to help, except for maybe Olivia.

"So bonehead. Will you finally tell us your secret hunting spot?" Olivia asked, giving me a hard time while lifting a spoonful of oatmeal to her mouth. She knew I wouldn't answer because there was no secret spot. It was just her way of letting me know she was thinking of me.

Olivia had lovingly stopped hating me and I had leveled up to the dislike category. Hence the loving pet name thanks to my skeletal armor. Perhaps I shouldn't have it cast at all times…

"Sorry, Farmer." I returned the favor. Her talent was nature magic, so it fit. "There's too much shade for anything to grow there. I'd invite you otherwise."

"With a green thumb, you can make things grow anywhere. Trust me!" she threatened; suddenly a flower grew out of my sunny side up eggs. Eh… It's in the yolk.

"That's very artistic," I mocked and praised her at the same time. It actually did look pretty interesting.

Plucking the flower from my breakfast, I just continued to eat. *Bacon and eggs! Did I mention there were biscuits and a side of bacon?!*

"Why are you begging to hunt with the guy that's all sticks and bones when you have these at your disposal?" Russ grinned as he flexed his now massive arms. He was genuinely impressive. That's what 100 Strength and 350 Constitution looked like, ladies and gentlemen. Constitution had a lot more to do with your size than you might think. Also, with his talent in Constitution, it translated as much to his toughness as it did his endurance. Just imagine a thickly muscled dwarf warrior... that was six foot tall and beardless.

The man had certainly grown into his position as the main tank of the group. Instead of the mostly tall chubby guy, he was now a block of muscle, thicker than anyone I had ever met thanks to his Con, with just a little chub left in his face and around the waist. With his blocky face and large build, he looked perfect for the part.

Because he had once been your typical overweight gamer, he was a little socially odd, especially around Olivia. He crushed on her pretty hard. Everyone knew it, whether they would admit it or not, but instead of being annoying it was hilarious. Not in the laughing at you kind of way, but the situation was comfortably awkward.

Olivia liked the attention, even if she wasn't exactly nice to him either. She was at least gentler with him than she was with me.

"Because I'm not having a 'cheesy' burger for my breakfast, Mountain Man," she barked.

I didn't see how she could get away with calling Russ cheesy while giving him a name like Mountain Man. Oh well. I slipped quietly out of this conversation thanks to Russ's good timing.

"Where are you hunting currently?" Aeris asked, bringing me right back into the conversation I was so close to escaping.

"Skeleton Sentinels. As you know, after Champions the different kinds of skeletons start to mix in groups, but after that, about five rooms deeper, there is a large room with the ceiling so high you can't see it. At the far end of the room is the bone palace I mentioned with its locked door. That's where you find them. They are about level 230."

"Yeah. Just Sentinels. They are nothing to me. I just fight them because if I win they give free foot massages," Olivia jabbed.

Quickly I added, "When you have boney feet as I do, can you blame me?"

Everyone laughed, including Olivia.

After a few more minutes I had cleared my plate. It was time to get to work. I stood to go.

"Don't forget to give me some of your sunshine before you leave," Travis jested, adding to the awkwardness.

When I finished healing everyone with Intermediate Heal, I wished them luck and headed from the dining hall after depositing my dish in one of the busing bins on the side of the room.

As I left, I healed everyone else that happened to be there, which was about 5 or 6 other players. Only one of them looked at me oddly. I didn't have to explain anything to him though because his friends did that for me. They had started showing up any time I met with my group.

The word was getting around so more people were starting to get the idea when I would be at the base. There was even a large group that just happened to be there the same time I was around at midnight, so they could manage to hunt late into the night.

Traveling to where I was currently hunting took me almost an hour if I didn't rush. Normally I would power level my spells on my way to and from that area. I continued that practice today.

The books I bought had proved their worth to help keep me sane during my long hours alone. More than that, I would have given the 90k for just one of them if I knew they would be this helpful. The knowledge inside was like throwing fried chicken at a starving teenager. Lifesaving and tasted awesome too!

The theory behind how the magic worked was the key that unlocked a new world of possibility to me.

Though the new information on Blue Magic wasn't as life-changing as Light Magic was, nonetheless I was enlightened. The prerequisite to manipulate the mana of a spell was 100 Intelligence, which I had. This book guided me in doing things like changing the shape of Alpha Bolt. It allowed for me to compress the bolt, while using less mana, into a small, bullet-like projectile.

A bullet was my idea. The book described an arrow, which seemed like a lot of excess energy for the shaft. Because of its smaller size, a bullet also flew at enemies faster than a normal Alpha Bolt and actually did slightly higher damage if my aim was good. It could be difficult to hit unarmored skeletons though the practice was good to improve my accuracy. Also, because the mana used was only about a quarter that of a normal Alpha Bolt, I could fire a bunch of them much quicker, greatly upping my efficiency.

Each time I manipulated mana and used it a few times, it would develop a new spell which I was able to name, making it easier to utilize. Alpha Bullet was one such spell.

Flamethrower easily became Fireball, but still had to be fired out my mouth.

As I headed through the lower rank skeletons and zombies, I roasted me some undead baddies just for the fun of it. I had yet to figure out what I enjoyed the most, the area of effect of Flamethrower or the explosiveness of Fireball.

I could also do things like cast Skeletal Warrior's Shield and direct the hard bone to form over a normal shield, just as Skeletal Armor formed over my leather armor. The same went for my scepter, except it insisted on giving my scepter a sharp pointy Mohawk. I was fully covered in bone except for my head. This would help save the durability of my items and add to their effectiveness.

With some trial and error, I was also able to charge my defensive spells just as I did Alpha Bolt and Heal. This would more accurately be called channeling. This added to my mana per minute cost, but in emergencies, it could be useful. I now had Skeletal Plate Mail ready for emergencies, which was a charged Skeletal Armor. For some reason, Fluid Body and Fluid Mentality were not able to be charged. They both maxed out at 33% physical and magic reduction and didn't have stages like my Heal spell did after you reached level 100. Their mana per minute cost had become almost nothing.

Also, there were over two hundred spells mentioned in the blue magic book and the location of the creatures that gave them. It even included a map. Some of them were worthless or just plain odd, like a spell to make your tongue super sticky and flexible so that you could catch things like a frog. Others were on my wish list of things to track down.

I wasn't sure I could pursue anything in the book now because, at the end of the Mistress's labyrinth, the same place I was going now to fight Skeleton Sentinels, the dungeon just seemed to end. A large palace with two large locked double doors made of pearl white bone stood blocking the way. These bones weren't from anything I had ever seen because the ones used were taller than I was and as thick as my leg. There was no getting through them.

There had to be a way though. How had the Lich happened to get in and meet with the imp?

Another thing the book gave me was a general idea of how large the underworld really was if I ever got outside the Leveling Tunnels. It went on for literally thousands of miles in all directions.

What was obviously missing was any path to the world above.

The book on light magic was even more eye-opening. Light magic wasn't really considered an element. That was why I had no skill tree to speak of like the elemental mages as I leveled up. Most everything you could do with light magic required that you manipulate the one spell Heal. With 100 Intelligence you had access to nearly every light spell you could imagine just because you could manipulate it. Who knew how long it would have taken me to figure this out without a magic book…

First, there were the damage and healing spells.

Normally when you Heal someone or yourself a type of mist envelops the person and they are healed as a whole. It is also possible to manipulate this energy into something like a condensed stream to heal individual body parts or damage them in the case of the undead.

Another use is to turn it into a bolt just like Alpha Bolt. I was also able to turn this into a Health Bullet which flew at high velocities as well but was actually too dangerous to be used to heal someone. The speed of the energy's impact would actually harm a living creature. I knew because I shot myself in the hand.

Just imagine a man in layered bone armor pointing his hand in the shape of a gun at a well-armed skeleton. Dropping the hammer by lowering his thumb, a small golden bullet soars at the monster's skull, piercing one side and exiting the other. Why fire it out of my finger like a pretend gun? I could just as easily fire it out of my palm, but why would I? *I got bullets, bro!*

When I reached the Skeleton Warriors I switched from fire to Alpha and Healing Bullets. Though in some cases they were harder to hit, firing bullets at anything can be a blast. These little rounds could even pierce their shields if the angle was right. I wouldn't say they were as powerful as real bullets though just because the pressure I could build up with magic just isn't as powerful as a gunpowder explosion. The velocity isn't nearly as high.

Health Bullet was only the beginning though. I now had a Health Bomb that was an area of effect spell, basically harming or healing. Depending on if you were living or not, everything in about a 10 foot radius was affected. It was an expensive 500 MP though. Lesser Health Bomb was 200 MP. Not that bad with my buffs, but still high considering the amount of damage it does. I'd have to level this one a lot to make it worth it.

As I reached the Skeleton Archers, there were about four standing close together.

I fired a Lesser Heal Bomb off, hitting the one in the middle.

The skeleton that was hit became airborne shrapnel. Another skeleton was killed instantly from the extra bone flying in the air. The other two skeletons were just blown back. A few bullets took care of them.

Next were buffs and debuffs.

All this time I had been sitting on insane power that I didn't know I had. The buffs worked in a way that I had never seen in a game. For starters, a light magic buff worked by casting Heal on a specific bodily system and directing mana to that spot without stopping the flow. The constant flow of mana to an area didn't just heal but enhanced it. There were only four systems.

The mind. When healing magic was focused on the mind, it would give an increase in Intelligence and Wisdom: Lesser Mind Buff and (Intermediate) Mind Buff.

When it was focused on the muscular system I was given an increase in Strength and Dexterity: Lesser Muscle Buff and Muscle Buff. I was able to confirm that I could further isolate my channeling to my legs or arms if needed, but buffing the entire body was actually more cost effective.

When it was focused on the skeletal system I was given a boost in Con: Lesser Skeletal Buff and Skeletal Buff.

Finally, you could focus it on your internal organs. This could both cure and give resistance to poison or mental effects like Pain. Lesser Organ Defense and Organ Defense.

Only a crazy person would cast Pain on themselves. *You dare call a man fully decked out in skeletal armor crazy? I'm talking to myself.*

Now, I only cast Lesser Pain instead of Intermediate, so my insanity was to a lesser degree.

With the buff, Lesser Organ Defense activated, Lesser Pain didn't even take hold. I was literally immune to it. That was when I went completely crazy and cast Intermediate Pain. With Lesser Organ Defense I wasn't immune, but the 10-second stun turned into a 5-second muscle flexing exercise that hurt a lot. It was not debilitating though. I would have been able to struggle through it and fight if I had to. With Intermediate Organ Defense Intermediate Pain lessened the effects of the stun greatly to where I could fully function, even if it was annoying for 2 to 3 seconds.

So how did these buffs work out practically? They were all mana per minute spells. Not to mention they were also fairly expensive when added up. Buffing each system with Lesser Heal cost 100 mana per minute for each system and a total of 400 base MPM. This gave each attribute a +25 buff.

Intermediate buffs were on a whole other level. they cost 300 mana per minute for each system or cost 1200 base MPM total for all four systems active at once. The effects couldn't be ignored though. Instead of +25 to all stats, I received +75 to all stats.

You were talking to a caster that could take on a brown bear with one hand while holding a frappuccino in the other; a mocha frappuccino with whip topping. I didn't give in to the desire to bash some skulls often because there would be fewer opponents to level my spells on. Then I would have to wait for them to respawn.

With all my buffs combined, I decided to give it the nickname of *In the Buff!*

These light magic buffs became debuffs if I cast them on an undead monster. To initially cast it I had to be close. Since most of the enemies I faced were skeletons or non-humanoids I had to focus on what to direct the buff upon.

Skeletal Defense became a debuff called Brittle when cast on the undead, making fighting Skeletal Sentries easy. It was like debuffing their Constitution by 75 attribute points.

Over the next two days, the mana per second cost of In the Buff became manageable. Since I only had the Mana Per Minute to level up a few of my buffs at a time, it took longer than it would have if I had enough Mana Per Minute to keep them all active. But now, it had all been worth it. I was prepared for war.

Out of my Mana per Minute buffs, currently I had Fluid Body and Mind that each cost 12 Mana Per Minute each, Skeleton Warrior Shield and Sword enveloping my shield and scepter costing only 5 Mana Per Minute each, Invisibility costing 20 Mana Per Minute at its maximum level, Skeletal Armor costing 60 Mana Per Minute with its level maxed out, Intermediate Mind Buff costing only 36 Mana Per Minute maxed out, Intermediate Organ buff still costing 62 Mana Per Minute at level 46, Intermediate Bone Buff costing 102 at level 29, and finally Intermediate Muscle Buff costing 110 at level 21. For a grand total of 424 Mana Per Minute to keep my buffs running. With my current 598 Mana Per Minute without buffs, I was easily able to sustain this now with mana left over.

Thanks to constant buffs my Heal spell had begun leveling much faster even at the Intermediate level. Heal was at level 98, almost to the Advanced rank.

It was going to be a good day. Today I should reach Advanced Heal and 1000 Wisdom. It was almost time for a huge jump in power. The last 5 days hadn't been easy, but the 100 plus hours of hunting were starting to bear real fruit.

***

Moving on to the next room, I was closing in on the last room of the Mistress's Labyrinth, about two rooms from the Skeletal Sentinels.

The Skeletons in this area were in mixed groups of bashers and archers. Just because I was in the mood, I was sniping them one at a time with Health Bullet from afar. It was a quick way to whittle them down without much effort.

I noticed something was off. Spending so much time in this place had made me at one with it. A large number of groans and the shuffle of feet in the distance made me consider a possible elite monster, but there was nothing I had faced that sounded so large.

In total stealth mode, I headed toward the noise, avoiding the skeletons nearby. With my concealment cloak and boots, 80% of the sound my footfalls were making went unheard. *Just a quick stroll through the labyrinth. Nothing to see here.*

When I reached the entrance to the next room, I approached it from an angle to see as much as I could in the low light with my light orb off. It wasn't necessary. There was so much light coming from the next room that the doorway nearly glowed.

Even from an angle, I saw what was making such a large racket. There was an army of zombies.

When I say army, I mean they were lined up in formation with helmets and wielding weapons. With Creature Observation, I saw that even the Zombie Foot Soldiers were level 320. That was close to 100 levels more than the highest mob I had faced before.

Suddenly, I was unsure I trusted Invisibility enough to remain standing there. Before I left, I used Creature Observation one more time to view the Creature Sheet of a Lesser Zombie Sergeant that was level 511. My Healing Bomb would be little more than a fart to them.

I fled.

In the room directly attached to theirs I kept my pace so that I wouldn't lose invisibility, but after making it to the next room I ran. The danger that I had been afraid of was finally here. From the looks of it, after all my progress, I had failed in my mission to get strong enough to protect anyone. Survival was the next mission. Perhaps it would be enough.

With my buffed stats and the ability to heal myself, I didn't stop. In less than twenty minutes I made it the approximate five miles to the base.

My immediate action was to warn everyone, so now with my Invisibility off, I shouted, "We are being attacked!"

CHAPTER 16 - FLEE

The members of my old group as well as a few unfamiliar faces raced into the hall from the dining area. Thankfully they hadn't left. Six other people joined us.

Aeris spoke first. "What's happening?!"

"There is an army of Zombie Foot Soldiers," I said, catching my breath and Healing myself to help with the recovery. "Their levels start in the 300s! We have to run! Gather everyone you can!"

I pushed past them and yelled at the imps in the dining hall. "Get the Mistress! We are being attacked!"

The imp who knew me had already left the counter and nodded as he accessed the magic entrance to her living quarters.

"Are we missing anyone else in the base?"

"Nope! Everyone else is out hunting," called Travis, who was heading out of the barracks.

I saw Lydia had joined us near the back of the group with Chris. That was a relief.

"We are heading for the first slime tunnel. Stay close to those you are used to fighting with. Aeris, throw me a group invite."

It was quick coming and I accepted. Everyone was soon grouped into a 15 man raid group. More like a flee group. Just like that and we were gone. If only fast food was this fast back home. Maybe all you had to do was make the fast food workers scared for their lives.

"Alright. Follow me!"

A few voices threw out objections, but I didn't bother answering them. There wasn't time to debate.

By the end of the first room, there were already complaints that our pace was too fast. We didn't have time for it.

Thinking quickly, I turned and started spamming a Constitution Buff on all 15 people. I choose stamina over Dexterity because even if we were going faster, I didn't want to have to stop. It ate up the rest of my available Mana per Minute regeneration points, but it would be worth it if we made it out of here without having to face the army.

My higher level buffs made me overwhelmingly more powerful than average at this level. It wasn't fair to force them to follow at my pace, but I didn't have time for being nice. That could wait until later.

As everyone filed out into the next room through the narrow entrances I threw another Lesser Health Bomb for good measure.

My group stayed at my heels, and even Russ was keeping up with ease. If I thought about it that shouldn't have surprised me. His talent was in Constitution. Even without the buff, he could likely run longer than everyone there except for me with my buffs.

Zombies were easy enough to force our way through without much effort. Lesser Skeletons were just as easy. Aeris and Olivia took care of them for us all.

It was the first time since our first day that I got to see Olivia's magic. She was now on an entirely different level. Good. We would probably need her.

Her favorite spell seemed to be one where a single large vine with sharp thorns shot out of the ground or ceiling and grabbed and constricted the enemy. The vine pierced through the zombies, but crushed the skeletons.

A green energy shot from her wand and landed where the vine sprouted from. One after another, she seemed to cast them in threes.

"We are getting close," Travis said, taking the lead of our small mob of frightened players. His pace quickened even more and he raced into the next room ahead of us.

I moved to quicken my own pace when Aeris spoke up. "Let him go."

Nodding, I forgot one of his talents had been tracking. Okay, perhaps two people wouldn't have a problem running with me. It seems that his talent was more in-depth than it sounded.

Travis finally came flying back faster than I suspected was humanly possible as we reached Skeleton Warriors. His face was bleached white.

I let everyone slow to wait for him and cast Invisibility on myself as a precaution.

As I had feared, I noticed someone following him. He was cloaked in some kind of dark fog or shadow. It seems his movement had allowed him to be revealed enough that I had noticed him since I had been looking for someone.

Creature Observation told me it was a Dark Elf Scout, level 310. When he saw our group the dark fog started to fade into an invisible state. I cast my spell before I lost sight of him.

Travis ran past our group, still going at his insane pace.

Everyone else seemed confused when he raced by. This seemed to put the Dark Elf at ease since I saw no more movement. That is until his muscles started to flex violently as my Pain spell overtook him.

Pretty sure he hadn't been able to move from that spot, I started to cast Health Bullet. I didn't know if it would harm or heal a dark elf, so I immediately cast Alpha Bullet afterward. It was impossible to tell so I started casting Alpha Bullet non-stop.

Everyone else got the idea when they saw my little silvery projectiles running into a cloudy bulge of matter and disappearing out of nowhere. The noise of the impact was probably even more obvious. Besides a Wind Slash and a giant vine grabbing the dark elf, a long bolt of electricity surged by followed by a glowing shadow bolt type thing I suspected was dark magic. We pummeled the dark elf and he was dead before the 10-second stun gave out. His now visible body lay in an unnatural heap.

Basically, everyone in our mob got a chorus of Level Ups including me.

That means it was time for 1000 Wisdom! It was not something I could wait for. It could literally save our lives. I had received 3 levels from the experience bonus for being the first time killing a new species. No doubt the others had extreme jumps in level. Especially since the mob's level was so much higher than theirs.

At level 237, I now had 1003 Wisdom and saved the rest of my stats. I was considering getting every attribute to 100 for the bonuses I knew would come with it. That I would save for later. My bonus window populated.

Intermediate Mana Flow Understood

Mana rejuvenation is now calculated by 2 points of mana per minute per point of wisdom.

Total mana multiplied by 5. 1000 base mana is now 5000

All spells cost 40% less mana to cast.

All spells are 40% more powerful when cast.

My base mana regeneration had just gone from 598 to 2000 MPM. That was over 3 times more. And my base mana went up 5 times more than before. *Slime muffins and goblin dumplings!* Eh… On second thought, even ranch dressing couldn't cure that grossness, but my excitement still stood! Wisdom had been a wise choice.

Novice Spell Mastery

All spells at the Novice level now cost 5 MP/MPM or less regardless of level.

Not that novice spells were expensive in the first place, but my efficiency had just gone up to an insane level.

No time to bask in my new awesomeness, or to get the drops.

To my surprise, I heard Olivia. "I got them!" A spell she had cast entangled the body and dragged it over to us.

I nodded to her as she smiled slyly and looted the corpse.

Travis had soon returned to my side. *Quick little bugger.*

He must have had some kind of stamina skill because he wasn't even breathing hard. "They are marching this way. We won't make it to the slimes area."

Panic gripped at my gut like an iron fist.

"The tunnels!" came a voice from somewhere behind.

"Where?" Aeris asked.

A silver cloaked girl with short curly hair stepped forward. "Only about three rooms back. No one knows where it goes though. There were no monsters in there for like a mile, so we stopped exploring."

"Good!" I responded. "We'll follow you!"

With such a huge jump in my Mana Per Minute, I cast Lesser Skeletal and Muscular Buff on everyone in our group and we really started to run.

As we backtracked, I started to quickly reconsider my buffs with all my newfound mana and regen. Quickly, I charged up my Skeletal Armor to Skeletal Plate Mail, as I had named it. The bone just thickened to grant me more protection. It was now costing me 300 MPM, but I had a lot more to spare. With my attribute buffs, the added weight wasn't even noticeable.

Soon we were turning down one of many side passages that I had never explored. The room turned into a hall and the hall became a wide enough tunnel for us all to run in side by side. It looked like a huge mine that was likely carved out by magic instead of tools of steel and iron. There was no light, so everyone had their light orbs cast so that we could see as well as possible.

"I'll check," Travis called as he raced by again.

So we ran from an enemy army into the unknown.

***

It was just as the curly-haired girl said. After about a mile I had everyone stop. Travis had confirmed there was no one in here, but also that it didn't go much deeper either. There were a few offshoots, or side tunnels, so we turned down one and rested. After a Health Bomb, I mentioned for everyone to meditate or prepare just in case we were attacked.

About a third of the group had a talent in magic, a third in melee combat, and the others were similar to rogue classes. Two of the rogues were no use in a hand to hand fight. I had a tall wiry guy go with Travis and set some traps about 200 meters away that would warn us of any coming threat.

From this side tunnel, it wasn't even possible to see the main tunnel from our deep position. I went invisible to stay hidden from invisible enemies and considered casting Invisibility on everyone there. My mana regen would certainly allow it now.

I was also able to confirm that there was a very subtle glow of red around the traps. Whether this was from being grouped with the rogue that set them or my bonus from equipment to see traps I had no idea.

There was another thing on my mind. This was a huge opportunity.

As a blue mage, I either had to observe a creature to acquire their skills or have them cast on me to learn them. Already, I had seen two new kinds of zombies and my first dark elf. Sneaking in from behind the army to use Force Learn to try and learn some blue magic wasn't just a good idea, but the very reason the Mistress had given me Invisibility. I couldn't just let this opportunity pass.

***

I reappeared in front of everyone suddenly. A few people jumped.

"Aeris!" I said loud enough for everyone to hear, especially since everyone was talking in hushed tones.

She stood up from her meditation.

"I want you to take the lead. I'm going to check out the threat."

The glare she gave me warned that she wasn't happy. For a moment I thought I would have to say more, but she finally nodded.

"Travis," I called.

He was quickly by my side.

"Can you see through invisibility?"

"I can."

A sigh of relief escaped me. That was one ability I needed to learn, quickly.

"Keep a lookout, but don't leave this side tunnel. You are their eyes if any assassins find them. You know the drill. Call targets and crush anything that gets close."

After healing everyone one last time, I dropped my buffs on them because I would soon be out of range. About 400 meters, give or take 100. As idiotic as it sounded, I was heading back to danger to try and steal as many blue spells as possible. I also considered killing any stragglers, but then I shut my mind to that to not give away my presence. I'd avoid that unless it was necessary.

Chapter 17 – Theft From My
Would Be Killers

By the time I had snuck the mile to make it back to the main passageway the majority of the army had already passed. At the rear of the army was the same lich I had seen meeting with the imp I had killed, hovering about four feet off the ground leading the army's progression. Was he blind? Oddly, he was looking directly at the stone wall about 15 feet in front of him.

At the lich's side was a pale man with soot-black hair riding upon a golden throne with two molded gargoyles perched upon the tall back of the chair. The throne was held up by eight massive shouldered orcs on either side holding a railing along its base. Orcs?! Level 400? *Sweet! Fanboy moment!* Who doesn't dream about walking up to an orc and poking it with a sword?

There were about twenty other creatures: two massive ogres with a level too high to register standing at the rear to either side of the throne, four ghoul spellcasters, also too high of a level, and a zombie general that was about 12 feet tall in greasy chainmail. The grease I feared was from rotting body fluids. I wasn't sure how they expected to get the large platform the pale man sat on through the small doorway to the next room.

On the other hand, how had they gotten into the room in the first place? The other wall was intact and there was no way the platform would have been able to fit through even if they broke it down into smaller pieces.

This was only part of the army. Creatures were still funneling through the doorway, filing in behind the lich and the guy on the throne. No wonder why their progress had been so slow.

Since they were held up, I'd begin. Casting Force Learn kept me mostly ethereal, but I was ready to run.

I stood in a side room that would make it easy to side step out of sight after casting. My target was the pale dude on the throne.

When I triggered Creature Observation on him as a skill, the only information I received was *Vampire*. His level was too high for my skill to display it for me. Next, I cast Force Learn.

Too bad I hadn't cast it on the dark elf earlier. That was a missed opportunity that would not happen again.

Part of me feared that Observing a high enough level creature would alert them to my presence. Thankfully, no commotion came from the overwhelmingly high-level vampire, nor did I explode from some spell cast in response. It seemed I hadn't been noticed at all. The Mistress hadn't been lying when she said this form of invisibility was among the most powerful.

Astonishingly seven trigger windows had popped up the moment I cast Force Learn. Sadly, the first six had the same message.

You are unable to learn this spell at this time.

Thankfully the seventh window had better news.

Wait. What kind of joke was this?

Teeth Whitening

A passive spell that will ensure your teeth stay healthy and white. This spell costs no mana but will cease to work if the user dies.

Seriously? Did this just keep my teeth magically clean, or did it help with bad breath too?

With my attention back on the party before me, I was just in time to see the lich place his hand on the stone wall and cast a spell that made it turn to translucent fluid before my eyes.

The rest of the lead group passed through the wall like it wasn't even there. My mouth dropped. How powerful were these guys? They were crazy enough to go up against the Mistress so I imagined they must be pretty powerful. I had a feeling I was about to find out my 237 levels were little more than an advanced newbie.

I followed carefully, taking my time and only using Force Learn when I was behind the safety of a side passage.

My second target had been the lich. He had over 70 trigger windows but none of them were learnable. *Insane!*

A dark elf was next. Even with the earlier lost opportunity, I'd get to learn all their secrets!

Shadow Step

Manipulates shadows to make you difficult to see.

Another stealth skill that wasn't as good as the one I had. If it was the same one the dark elf used, I would prefer to be in an ethereal state than a foggy one. The fog would be helpful in low light settings, but in the mild lighting of the Mistress's labyrinth, it had given him away.

The zombie general gave one spell as well.

Stench

Invited to an undead block party? Here's the latest in aromas to die for! Now is your chance to smell like all the cool corpses!

Okay, maybe it didn't actually say that, but you get the picture.

The only other creature that gave me any blue magic was the ghoul.

Lesser Wail of the Banshee

Sonic damage expelled through one's cry. Dead mages who are resurrected for whatever unknown evil become ghouls and have this ability naturally.

Finally, a useful spell! Just like taking candy from a banshee! Actually, I had a feeling real banshees were pretty high level and would probably whip me like a cupcake in need of icing. There was no time to test anything, so I stuck with what I knew.

It seemed that these creatures were difficult to learn blue magic from because they were of such a high level in comparison to me. *Bummer.*

When the army of about 250 reached the realm of the Decrepit Skeletons, a shiver shot down my spine. The entire area had changed. Before, there had been the typical large stone room with countless side rooms. The ceiling was now nearly impossible to see, reaching at least 10 stories high. Walls that had been separating each of the large rooms had been knocked down, or blasted away, leaving a flat battlefield that was at least half a mile long. Any side rooms were also non-existent leaving rough jagged stone to either side for walls.

I couldn't decide what took more strength. Decimating a number of walls and side rooms in a few minutes or liquefying walls to allow someone to pass through.

Suddenly, I felt very unsafe. Many of these creatures were too high a level for me to even determine. The highest level Creature Observation would register currently was in the 700s, about 500 levels higher than my own.

Should I try and make my way to the Mistress's line or just flee and head back to camp where my friends were?

The answer was soon answered for me. For the first time since being kidnapped, I received a pop-up requesting permission for someone to whisper to me with magic. When I accepted, I immediately heard an unfamiliar voice in a frantic hushed tone.

"Elorion. My name is Richard. Aeris wanted me to tell you we are in trouble. About 30 zombies are marching our way. Somehow they found us!"

"I'm coming!" I whispered in panic.

"They are here!" he responded. The connection cut off.

Backing out of the entrance of the newly constructed room, I started to sprint at full speed when I was at a safe distance from the army. Why had I left their side? How had the group found them in the first place? My group was at least a mile away from the main hall. They had either followed us, or had some really good scouts.

To increase my speed even more, I charged up Muscular Buff by 500 MPM. The excess mana gave me an extra 125 to strength and dexterity. I ran like a mad skeleton cheetah standing up!

***

I almost missed the turn I was going so fast. Another mile to go.

Almost as soon as I entered the tunnel I heard the clash of weapons. Pumping up Muscular Buff with another 500 mana only gave me another plus 25 to stats, so I lessened my mana use to what I used before. Charging had a limit it seemed. Wasting mana was not an option either if I was going to be useful to my friends when I arrived.

The mind does odd things when you fear your friends might die or are already dead. Try as I might to block out all the images of gruesome deaths my imagination was taunting me with.

As I neared, I readied the largest healing bomb I could manage. If you call a compressed barrel-sized yellow energy ball manageable. It was like trying hold down the lid on 1000 starving, caffeinated guinea pigs in a trash can. The energy itself didn't want to stay put. When the side tunnel came into view I had 3000 mana ready to go. Thankfully it hadn't exploded, taking my arm with it.

I was only just barely able to see over the heads of the 30 odd zombie soldiers that my group had wedged themselves into a narrow space between two large boulders to let the tanks hold them back from the rest of the group as they lobbed spells at them.

Olivia had large thick vines tangled from ceiling to floor narrowing the entrance to their hideout even more. Spells flew even as I rounded the corner.

Afraid the blast from my Heal Bomb would be powerful enough to hurt my teammates, I tossed it at the rear of the 25 zombie foot soldiers still left standing. With so many monsters of level 300 and above, I was surprised anyone was still left alive to save.

The tunnel lit up like the surface of the sun, blinding even me who had been clenching my eyes tightly in preparation for the explosion. There was a large pressure that knocked me back. A literal zombie foot flew at my head, nearly knocking me over. Zombie shrapnel flew everywhere.

A chorus of level ups floated up from the floor. With my vision refocusing I saw most of the zombies were not just dead but left in pieces. A few were still alive, but as the others recovered, Aeris's Wind Slash and a dark bolt finished off two more.

The only mob that remained standing was a level 391 Lesser Zombie Sergeant. This guy wore some slimy scale mail and stood about 7 feet tall with a skull cap protecting its weak spot.

There were some humans scattered on the floor in front of him, but they seemed to be moving. Although a familiar face, Russ in his thick leather armor, stood facing the large zombie alone. The Sergeant held him by his leather vest. They were both weaponless.

In a motion too quick to interrupt, the zombie threw a devastating right cross, striking Russ square in the face. It was a miracle his head still remained on his body.

All I could do was react. I healed Russ as quickly as possible.

The zombie hit him again.

Healing magic flowed from me until he was fully In the Buff, and even then I had to keep healing him. I was afraid to stop because the blows came one after another.

A hand of Russ's reached up and grabbed the collar of the zombie Sergeant. With as much insanity as humanly possible, Russ pulled the zombie to him with all his strength and pummeled the undead face with his forehead.

With a bloody grin, he looked up at the Sergeant that towered over him. He was stunned.

It gave me the opportunity I needed to debuff the zombie's Con with a Skeletal Debuff that was generously charged.

Russ stepped into his next blow with all of his weight and pulled the Sergeant to him once again. He head-butted the highest level mob any of us had fought, this time staggering him.

Anyone that head-butts a Zombie Sergeant in the face has my respect.

Before I could even add my own attack, the zombie was cut off from Russ by a large vine and a gust of wind sent him back a few meters. Electricity, a dark bolt, and a wind slash joined my healing bullets as we pummeled the monster as a team.

Russ now had a shield user to his right and a poleaxe guy to his left. They stood with him to block the monster from their group behind them. It was unnecessary.

The Sergeant stood against the onslaught for perhaps a full minute. That much defense and HP was boss-like. Olivia and Aeris were instrumental in making it nearly impossible for the creature to move. I for one now had enough mana that I tried out a new spell that I invented on the fly, Light Magic Machine Gun. It was little more than rapid fire mode for Health Bullets.

When the monster died Level Ups streamed up like a fireworks finale.

Ignoring my pop-up windows for now, I hurried through the mess of bodies lying across the floor and healed anything that was living. It was a long number of minutes, but I was finally delighted to find we hadn't lost a single person.

CHAPTER 18 - CURIOSITY KILLED THE HUMAN?

Even covered in zombie goop Aeris ran up and hugged me, Skeletal Plate Mail and all.

"One minute we are struggling to hold them back, and the next there is a blinding light and a dead man's ear flies into my mouth! What in the underworld was that?!"

"Health Bomb." I grinned. "With 3000 mana!"

She hit me harder than was good for her hand. It would bruise. I healed it for her.

"You can't just up and leave again!" she insisted.

It couldn't be helped, I teased her. "Why not? You have Russ."

A choked chuckle came from behind Aeris. Olivia was waiting to speak with her as Aeris chewed me out.

The timing couldn't have been better.

"600 Con!" Russ bellowed. "You stinky, rotten, wimpy little zombie men ain't got nothing on me! You will be crushed!"

I believed him. His girth and overall size was twice the size of any bodybuilder I had ever seen. It wouldn't surprise me if he weighed 400 lbs. As for his chub, he had the build of a world's strongest man competitor. There was no doubt about it now. He was a true-hearted tank.

Regardless, how could he possibly be alright after getting beaten within an inch of his life and almost dying? What was the first thing you think of when you almost die? Check your status screen for your rewards?!

I grabbed Aeris's hand and gave it a squeeze. She was obviously not going to take no for an answer so I told her, "I will stay with you for now."

Heading over to Russ, we congratulated him. He was happy to show off his stats.

Stats

Strength – 233

Dexterity – 41

Constitution – 600

Intelligence – 46

Wisdom – 24

What really surprised me was his level though. 143... He had gotten at least 10-15 levels without doing any of the killing.

Seeing him change almost made me want to up my Constitution, but there was no guarantee I would grow the way he did. His talent was in Con, so I doubted 600 Con for me would equal 600 Con for him.

Suddenly, I noticed the odd vibe coming from a number of the people around me as they checked their status screens. Everyone was in an odd form of gleeful shock.

The rest had skipped their status screens and were looting the dead bodies.

After finishing off about 25 zombies between levels 300 to 350 and the captain that was level 391, it shouldn't have been as much of a surprise that everyone had leveled quite a bit. Then I looked at my own status screen and suddenly felt like my body disappeared and all that was left was a grin. In other words, I had just gained 18 levels… I was level 257.

It was thanks to the bonuses for killing two new monsters for the first time, but that was only where it began. I had 9 different pop-up windows indicating I had killed a monster 100 levels higher than my own.

I had gained the most experience because I had done the most damage. Just for being in the group they would get experience, but if they had also participated in the fight, then they would have earned even more. Power leveling them was looking like a very real possibility.

The last window was the best at of all of them, but it wasn't related to leveling.

Healing reached Advanced Rank!

Advanced Healing

Base Heal of 5000 at level 1.

Cost 1000 MP per cast.

Crazy undead monkey stink! The cost was high, but my damage potential just became ten times stronger!

Talk about good problems to have. Just one battle and suddenly I had an additional 90 attribute points to spend, plus the 10 I already had saved. This gave me a lot of options. If I followed the Head Mistress's advice blindly I could pump everything into Wisdom and be that much closer to 10,000 for the next bonus. It was so far away though.

The benefits of going just Wisdom wouldn't only come when I reached the bonus. If I put everything in Wisdom I would have a regen rate of about 2200 Mana Per Minute.

Another option was pumping everything into Intelligence. This would also only slow down my progress to 10,000 Wisdom by 5%. If I had 1800 levels to go until that next bonus, it would only take 100 extra levels to get the Intelligence bonus.

Was it even possible to reach that high of a level though? I had no idea what the level cap was or if there even was one. The Head Mistress had mentioned 10,000 in her explanation, so perhaps that was a clue. What level was she I wondered?

There was also the option of getting Constitution, Dexterity and even Strength to 100 for the bonuses. The best thing about it would be that I didn't have to wait. For 83 points I could get Constitution and Dexterity both to 100 for the bonus. It would take 136 for Constitution, Dexterity, and Strength. Constitution and Dexterity seemed like no-brainers, but did I need Strength for anything? With my buffs, I was already really strong. For survival's sake getting the bonuses at 100 seemed like the wise thing to do.

I began by putting the needed points to get Constitution to 100.

Durable Body

Instead of 10 HP for each point of Con, you will now receive 25.

All damage taken reduced by 5%

Enhanced Endurance

Stamina doubled.

25% less stamina used.

Toughness Synergy

Because of the close relationship between Strength and Constitution, your high Con now reflects this. Every 5 points of Strength acts just as 1 point of Con would.

Seeing my Health Points increase from a base of 590 to 2500 in an instant allowed me to relax more than I had been able to in days. With the additional 800 HP from items, I was at 3300! I hadn't even realized I had been so uptight. The increase in Endurance and the relationship with Strength were nice little bonuses as well.

The large increase caused me to take a second look at Russ. With his 600 Con he had just over 25000 HP and if my calculations were right, 10000 of it was because of his talent. If his HP was calculated like mine he would have had closer to 15000. He really was a monster.

Dexterity came next. I didn't hesitate.

Light Step

You have surpassed the normal human limit for agile reactions. Due to this, it will seem to others as if you float off the ground when you run.

Speed Increased by 20%

Quick Reflexes Increased by 20%

Speed Synergy

Due to the relationship between fast twitch muscles responsible for Dexterity and how they help when lifting heavy objects, for every 5 points of Strength, it will be as if you have an additional point of Dex.

Seeing the bonuses from Con and Dex, I was convinced getting Strength to 100 would be worth it for 53 points. I dumped the 17 points I had left into Strength and would finish it off soon.

I was also leaning toward getting Intelligence to 1000 before aiming for 10,000 in Wisdom, just because of how far away from 10,000 I really was.

There was so much about me that had just changed that I didn't have the time to fully realize just how much. Examining my arms and abs, I looked and felt like an amateur bodybuilder.

Glancing at Aeris, she was far too busy considering her own character progression for her to notice me. Taking in the rest of the group, they were the same. Zombie goo and all, everyone was still studying their screens.

Next, I considered what Advanced Healing really did for me. I cast Advanced buffs on my Intelligence and Wisdom. It gave me an incredible +300 to each stat. This increased my Mana Per Minute, Max Mana and my damage. With that, I was able to go Advanced *In the Buff!* +300 to all stats literally made me 3 times stronger.

Aeris had finally noticed me after applying the spells.

"How'd you do?" I asked, overlooking her newly red face.

Her mouth opened to say something, then closed as she took me in. She shook her head then responded, "You have no idea." She smiled slyly. "I don't think we should hide any longer. This is an opportunity we can't afford to miss. We were only able to take out a handful of them before you came, but I think we may have been able to pull it off if it wasn't for that Sergeant. And now... With you here, I think we should seriously consider fighting." Her eyes seemed hungry.

The sudden jump in levels and power sent a cloud of Level Up stupor over the lot of them. Everyone wanted to face the army now even after I told them there were 250 of them; many of them twice the level of the Sergeant. It took me five minutes to convince them they weren't strong enough to fight them face to face. I gave in when they came up with a compromise.

I deactivated Advanced Muscular Buff, which gave me enough to cast Invisibility on everyone. Skeleton Plate Mail I also scaled back to Skeletal Armor. This gave me enough Mana Per Minute to recover if I needed to if we had to fight.

Travis was excited to scout out the battlefield with his new stats and return to us covering three miles in seven minutes!

"The battle is going at full force. The mages on both sides are using zombies and skeletons as foot soldiers and healing or resurrecting them. There are no signs that either side is winning."

"Very well," I replied.

The plan was to wait at the rear of the battlefield and only attack injured enemies as they retreated for some easy experience. We had agreed that we would only attack a Lesser Skeletal Sergeant or lower.

Thankfully the troops seemed to all be controlled by magic, so I doubted there would be any retreating. Our group was made up of too many power-hungry gamers. This was not a good idea.

Everyone spread out in their smaller groups as we had planned. The attacking army had advanced a quarter of a mile across the battlefield. We were technically safe for the moment since everyone was shrouded in my Invisibility spell.

It was a light show of lightning, ice, and fire. Spells were hurled down on the opposing armies from both fronts.

Our view was very limited from our distance, but everyone was satisfied that we hadn't been seen. The lich at the side of the vampire was directing the zombie army. Even now the vampire had yet to rise from his seat. It seemed the battle was little more than a spectator sport for him.

The skeletal force aligned against him was smaller in number, but the Skeleton Legionaries were higher in level—at least in the 400s or higher. There were also Skeletal Captains in the low 700s. Many were too high of a level for me to know for sure.

Just as the Vampire had his Zombie General, the Head Mistress had her Skeleton General who towered over the battlefield. He had two large horns of a bull sticking up from his bone helm and his level was too high to see. His armor itself looked familiar because I was wearing its lesser counterpart. Immediately I cast Force Learn.

Your Skeleton Armor has evolved to Skeletal General's Defense.

For an extra 200 MPM, I now had a sure fitting bone helm similar to that of a samurai Kabuto with two horns reaching up to either side of my head. The armor now fit me head to toe, with a skull covering the majority of my face, the jaw missing, and I peered out of large eye sockets that barely hindered my vision. I couldn't wait to try and buck some low-level zombies with my horns. There was no way I wouldn't at least try it.

After twenty minutes of back and forth, the constant death and resurrection of zombies and skeletons was getting boring. We weren't the only ones who were tired of the stalemate. The vampire finally stood up from his chair.

In the blink of an eye, black cords shot out of the pale man's hand and sucked the life out of his own zombies. It took less than a minute before they all lay motionless.

The skeletons stopped where they stood in response.

A male's tenor rung out. "Dearest Lilith!" the vampire called. "How rude of a welcome you have given us!"

I could almost hear her snort from a quarter of a mile away. "You bring the stench of rotting flesh into my realm and you call me rude?!" she rebuked.

"Oh yes! I have forgotten your sensitivities! You are still very much attached to your flesh!"

"Enough!" she demanded. "You dare attack me?! Your superior?!"

"Head Mistress or not, you are a succubus, Lilith! Talented?! Sure! But you are a lesser being despite your many talents! Swear your allegiance to me and I will let you live! If not… Either way, you will stop this abomination of fraternizing with the human world! Though I do applaud your creativity! Today I will take my rightful place as your master or drain the power from your lusty corpse!"

A similar black cord proceeded from the Mistress's hand and leeched the power from her own skeletons. Even her general was drained.

"Come then, child! Today I will teach you an everlasting lesson!"

The sudden intensity of power radiating from the pair sent the orcs and dark elves running for an exit. They were the only creatures that weren't already dead or leeched to death by the black cord spell.

I suddenly felt like throwing skeleton bones against the wall as hard as I could. *Idiot!* How had I let everyone talk me into doing this? 14 other newly leveled up ex-gamers had new power to test on creatures that looked at us like steak with legs, covered with BBQ sauce.

An uncoordinated mob ran right toward us, making for the exit behind us.

Chapter 19 – A Master's Duel

I counted two dark elves and eight orcs coming at us without any formation or clue that we were in their way. Besides the obvious danger of having eight level 400 tanks heading right at us, I feared there might be stealth users that I couldn't see. Being invisible myself didn't make it possible to see others that were invisible.

The orcs were probably not weak to Light magic.

A Health Bullet hit one in the shoulder, knocking one off balance but little else. It was confirmed my Healing spells wouldn't really affect them. *Alpha Bullet it is.*

My attack set off the rest of my group. Spells flew, bows sang, Russ ran to the center of the exit with two other guys not nearly as big as him, and a few rogues inched to better positions at the flank of our ridiculously small defensive line.

Multiple strategies played through my head in a moment. Logic came so easily to me now and my wisdom attribute was obviously doing more than just affecting my spells.

The selfish approach would be to try to kill every single one of them without anyone else getting the last kill. This would give me the most experience.

The selfless strategy would be to buff everyone else and go into full heal mode. It might even be the only approach where everyone would survive. One Orc was twice the level of any of our bashers. Heck, they were nearly twice my own level.

Because of the danger, our only hope might also be to do as much damage as possible as quickly as possible. Going into healing mode might get people killed.

There was one thing I could do quickly before the Orcs reached us. They had just noticed us after I had cast a Health Bullet. I turned to the two fleeing dark elves. They were only about level 300.

I formed up an Advanced Health Bullet for the first time. It cost only about a fifth of the 1000MP, making it efficient and deadly. With over 40% spell strength increase from Wisdom bonuses, 20% from Intelligence bonuses, and 50% from my scepter and their weakness to light magic, it would be devastating.

Instead of firing quickly, I took a breath to aim.

Both of the dark elves had the same reaction when they saw us. A knife was drawn and they tried to go invisible.

Releasing my first bullet, it carried much more acceleration than Heal or Lesser Heal was capable of.

It tore into the center of the dark elf's skull. *Head shot!*

Other attack spells bombarded the dark elves as well. I wasn't the only one who thought to get them out of the way first.

I didn't wait for another reaction, but immediately fired another Advanced Health Bullet when I saw it hit.

It seemed like it was going to miss high. The dark elf was falling after my first bullet had hit.

Instead of missing it hit him in the temple, finishing him before he hit the ground!

I didn't change anything when attacking the second dark elf. My Advanced Health Bullet finished him by sniping him in the neck.

Turning to the Orcs, Olivia went all out casting a spell like her vine entanglement, but this was no small control spell. A small forest rose out of the ground at her beck and call. Not only did it entrap their legs but it dragged the lot of them together into a huddle.

It only momentarily hindered the massive green orcs. The average one was the size of Russ and it was obvious their strength attribute was at a stupid awesome level.

It was time to decide. Instead of choosing to just heal or attack, I would roll with the situation. My first course was to buff our tanks' Constitution to the Advanced level. I didn't believe that an additional 300 Strength would help them do enough damage against the incoming squad to make it worth the mana, but making them able to take a few more punches could be a lifesaver for all of us.

Then my mouth dropped as I learned how much I had been underestimating my group.

Our casters unleashed what they were really capable of. Before the first Wind Slash struck, two other spells reached the orcs first.

A makeshift thundercloud formed above them and a bolt of lightning took advantage of their close proximity.

In utter defiance and in the face of the superior enemy, a giant black shadow in the shape of a hand hovered over their heads for no more than a second. It was the size of a truck.

It slammed down to the earth, driving the orcs into the ground. *What in the Underworld was that?!*

Aeris's wind slash was obviously charged—instead of the thickness of a sword blade, it hurled forward like the blade of a massive battleax. It sunk into the group at the knees, blood spraying, tying my throat in knots.

There hadn't been many creatures we had fought that seemed really alive. The orcs were close enough to human that it seemed more real to see them get hurt. Not that it slowed me down.

A moment ago the group of orcs had been tearing through Olivia's vines like children pulling up grass, but they were now staggering, some holding injured limbs or taking a knee.

Multiple spells hit them from all sides.

I prepared an Alpha Bomb, pumping 2k MP into the spell. *Time for some experience.*

It was clear that the power of this group had incredible potential.

Our tanks were no longer bracing for a fight, but watching us casters while scratching their heads. When Russ crossed his arms like it wasn't fair, I snorted, releasing my spell.

The concussion of Alpha Bomb sounded like a small thunderclap when it connected. Orcs were blasted off their feet and flew outside of the radius of Olivia's forest of entanglement. Orc and vine were left in pieces. Not a one of them was left alive.

Despite the cool effect, I was pretty sure I had only finished two or three of them. The rest had already been dead. *No bonus experience for destruction?*

Level Ups streamed from the floor.

The power our mages had together was mind-boggling. I now believed Aeris when she said that they could have probably taken the zombies from before if it wasn't for their Sergeant.

Scanning the battlefield I didn't see any others coming our way, but still feared possible stealth users.

"Watch out for rogues! There might be some invisible enemies left."

"It's clear!" Travis called. "I was able to see through their stealth before. I think it's safe."

"Still! Let my invisibility spell take effect again! Don't move too quickly or you will stay visible! Just to be safe!"

Everyone took my advice as I released Advanced Skeletal Buff on the tanks.

I saw Aeris and Olivia hug each other in victory and two other casters dogpiled them. The one with a brown mess of hair and a smug grin was the lightning mage, and a skinny redheaded guy with a black robe looked back at me. This was the guy that cast the giant hand dark spell. There was no way it was a normal spell, right? He nodded to me with dorky awesomeness!

I couldn't help but give the guys a round of knuckle bumps. *Gamer mage dudes unite!*

Of course, our tanks weren't exactly happy it was already over. They celebrated anyways. It was all short-lived, however.

Enormous energy was radiating from the Vampire and Head Mistress and was only growing. The first attack, a black ball of energy, shot from the Vampire's hand.

The Mistress waved her hand and the attack exploded ten feet from her head. The concussion caused a thunderclap and knocked half of us off our feet. From her side of the battlefield, she was at least 500 meters away. We ran.

Stopping directly on the other side of the stone wall wasn't an option. The wall was shaking.

It didn't have to be discussed. We ran two more rooms before we finally stopped. Even from there the concussions seemed to send our internal organs trembling.

Sitting, I began to recover my mana through meditation and let it max out. When I was fairly confident nothing was following us, I released everyone's invisibility. It seemed the danger of any additional mobs had passed, and those that we might have missed would have likely run back home instead of trying to get a solo kill before we could respond.

"What are you doing?" Aeris demanded. She already knew how I would answer.

I hid behind a foolhardy smile and replied, "I'm going to go watch."

Before she could object, I activated Advanced Muscular Buff and charged Skeleton General's Armor up to Skeleton General's Full Plate Mail. I didn't quite reach Russ's size, but with the armor, I looked far more intimidating.

The only parts of me that hinted that I was actually human were my mouth and eyes that showed from behind the skeletal mask.

"It's okay, Aeris. I have to be there to see if I need to warn everyone if she loses." Hesitating, I added, "I need to see what we are really dealing with."

She gave in. "Fine. Go. You owe me though."

I did hate to leave her like that, but it was time to see how far I had really come and how powerful these centuries' old monsters really were. No more illusions.

Entering the room where the duel raged on, I was able to stand against the worst concussions from this distance. I dared to approach off to the side by the roughly carved out wall until I was a little over 100 meters from the action. I remained invisible, though I was pretty sure at least the Head Mistress had some form of spell that could detect me. My vantage point gave me the opportunity to really watch the battle.

Under the Mistress's feet was a river of flame that licked as high as her chest. It was no doubt a spell cast by the vampire to do her harm, though it seemed to have little effect.

If I had to guess, I'd say the vampire was winning. He stood upon a pillar of ice a story up and was completely encased in see-through ice. There were fifteen feet of ice protecting him on all sides from every angle. Inside he had space to move. His hands wove spell after spell. His favorites seemed to be dark magic bolts and fire.

The Head Mistress fended them off with an energy shield of some kind and didn't seem to be able to do much else. It did not look good for her, or for us.

A massive funnel of wind came down from above the succubus. The twister was stopped a few feet from her head by the Mistress's invisible dome.

"Do not interfere," warned a sudden voice to my left.

Even though I was invisible the voice was directed right at me. I nearly jumped out of my skeletal armor.

"Yes. His Majesty would not forgive any interruptions either," came a voice from my right.

Looking frantically to either side I saw the vampire's lich to my left and the Mistress's lich to my right. They both looked nearly identical, hunched over with dark cloaks completely covering their faces. Even though they were both hovering about a foot off the ground, they were still only as tall as I was.

"You are the old man?" I declared to the Mistress's lich. His size and posture were the same.

"Yes," he replied.

Then I remembered the danger I was in. Before the vampire stood up, these two seemed to be doing all the fighting themselves. Why exactly was I still alive? "Is there a reason you two aren't fighting each other?"

"Our contracts only state we fight on our partner's behalf."

"Contract?"

"The young one has many questions," the vampire's lich observed.

"Young ones do," replied the other.

So odd. They were just fighting each other minutes ago and now they were speaking like two old men meeting over breakfast. Or was this their dinner entertainment?

"May I ask a question?" I dared.

"Yes, you must."

"Must," echoed the other.

Well, if that was the case. "Do you have any Blue Magic you can teach me?"

***

Sitting in the middle of the most dangerous moment of my life and I dare to ask for free stuff?! You better believe it!

"You are watching two masters. Observe all you can. Learn all you can," the Mistress's lich answered.

"Yes. The battle before you will serve you the best. Steal every secret that you can. There is no moment more vulnerable to any creature than the moment they die. Cast Force Learn then. You will then learn the most."

Blah! If there was only an imp around to hit in the face. My fist probably wouldn't even break now with my buffs. Of course, I should be casting Force Learn on everything in sight! Even if it doesn't give me any more Blue Magic, perhaps with enough time it will unlock more.

I guess I should give myself a break for being surrounded by two liches that were probably powerful enough to kill me with their pinky toes. Not to mention that a literal magic wielding vampire was a football field away and encased in an ice cold glacier he wore as armor. Oh, and the thousand-year-old succubus that was wading in a pool of fire as if it was a hot tub.

Because it seemed I had learned everything I could from the vampire, I cast Force Learn again on the Head Mistress.

"Human, you are doing it all wrong. Put some mana into it."

"Like charging a spell?"

"Yes."

I couldn't say I was surprised that it could be charged. The fact that there were certain times that my targets were more vulnerable was an even bigger discovery.

"What other situations are the best times to cast Creature Observation?"

The Mistress's lich sighed. "When a creature is injured. The worse the injury the higher the likelihood of you learning a spell. Their weakness decreases their natural defense for mind effecting spells. When a creature is sleeping. When a creature is starving. And finally, when you are watching someone cast the spell you are trying to learn. It's best to funnel mana into the spell version of Creature Observation for this more traditional method. This way you can observe it over a period of time."

You can funnel mana into Force Learn? *How? Wait...*

I let mana gather around my eyes as normal when casting the spell. This time when I released it I didn't let the flow of mana stop. So simple it was silly. I became slap happy, upping the MP usage to 100 MP a minute, then studied the fight before me more closely.

Time seemed to slow as the scene before me became clearer. It felt like I was standing in the middle of the contest immune to any damage and standing as judge of how well the competitors were doing.

Hundreds of pop-up windows appeared before me from casting it on the Head Mistress for the first time. As I feared, most of them just warned me that the criteria to gain the spell from her weren't met, which I was able to close in bulk. There were still a few that I was able to glean from her, though.

Cleanliness

Use mana to clean your body. Its ability to clean and disinfect grows with level. At the highest level, this can even be used to cleanse bacterial diseases.

It was the same spell the Mistress had used on me to clean me up when I had warned her about the lich. For some reason, I felt embarrassed learning this one. Why had I learned it now anyway? Had she just cast it on the vampire? I hadn't noticed if she had. Was she planning on insulting him to death?

Ice Shard (Novice)

A large ice shard is propelled at your enemy. The number of shards and your ability to manipulate them grows as it levels. One additional shard for each 10 levels while in novice rank.

Well, at least Shard was obvious. It was one of the few spells she cast periodically, although why she was attacking ice with ice I couldn't say.

Only two spells in close to 300 windows? In comparison, the vampire only had seven windows to click through. I didn't learn anything from him this time around. Maybe he just didn't know blue magic, but these were his natural skills that fit the criteria for blue magic. Could he really even compete with her? Something felt off. Was he really winning?

As fire and dark magic continued to bombard the Head Mistress to wear her down I decided it was worth asking.

"Who is winning?"

"The Head Mistress has won," the Head Mistress's lich replied.

Quickly after, the vampire's lich replied, "Very true. It's just a matter of time now."

"But it looks just like the opposite."

A single bony finger pointed up. My eyes followed it to see thousands of what I suspected to be the very Ice Shards of the spell I had just stolen from her. The shards were gathered behind the vampire, so he probably didn't even notice them.

Doing a double take, I just realized the lich on the losing side was still standing here. Why wasn't he fleeing for his life if he believed the Mistress was going to win?

Instead of fleeing I readied Force Learn to cast the moment one of them died just as the liches had said.

"Wait for it. The threat is imminent but the damage has not yet been done," the vampire's lich warned me.

"And use more mana," the Mistress's lich added.

I already had 500 mana prepared. Not enough? How about 2,000. I let the spell slowly gain in mana; the energy around my eyes was overwhelming.

"More."

Fine. If 2,000 wasn't enough, how about 5,000.

"Good," was all the Mistress's lich said.

It felt as if my eyeballs were commissioned with trying to hold back the sun. It wasn't exactly painful, but that amount of power around my eyes had the very real likelihood of killing me.

Another part of me wanted more. My body lusted over the potential of what such power was capable of. The idea of magic and the reality of it couldn't be compared. I loved it. The way it felt and how it enabled me.

The ice shards were released. A sudden cone of sharp ice shards arrowed toward the seemingly impregnable glacier defense. If the vampire did die, I really wanted that defensive spell.

It didn't make sense to my gamer brain. Why attack ice with ice?

The vampire's defense was tested.

Before my eyes, the glacier turned into a fountain of ice chips and slush that flew in all directions. It flew so far that it ended up covering the two liches and myself. I was still able to see the vampire clearly because I was viewing him magically with a charged Force Learn.

The spell was so powerful that each ice chip seemed to fly in slow motion. The millions of them were clear and visible. I could have stopped what I was doing and studied each one individually. But there was no way my attention could be swayed. I was crushed under the weight of the powerful magic that I was watching unfold.

The ice shards ate through the fifteen feet of ice and pierced the vampire through the gut before the majority of the shards had even started moving.

"Now!" both the liches screeched as the ice spears started to extinguish his life.

You don't have to yell! I wanted to scream back, but instead, I unleashed Force Learn on the dying vampire.

An avalanche of energy entered my vision. It was as if my spirit was thrown from my body and pummeled the vampire with vision itself. I was no longer outside of him, looking upon a dying monster, but had pierced into his very soul, his magic itself, and saw all that he was.

Learning new magic no longer mattered. I wanted to stay and dwell in the ancient creature. His lust for blood wasn't just a lust for refreshment, but power! The power he had already drunk from thousands of other souls was there. It touched me. Not on my skin, but it was suddenly a part of me and we were one.

Chapter 20 - Loot!

As if it had never happened, I was driven back into my body and knew the vampire was dead.

The four Blue Magic spells I had not been able to learn from him before became mine!

Bat Form

Capable of turning into a bat form. All spells and stats remain available in this form, but the stronger you are the larger the bat. Stealth becomes harder the higher the Strength and Constitution, but Invisibility is possible.

Cold Resist (Novice)

The ability to resist cold damage. This skill grows as your spell levels and increases in rank.

"The vampire was resistant to ice?!" I shouted, not really sure why.

"Yes," the vampire's lich responded. "She finished him with ice magic to show her superiority and crush his spirit the moment before it took his life."

The other lich mused, "His only real hope was to catch her off guard and that didn't happen."

I found myself trembling once again as I learned more about how powerful our kidnapper really was. Just minutes ago I was thinking we had grown powerful; far beyond what our levels spoke of. But in comparison to what these monsters were capable of, we were less than newbies in comparison. No, what are newbies in comparison to a being of true power? She was beyond me, beyond us all. How was I ever going to kill her and get home?

If I did ever get home, she could slaughter the entire world of men just out of spite before taking me by force again.

Shaking my head to regain my senses I put my mind back to work to forget my horror.

Vampire's Might

Novice Blood Drain evolves into its truest form. By draining a creature's blood, the power gain can be applied to Heal, Mana and attribute points. Must continue to consume blood for your power to not fade over time.

The power I had felt when I had cast Force Learn on the vampire came back to me. It was terrifying. I was determined to never use this spell if it caused me to lust so intensely for the power that came through blood. Even as the thought entered my mind, I knew I would never be able to hold myself back. Had my search for power just changed me? Was I now a vampire?

Fear

An aura of bloodlust terrifies all of those caught in its influence. Its effects grow with level. Does not affect those with a strong will, rage, bloodlust or high focus.

What if I wasn't a vampire, but I was still able to gain power as they did? Without the bloodlust, this might be the very thing that makes it possible for me to not only survive but grow powerful enough to get my life back.

The pillar of ice melted away as the Mistress strolled up to the now lifeless corpse of what was once the vampire. Even the water evaporated before her red heels touched a single drop.

The vampire had been pierced so many times it was impossible to even tell what creature had once stood there. She held out her hand and the same dark cord that had drained the energy from her undead minions reached out and drained him of his body's remaining power.

Even though I didn't know the spell she cast, I felt a star's worth of radiation leave his corpse and enter her.

I was too frightened to cast Force Learn on her.

Both liches floated towards her as if they had been summoned.

There I stayed, keeping my distance. Her power was now clearer than ever.

As she turned to leave, her eyes stopped on me and she studied my still invisible self for a few seconds. I wasn't even a cockroach to her. I was more like a hamster shrunk to the size of a cockroach that could only try and harm her with cuddles and stink pellets.

I dropped Invisibility, even though I knew she could see through it, and bowed my head. For some reason calling out "Good fight, Head Mistress!" didn't seem appropriate.

She smiled wide, looking genuinely happy at the turn of events. As she headed in the direction of her home she skipped like a schoolgirl. The liches both followed in tow. Why the vampire's lich was still alive gave me pause, but it was clear the liches were not just another monster. Not even a boss. It worried me that in some ways they might be more dangerous than even the Mistress. The fact that she kept one around proved they had their uses.

They stopped at the entrance of our home base well out of hearing range and began a conversation I would have loved to get an ear in.

Though I should be terrified, I didn't let the vampire's corpse being left there escape my attention. I had not forgotten that feeling of power I had when observing him. The situation demanded I try. Seeing the Mistress's power terrified me. I wasn't normally willing to drink blood, but if it was the only way...

I approached the vampire's mangled body. I took a deep breath before bringing up my hand. I willed Vampire's Might to take effect.

Red smoke rose up from the corpse and gathered at one point, creating a cloud. It compressed until the cloud was one large fragile globe of blood. It took only seconds for it to gather. As soon as it did, a stream of it rushed at me from its center. It touched my palm and violated me by magically entering into my system. Power filled me.

Whether the Mistress had left some power in the vampire's corpse, or the blood itself contained its own power, the thousands of creatures that had died to supply him power were now mine.

The veins in my body seemed to swell, pulsing with power. My heart beat harder than I had ever experienced. It was like it was rejoicing by drumming its beat with an intensity it didn't know was possible. I knew then that I was different and I would never be the same. No longer was I human, but I wasn't a vampire either. I was a true to life Blue Mage. Through magic, I was becoming more than human. In time I would be both creature and man. A monster ruled by the humanity inside me.

I didn't have to become a blood drinker! Flexing the muscles in my arms and chest, I basked in the power I felt, but fear started to rise up. Even if I didn't lust for blood in the way a vampire might, I couldn't deny that receiving power through Vampire's Might was intoxicating. It might be just as dangerous. There was also an additional pop-up I received after casting it.

You have fully drained a Master 200-Year-Old Vampire!

Because of the purity of the source the benefits will be 100x that of a basic creature, plus bonus stats depending on the target's personality and talents while living.

+10,000 HP

+10,000 MP

+50 Str

+20 Dex

+50 Con

+200 Int

+100 Wis

Note: These stats are permanent as long as you use Vampire's Might at least once in the next 7 days and once a week after. If you do not find another creature to drain within the next 7 days these stats will be lost at a rate of 3.33% a day until the end of a full month when your stats will return to normal.

As you drain targets, the benefits you receive will depend primarily on the purity of the source. Once your stats have reached a certain level, you will not be able to drain from low-level creatures to improve stats, only to sustain them.

If no stats are lost in a year's time, they will become yours permanently without having to continue to use Vampire's Might. All attribute gains through use on multiple targets of Vampire's Might stack. The one-year timer does not start over with each gain of more stats. Each creature drained starts a separate timer.

Holey Vampire underpants! Did I just gain 140 levels worth of stats?! Everything just got a bit more complicated.

Okay, breathe.

After a few heavy breaths, I settled down. This was a good thing, but also dangerous. If the Head Mistress, and all high-level creatures, commonly had skills like this besides just the ability to level up, then how powerful were they? If spells like Vampire's Might were rare, would this give me the ability to compete with them and possibly catch them?

A second pop-up was in regard to my strength reaching level 100. I had gotten the bonus even though the stats had come from Vampire's Might.

Heavy Lifter

You are now able to lift things 10% heavier. Because it is so much easier for you to handle lighter weight, all damage with melee weapons is increased by an additional 10%

Intensity

You will now have the ability to increase your focus at will at a cost of double stamina use to add 25% damage and 50% aim to every melee attack.

Full Body Synergy

Strength, Constitution, and Dexterity all work together through muscles, tendon, and bone. Because of this relationship and the improvement of all three, it will be as if you have an additional +25 in all three attributes.

Additional +1 to all three stats for every 5 points put in each attribute equally. Example: 5 Str = 1 Con and 1 Dex.

This +25 is included in all damage and skill calculations but does not apply to Leveling Bonuses.

I looted the vampire's corpse! To my horror, most of what the vampire carried was as destroyed as he was. All that I could recover was a golden ring with a nickel-sized blood ruby. Sadly my identification scroll couldn't identify it. That was interesting in itself. It was the first item that I wasn't able to identify with the scrolls.

Turning to the corpses of the rest of the creatures scattered around I hesitated. Should I really drain them all? I feared that the rest of my group would find out what I was doing. Would they look down on me for it?

Looking back, I didn't see anyone that had re-entered this room.

If only skeletons were left out of the zombies, ogres, ghouls, dark elves, orcs and the vampire, how would they react? Shaking my fear away, I remembered that they were gamers. They would understand. At least, that seemed reasonable.

No doubt they were on their way already, so I got to work draining everything. It was a fairly quick process. I wondered if it took longer if I tried to use it when the creatures were alive. The orcs, zombies, ghouls, dark elves and ogres only gave a fraction of the bonuses the vampire gave.

It was interesting seeing which creatures gave me the most stats. Dark elves and orcs gave me more than any of the undead creatures except the Zombie General.

Overall, I gained the following stats.

+14,741 HP

+11,277 MP

+66 Str

+37 Dex

+71 Con

+207 Int

+103 Wis

The undead and orcs gave Strength and Con. The dark elves gave Dexterity and the casters gave Intelligence and Wisdom. It was all pretty logical in the stats they gave.

Should I start dressing like a vampire? A vampire with Skeletal Full Plate Mail. After all, my teeth would always stay nice and white, I mused. The stats would be permanent unless I didn't drain anything within the next seven days and then once a week after. I didn't think that would be a problem for the year required to gain the stats permanently. There were lots of creatures besides skeletons available for me to fight, so I'd just make it a point to drain things on my way to and from my hunting trips.

As I drained the Zombie General something very interesting happened.

You have unlocked the nature of the Undead and the magic that brings them to life!

Blue Magic - Undead Dominance (Novice)

Unlike Raise the Dead, you are able to both bring the dead to life and command those that are already raised unless the being is directly controlled by the necromancer. The level of undead you can control or raise depends on the level and rank of the spell.

So this is what all of those *you better understand the undead* notifications were about. Considering our base was an undead haven it was perfect. Icing on the cake!

***

My group joined me a few minutes later. There were still about 30 zombies I had left to drain. Well, and of course the skeletons remained untouched since they had no blood to leech.

"What are you doing?" Aeris sounded shocked.

The bloody strand that came from Vampire's Might, connecting me and the blood, was already gathered from a zombie and was beginning to fill me.

With a sigh, I looked at her. "I gained a spell from the vampire that lets me drain creatures of blood and gain stats. And no, I don't have to drink anything! It's only a spell," I insisted before anyone asked.

"That's totally gross, Skeletor!" Olivia butted in, ignoring my insistence.

"Seriously!" Travis ran up to me and watched as I finished draining the zombie. "I always wanted to be a vampire!"

"What?!" Olivia turned on him.

He just grinned at her, placing his fist on his hips, standing like a superhero.

"So he likes to drink a little bloody Mary... or bloody Matt, Bob, Sue, and Jose or whatever these zombies' names were. Aren't you guys forgetting something? Loot!" Russ shouted way too loud for how close he was to us.

Any attention to my new spell was forgotten immediately for the promise of rare equipment, which had suddenly become common. Only Aeris hesitated, looking at me with concern for another second longer before the call of loot beckoned her.

It was then I realized that I had been so lost in considering the positives and negatives of draining and devouring that I hadn't looted anything else besides the vampire. *Progression fail! And I call myself a gamer?*

I stopped what I was doing even though the zombie wasn't fully drained and ran to the where I remember the ghouls being. Only a cloak and short staff the size of a baseball bat was left on the now skeletal mages.

Drew had already looted at least two of them himself. Greedy Lightning Mage!

What was I complaining about anyway? I had just gained an insane amount of free stats!

I wandered to the Head Mistress's side of the main battle line where the skeletons had fallen. The skeletons I hadn't paid much attention to and most of the group hadn't reached them in the looting spree. Only Mel, our redheaded dark mage, was already there. He seemed to be looking down and considering something seriously as he stood over the Skeleton General.

What was there to consider? The two-handed sword the monster had wielded as a one-handed weapon was obviously one of the highest quality I had ever seen. A silver wire handle with large silver gothic fangs for a cross guard and glass finish had a soft glow to it. No doubt it was magic. Was something wrong?

"Hey, what's up?" I asked.

"Elorion!" He jumped. "You uh… you really sucked blood from those mobs?"

"Drained is more like it. No sucking required."

A faint smile appeared on his face and was gone as soon as it came. "I, uh."

"What's wrong?"

"I… What do you think of necromancers? I'm not sure what everyone will think…" He looked down, not willing to meet my eyes.

"Well considering the Mistress and Vampire dude had their own army of undead, I think everyone will be happy to have the undead on our side for a change. I have a new necromancer type spell myself but haven't gotten the chance to test it out yet."

With a look of relief, he finally dared to look at me to make sure I wasn't mocking him.

I just shrugged.

"You're a necromancer too, huh?!" A grin found his face. Suddenly he was talking way too fast.

"Not exactly. I'm a total necro newb. I only have one spell."

"Ahh. Let me know if you need any pointers. My Summon Undead reached intermediate."

Not mentioning to him that my spell was Blue Magic and not Dark, I agreed I'd have some questions for him later. It would be a good opportunity to learn about Dark Magic anyways. He had just squashed a number of high-level orcs with some ginormous dark hand spell no one had ever seen. I didn't doubt his ability for a second.

When he bent down to pick up the Skeletal General's loot, I started to turn to look for different bounty, but I stopped short. Mel wasn't grabbing the amazing sword. He grabbed the General's skull, which was the size of a bull's head. He stepped on its neck and started to pull. I just stared at him for a few seconds as he tried to yank its head off.

A look of dread came over him as he noticed me watching him. Must be for some Dark Magic I decided and walked up to give him a hand.

I motioned to the skeleton's neck as I grabbed the general's sword that was far too big for me even with two hands, but my strength made it wieldable. His excitement returned.

With a single swing, I was able to decapitate the skeleton.

"Jackpot!" he cried.

Why he was so excited escaped me, but hey, if he needed the bones and I needed the blood then we might complement each other while hunting. I suspected I would be spending even more time with everyone in the coming days anyway. They were far more powerful and had proved we could take out some fairly high-level creatures as a group.

He put the giant skull in his inventory and pulled out some chainmail to discard, thanking me for the help. Why was he just taking the skull? The dropped sword that I held he had completely ignored. So I happily took it.

It was then that Skyler and his group entered the battlefield, coming back from their hunt.

"What the? What happened?" he said, staring wide-eyed.

The sledge boys and the casters were just as shocked. It was obvious they had been completely oblivious to the battle, or that an army passed right by them. They must have been in a side dungeon.

"Is that what I think it is?" the chestnut-haired rock mage asked. She rubbed her hands together in greed.

"Dude!" Skyler called before he rushed forward,

He reached one of the zombie's corpses at the rear of the defeated army and stooped over to grab a helm.

An oppressive barrage of energy soared over my head like a world-ending comet had just shot past.

Then I looked to see the Mistress floating above Skyler, staring down at him like he was Thanksgiving dinner. "What do you think you are doing?" she said. Her voice was sharp, but playful.

Skyler fell back, his mouth agape as he looked up at the predator above. No words came.

"Every one of these humans helped with the battle," she said, motioning to us with her arm. "They are welcome to take what they please. But you and your friends weren't here."

She slowly drifted closer to him, until she was nearly standing on his gut.

It wasn't what she was saying, but how she was saying it that made me weak in the knees. Her tone was almost flirtatious as if her deepest desire was for him to continue doing what she was asking him not to do.

Something in what she said stole my attention. How had she known we had all helped with the battle? A glacier had literally stood between her and us. How she did it was not as important as what it implied. Either she had the ability to sense the unseen, or the original spell she had cast on us to leech our excess energy could act like a super GPS.

I couldn't see her face since I was standing behind them, but I imagined her licking her lips. It seemed in all the excitement, the succubus part of her she had been suppressing was now unleashed.

"I don't tolerate thieves." She giggled. Raising an open hand, she hovered there motionless for a long moment.

I dared to hope that she would let him go after scaring him speechless, but then she closed her hand.

As if an invisible giant had reached out and grabbed him, he rose off the ground, his arms and legs bound with invisible chains. With a single movement of her hand, he flew off, stopping in mid-air ten feet to her side and hovered there.

"Come, my lovely humans. Gather around."

At her word, the enticing draw I had felt from her the night I had warned her of her imp's betrayal grabbed a hold of me. It wasn't just me that seemed to be affected. My sudden desire for her overcame my fear, and I found myself obeying her summons.

When we were all lined up with her facing us, she looked upon us with enamored eyes.

Even though I was conscious of it, I was entranced.

"You have done so well. Beyond what I had expected in such a short period of time."

Her words pleased me, even though I knew my real concern should be Skyler and whatever she planned to do with him.

"You will all be rewarded for what you have done. This area," she said, with a wave of her hand, "will be rebuilt. You will each be given your own room and access to builders and contractors. There are those among you with crafting talent. If you raise the funds, I give you full reign of building up this area however you so desire. Carefully consider your options.

"I will leave you now. It's a time to celebrate! Do enjoy yourselves."

She looked back as she turned to go, adding one last thing. "Elorion. Do come see me when you have a moment. Once again you have warned me as danger approached my door. As I promised, I have a special reward for you."

She flew away at a leisurely pace with Skyler in tow.

When she disappeared into the next room, her spell's effects lessened and there was a sudden uproar.

"We have to rescue him!" one of the sledge brothers roared.

"How?" asked the much more level-headed earth mage.

A passionate jumble of ideas and objections started to be tossed back and forth.

I ignored them. The illusion of the last week dissolved, and it was clear to all that the Mistress was nothing more than a monster.

It wasn't anger at the injustice that Skyler had been taken, nor betrayal that the Mistress couldn't be trusted with the deal she had given us that bothered me the most. It was knowing that all that the Underworld provided could be taken from me so easily. My talent with Healing and Blue Magic, my Invisibility spell and the power I had leeched from the vampire and his army. I wasn't sure if I should feel ashamed, but if I was honest with myself, I loved this new life. The Head Mistress threatened it and I hated her for it.

I really needed to punch a succubus in the face right now.

Shaking off the thought, I knew there was really only one chance of saving Skyler. I needed to go speak with her. Now.

How do you tell a succubus who is a self-imposed vegetarian to not indulge when she finally gives in to her desire to eat meat?

It was then that I noticed Aeris was staring up at me. "You're going?"

All I could manage was a nod.

"Save him," she replied, unable to look me in the eye. Before I knew it she was hugging me at the waist, and just as quickly walking away.

"Go!" Olivia demanded. "We will hold these idiots back."

She wasn't kidding. Russ and our tanks were literally standing in front of Skyler's group as they tried to push through.

Seeing their dangerous reactions helped cool my own head a bit and focus. Anger would do me no good where I was going.

With a sigh, I turned to go.

"Stay alive, Skeletor!" Olivia called.

I held up my hand so that she could see that I heard her and marched to the Mistress's dinner. I just hoped I wouldn't end up as the main course.

CHAPTER 21 – A SUCCUBUS'S REWARD

I didn't bother asking the imp to take me to the Head Mistress. As foolish as it was to make it known that I had overheard the imp, I stopped at the part of the wall that had opened to the imp before and spoke the word I heard him say. "HidaGrach."

Silently, the wall parted and folded in to reveal the staircase I had taken before. I began the climb up to the domain of my schizophrenic kidnapper.

It was my second time in this hall since I had arrived. I allowed my advanced buffs to remain, but let my skeletal armor remain uncast. She had already seen me in the armor and with my buffs. Removing the armor seemed respectful. Keeping my buffs felt like self-preservation. It would hopefully remind her that we were worth keeping around.

In most games, there was a limit on how high of a level you could reach and how powerful you could become. That didn't seem to be the case in the Underworld. There was no indication there would be a cap to the progress we could make. Levels were only one way to progress. The spells like Vampire's Might and the spell the Mistress had used to drain the vampire's energy looked very much like an unending source of growth if you could manage to live long enough.

How powerful could someone become in a thousand years? Were there those that were a lot older than her? Insanely powerful was an understatement. It took no effort at all to approach her with a renewed dose of humility.

There was no need to knock when I reached the golden double doors to her quarters. They stood wide open.

The Mistress sat cross-legged on her throne while two familiar succubi that had been here on my last visit sat on the couch to either side. Skyler was missing. Was I too late?

This time the three of them were dressed in lavender togas. The Mistress had a golden Olympic wreath sitting on her head like a crown. The two lesser succubi wore a generous amount of clothing in comparison to last time. I was surprised they weren't looking at me like I was the main course. As I entered the room the lesser succubi both stood and motioned for me to sit.

In place of the table that had held the slain dark elf was a red cushioned seat. I sat there as directed even if it seemed small for my new size.

As the two succubi sat back down, the Head Mistress looked me over. I would like to say that there was no squirming on my part, but that would be an over-seasoned lie. She towered over me from her throne. Even if she looked to be in a good mood it was intimidating.

Bringing her hands together before her, she looked me in the eye.

Without lowering my gaze I bowed my head, not really from respect, but my nerves were fraying at the edges.

The three of them giggled together.

"Elorion, my dear. This is the second time you have warned me of a threat. It pleases me you survived Lord Darius's little visit. And you have grown so much!"

I would bid my time before asking about Skyler. My only hope was that she could be convinced it was worth keeping him alive. Bursting in here and demanding him be released was probably the most certain way to fail my mission.

"Such a fine boy," added the succubus to her right. She cocked her head to the side as she stared at me.

"Sister," the Head Mistress rebuked sweetly, then turned back to me. "You have grown much stronger than our last meeting. I hope my gifts have proved useful. Congratulations are in order."

With a swallow, I found my voice. "Thank you. And on your victory as well."

"Oh yes! It has been a decade since I had such fun. There is no race I take more joy in putting in their place then the vampires." She rubbed her hands together quickly. "Which puts me in a splendid mood. As you may have heard, I will see to it that the area is renovated to make you all more comfortable."

I bowed my head to acknowledge that I did.

"Because of your actions, I think something else is in order."

"Sister!" The same succubus that had interrupted before inserted herself, while wrinkling up her nose. "There is some training that would do him well. The stench of his magic..."

It was the first time since the imp had discovered I had a talent in light magic that anyone had seemed to notice. This time she had really detected it from my smell. That was not a good sign.

"Very well. It will be your gift to him" The Head Mistress grinned. "I'm assuming you would like to do the pleasures yourself?"

"Oh, yes please!" she squealed with glee.

"Be gentle. Remember, he has been a big help to us."

I had no clue what they meant by training, but I turned my attention to the succubus who was going to give me the gift.

With the flick of her finger, a dark electric bolt shot out and struck me on the bare skin of my forearm.

The next thing I knew I had fallen out of my seat. A cold electricity bit into me, snaking out in chaotic little channels of pain.

At the same time, the hair on the back of my neck stood on end. *Was this the end? What was the point of them kidnapping us in the first place if I was just going to die when I had finally started to get stronger?!*

"Poor beautiful boy. Today's lesson is a bit painful, but a good one." The Mistress sighed happily. "Your light magic can strengthen your body, but it also makes you vulnerable to its opposite, dark magic. You see, since light and dark forms of magic aren't elements, they react differently than you would expect. Most things depend upon physics and the natural laws that govern us. This is not the case with light and dark.

"When they come together they both immediately begin warring with each other until one wins out. Since your magic is buffeting your body and literally filling you, the reaction between the two opposites brings your body into the mix, causing critical damage even if your power wins out. This is because you become the battlefield. The destruction they leave in their wake stays with you. The same happens if you attack a creature with dark alignment. They take critical damage even if they are more powerful than you."

Despite the pain, it was not something that lingered with me for long. My chest heaved and my arm hurt, but I was already breathing easier. The pain didn't hinder me from regaining my focus on what was being said; instead, it sharpened my mental clarity.

A simple clap of the Head Mistress's hands brought her explanation to a close. "Very good. Elorion. We do not cause you pain for our pleasure but for your good. Most creatures don't remember information well naturally, but they never forget how something makes them feel. This is a lesson you must learn or the first competent dark aligned creature you come across will slaughter you. And here's the danger. You are in the underworld. 80% of the creatures you run across will be creatures of the dark.

"You will also be able to smell them when you grow strong enough, but they can also sense you. Of course, if you remove your buffs, then the stench will be lessened greatly. This makes stealth a challenge, but with practice it is possible."

I was able to check my HP and saw my loss had been no more than 200. Pain must have been the point, for it was far from killing me.

"1500 years ago, humans had a powerful presence in the Underworld. Because of their religious traditions they forbade the practice of any magic but light magic. This also allowed them to master their magic quickly with a sole focus on one school. The number of humans along with the use of armor allowed them to get around some of their weakness. It was ultimately their downfall."

Recovering further, I found the strength to sit back, giving my hands and knees a rest.

"Their presence began as only an annoyance to the lesser lords. By the time I spawned five hundred years later, about a thousand years ago, the humans were wreaking havoc, conquering many of their dungeons and sacking the cities of their realm. This forced the Vampire and Orc Lords to intervene. A single family of Vampire Ancients wiped out the majority of the intruders except for the strongest. Their strategy was so simple that the humans who were left became easy prey to the rest of the Underworld."

My pain had lessened, but I feared healing myself to recover from the damage. Not letting the opportunity pass by, I looked the Mistress in the eye and asked the most obvious question. "What was the strategy?" My displeasure wasn't hidden.

Pity looked down on me from her throne. Then the unexpected happened. She stretched out her hand and white light came forth and surrounded me. "That should feel better."

It did, but I immediately noticed that it didn't heal my exhaustion, only the damage done to my body. My talent really was unique.

"Everyone still remembers the lesson the Vampire Lords taught the underworld that day. The humans became experts at crafting armor, but they left it without any elemental alignment that strengthens it against other alignments. They knew if they imbued it with light magic they would be weak to the dark. Steel is derived from the earth so it is earth aligned to a degree even if left neutral.

"The Vampire Lords took advantage of this and didn't attack the humans directly, but instead focused on their armor. They used a simple mixture of water, wind, and earth to quickly rust the armor and then shatter it with the person still in it. After the armor was destroyed, they switched to dark magic and finished the job. It is the ultimate example of why one must try to be a master of magic and not just a single element or alignment. Once this knowledge was made known, even the mightiest paladins had to go into hiding. In less than two years nearly all humans were driven from the surface of the deep."

As much as I wanted to hold a grudge against them because of the pain, this really was priceless information.

They lectured on the weakness of those that only used light magic, but didn't stress its strength. In one way it made me vulnerable. In another, she confirmed that 80% of creatures in the underworld were weak against my magic. That was huge. If I could find a way to get around my defensive weakness then there was real hope.

"What should I do?" I asked as I stood before her.

"For the time being, get the strongest armor you can find. And by all means, do not leave it neutral. If you survive long enough to learn multiple alignments of magic, which can be incredibly difficult, you will be able to change the alignment of your armor at will. It won't make you invincible, but even a lesser lord like Lord Darius would have difficulty killing you if you learn how to use elements properly.

"I'd recommend that you talk your friends into first building a smithy. It will take time, but I remember there was a human or two with the talent for such things. As they grow in skill and level up, they will be able to create more and more powerful armor and weapons. There are also relics and items of power in the underworld that you can use to level up the smithy and a smith's tools.

"This goes for all of the crafts. Everything from alchemy to enchanting, rune-scribing to tailoring, all must be mastered and their shops leveled up.

"Most importantly, don't let yourself become arrogant like your ancestors. Use every tool available to you. Every element, alignment, and magic has its benefit.

"Also, invisibility will continue to be one of the most powerful spells you will find."

"Thank you," I replied, swallowing back a knot in my throat.

"Now for my gift. What would you request of me this time?"

"I." *It was time.* "I would like to have Skyler returned to us."

She leaned forward in her chair, her knuckles white as she clenched the armrests of her throne. She glared down at me as if I had just spat in her face. Intensifying energy started to whirlwind from her.

"You want the thief?!" she said, her lips parting as if she was tasting the very idea of him.

I had to lean forward and plant my feet to keep from falling back.

"Calm yourself, sister," the bolder of the two succubi on her right said. Both of them started to pulsate energy to fend off her anger.

Not backing down, I replied, "Yes."

She was silent for a long moment. The muscles of her jaw clenched, released, and clenched again.

"Remember. It was you who swore off men, sister."

"But the human looks so large and juicy," she said. Her eyes were closed as her bottom lip trembled at the thought of him.

"There is a bodybuilder convention going on. Just say the word and we will bring half a dozen large ones."

"But it's not the same. Their steroids and starving themselves makes them taste like kale. You know I hate salad!"

With a huff, the Head Mistress turned to me. "Why do you want him?"

There were so many reasons, or excuses I could give, but what would actually convince her? What came out of my mouth wasn't what I expected.

"Because I love it here."

As one, the three succubi's heads twisted to the side like a bunch of questioning puppies.

I continued. "Eat—er, taking him will cause the other humans to be angry."

"This is good, sister. They will fear you," the not so bold succubus to her left said.

"The problem is they already fear you and are starting to respect you. If you do this you will lose that respect. Respect is worth more."

"Oh? I have found fear much more useful," the Mistress replied.

"Do you really want them to follow you out of fear? If they survive and grow powerful in time, eventually they might grow bold enough to challenge you. Yes, they might die as easily as the vampire, but then you would have to start over with more humans. But, if they respect you, then instead of challenging you, they will defend you.

"Either way, it's not like they need the motivation of fear. Did you see their faces as they looted the battlefield? Skyler, the person you arrested, was so motivated that he couldn't hold himself back. I don't want to take him from you. I just think it will be more beneficial for you, and for me, if you leave him alive."

Wording everything as if I was on her side put a bad taste in my mouth, but it was truer than I wanted to admit.

Her two sisters looked to her, nodding. They were taking my side?

The energy that was pouring out of her suddenly stopped. "You reason like a lich." She sat back into her chair with a sigh. "Very well. This will be my gift to you. Tell the humans what you will. That I punished him for his crime and he is now free. Does that please you?"

It felt like a thousand pound water balloon had been sitting upon my shoulders and had suddenly burst. I didn't really know what had just happened, but perhaps she was more reasonable than I thought. *Yeah right. Never trust someone that thinks men look juicy. Or like salad, for that matter.*

"And here. Take this key," she said, not hiding her disappointment. In her palm sat a six inch long skeleton key. By skeleton, I mean it in the most literal sense. It was made of polished bone.

"This is the prize for making it to the end of my dungeon. You have earned it months sooner than I believed any of you would. At the end of my labyrinth, you have likely noticed a tower made of bone. Inside you will find ten levels, each with its own set of guardians. Each level is progressively more powerful and aligned with a different element or magic form. At the top of the tower is a surprise. You will also find a door on the far side of the first floor. It will unlock once the first floor is completed. Through it, you will find the exit to the labyrinth into rest of the Underworld. From there you can pursue anything your heart desires, but only after you've earned it."

That meant we were currently shut off from the rest of the Underworld and everything we had faced up until now was of the Mistress's making—except the vampire. He was able to attack because of the lich's spell that turned the wall into something they could walk through. Did that mean I could learn a similar spell and bypass the trials of the tower? As I considered it I knew I didn't want to even if I could. Regardless of how sadistic the Mistress was, not everyone has a labyrinth designed to help them grow stronger. No gamer in their right mind would pass that up.

"There are many paths you can take. You have free rein to build your base below as you so desire as long as you can find or purchase the resources necessary. The underworld itself has many dungeons and secrets that can help one grow stronger. Will you conquer the first floor and try your hand out there, or climb the tower? I can't tell you what path is right or wrong, only that you must grow stronger. I have no idea if Lord Darius told others or if he kept it to himself. Eventually, his family will come looking for him. There may be other armies, larger and much more powerful ones, on their way here already. Or you might be safe for now. Most of those that pose a real danger to you live far enough away that it will take time for them to get here. In the underworld, peace never lasts forever."

I took the key as she tossed it, and she cautioned me, "Don't follow the mistake your race made a millennia ago. Respect all alignments. Magic in itself has no morality. Even the darkest magic can be used for good or the lightest for evil. If you know anything about your history you know how evil mankind can be."

With a nod of understanding, I inventoried the key and stood.

"Go. Your friend will be returned to you soon. I must eat something first, or at a glance I will be tempted to devour your friend." She turned to the succubus on her left. "Go fetch me the kale. Just make sure you bring plenty of ranch dressing."

My mouth opened, but I found myself speechless after how nonchalantly she talked about eating people. *With ranch dressing?* Instead of trembling with fear, I was disgusted. It was practically dishonorable toward ranch dressing. How could she?

Finding the three of them staring at me, I started scrambling and blurted out, "Thank you, Head Mistress. We will continue to grow stronger."

She moaned as if I was a child being sweet.

I left as quickly as my legs would allow without letting it look obvious that I wanted to throw a ranch dressing bottle at her and drown her in it.

Somehow, I had survived and even saved Skyler's life, although it seemed multiple people would take his place in her stomach. Any question that we were safe here had been answered. We were not. Every gift she had given was dependent on what she would get in return.

What I had said to her was true. In time the others could grow to respect and even defend her. But not if I could help it. I knew what she was really like. She could not be trusted with the wellbeing of the very creatures she most enjoyed to eat. We needed to escape.

Chapter 22 – Much Needed Nap

I woke up from my first nap in four days. Both my leather and skeletal armor was removed while I slept in the dark barracks. Most of my buffs I still had on so that they would level while I slept.

After some haggling, I had been able to purchase some shorts and a real cotton t-shirt for my nap. The goth dwarf merchant even had real sheets! Why? "Dwarves demand soft sheets!" he insisted. Did that make me part dwarf?

Before my nap, I had sold all the zombie armor and weapons I could carry. Twice. The looting basically stopped after I left to face the Mistress. After explaining she was punishing him but would return him soon unharmed, even his group settled down and returned their attention to the loot.

None of them dared try to loot anything from the battlefield after that. We found a way around this by looting the items ourselves and then handed them items we couldn't carry after our inventories were already full. There were so many items that it could hardly be called generous to gift them the items we handed them.

All the items I sold netted me an incredible 300k. The least of the items they dropped was better than all but the best that I had owned. Even after my second trip, there was armor to spare.

Two things kept me from grabbing more loot to sell. First, someone got the idea that we should save some of it in the armory that had been offered to us the first day. Secondly, it was decided that Skyler's group should get their pick of what was left. This was our gift to them, so they wouldn't fall under the Mistress's justice.

I just shook my head at the thought. *Justice? Maybe if it was the name of a new kind of sauce.* She would have likely dipped him in it.

With regards to the handful of rares that I now had in my possession, it was likely I would be able to sell them for more than what we loaded into the armory. I had held onto them until after getting some sleep.

Even though my nap had lasted only four hours, I felt like I had slept for a week. Even with the ability to restore fatigue, comfort and relaxation was a reward in itself. There is nothing like doing nothing.

***

Entering the dining hall, I walked into a conversation my group was having with the others that hadn't been there when we fled the base.

"Thank you, guys, again for sharing the loot," said Skyler gratefully. "Seriously, I never would have taken any loot if I would have known you guys had killed them."

"No problem," Aeris insisted kindly.

Skyler was no worse for wear than before he had been taken by the Mistress. He had swallowed the story of her doing it to punish him literally, since he was unable to recall anything himself. It seemed everyone was willing to believe it was justice and not her appetite that had been behind her actions.

All five members of his group passed along their thanks as they headed for the door. Each one nodded to me in turn. Sure they were thankful, but if they knew what had really happened…

No. I would tell them the truth when the time was right, but let them enjoy our newfound wealth and use it to grow. Long term it would make better use of our time. I hoped.

"Dude! Where are your clothes?" Travis mocked, finally turning his attention to me.

Everyone was still in their armor so they felt compelled to join him in laughter. They had a game of cards going as they snacked on fries. Yes, real french fries!

"These are athletic shorts, not underwear," I explained.

"Those aren't shorts. They're too-shorts," Olivia rebuked.

They were right if I was going to be honest. It was harder to get well fitting clothes when you were buff, especially when you had no experience dressing yourself while being so large. It was one of the few downsides to leveling up; a good problem to have I guess.

I just shrugged as my four closest friends in the underworld clowned on my farmer's tan. My thighs were pretty pasty white.

"We should take a trip to the beach," I recommended.

They laughed, but immediately all of our minds went to the same place. We would probably never see a beach again.

I had to get stronger.

After grabbing steak and pasta—and yes, it was drenched in ranch dressing!—I sat next to Aeris and Travis. The bench on the other side of the table was made up mostly of Russ, with a little bit of Olivia on the end. Russ was the size of a muscular brown bear. He even dwarfed Skyler now.

"It's great to see you with some more meat on your bones, bonehead," Olivia prodded.

To keep the good humor going I cast just the helm of my skeletal armor. "Who you calling a bonehead?"

Olivia almost fell off of the bench holding her stomach.

"Aeris! Put your boy in his place!" she screamed through her laughing fit.

"My boy?" Aeris replied, bright red as she looked to me for help.

I just grinned and played it off. "Mistress Aeris. Is that your bidding?"

"Well…" she teased back, recovering from the unexpected implication. "There is something. The merchants have new items on display…" Kittens and puppies don't have anything on Aeris's adorably elfish, large-eyed begging. We went shopping.

***

When we arrived to shop, the merchants had quickly restocked their shelves after we had come across so much more wealth from looting the armor. It seemed they had been waiting for us to get to this point. The items they had laid out for us to view had gone from 50k to 200k or more. Before, I had considered something with 50+ to a single attribute as a decent item. I had been way off. The tables were littered with as many items as they could possibly place on the tables and the walls were hung with items as well.

Browsing made it obvious the majority of the items had +250 to +500 to a single attribute or as much as +200 to every stat. Not just that, but even though the number of stats had gone up quite a bit, the price didn't seem to scale with it. The number of stats was nearly 10 times more than before, but the items cost only about 5 times more. That could only mean one thing.

These items that were becoming available to us were actually common in the Underworld. That meant that we hadn't even gotten to the good stuff yet. I assumed the reason the items we had been dealing with cost as much as they did was because of the markup. Basically, the merchants had to make enough money for it to be worth it for them to have a stall here. Now that we were leveling up, that meant they expected us to start making some real money and the items they would be selling to us would make a nice enough profit that they didn't have to compensate.

Aeris grabbed my arm, not even realizing how tight she squeezed me. She was like a floundering fish that had seen the water for the first time.

It occurred to me it was about time we had that talk she had mentioned to me. Should I tell her about what had really happened with the Mistress? I decided I trusted her enough, but would it just be a burden for her?

I started second-guessing selling my rarer drops. But when I saw the bookshelf up against the wall at the halfling's stall I started salivating. Over 200 books stared me in the face. I had a feeling there were bound to be more expensive ones than had been available before. Asking him to hide the bookshelf until he saw me later probably wouldn't go over well. Scanning the titles, I looked to see if there was anything I simply had to have no matter the cost.

Everything was there from elemental compasses, magic theory, history, maps, alchemy, blacksmithing, scavenging for food, a set of encyclopedias, and even a book on dating all the different races in the Underworld. I hoped they stuck to just humanoids at least. Most of them seemed worth it, but I didn't see any must-buys yet. I was convinced I did want to find out how difficult it was to learn a different school of magic. Not that I could probably ever compete with someone talented in a different element, but being well rounded for any situation seemed like a no-brainer.

After selling her drops Aeris began removing her leather armor.

How was a man supposed to stand there while an extremely attractive girl in cosplay took her armor off to try on new clothes?

"Help," Aeris grunted as she tried to pull off her leather vest.

With my new strength, the job was easy enough. I grabbed the shoulder pads on either side and lifted. It nearly popped off of her. It was a tight fit around the shoulders. She had a thick cotton shirt without any sleeves. The thicker shirt bunched up as I pulled, showing a small portion of her tummy. Whether she had earned her six pack here or before she came, it caught me off guard. I didn't normally associate abs with casters. She was fairly petite in build, but also lengthy and her muscle definition was firm and taut. She did have a talent in Dexterity.

Looking away, I did my best to hide that I had seen. In truth, I was afraid if I kept looking I would start staring, get caught, and then become known as the Underworld Peeping Tom. That's just not a good title to have hanging over your head.

"Thanks," she said, completely oblivious to my predicament because she had her eyes on something shiny. *Who can blame her?*

Taking the vest off my hands, she placed it in her inventory and went on to try on the new armor she was considering. When she motioned for the dwarf to let her try the Constitution focused plate mail I almost fell over.

The strangest thing from my observation of the armor's stats was that even plate mail didn't seem to limit a spell caster's ability to cast spells. At least not directly. There were a few practical things that would likely affect it. If you used buffs like I did, the armor would have to be fitted to me in a buffed state, because steel didn't stretch. Also, how would an element aligned armor react to elemental spells you were casting? Or what if you tried to wear a dark aligned armor when you had a light magic buff. Would it be like wearing magic acid and cause damage at the touch?

Plate mail also took a good bit of time to put on properly. When the full helm with a face guard finally slid down over her face I was looking at the best outfit in the history of cosplay. The steel was polished and shaped with a lady's figure in mind. The utilitarian design of it gave it an edge that most cosplay missed because they are mostly concerned with looking amazing. This just looked real.

"So?" she asked, slightly muffled from behind the helm.

"You look hot."

Her sudden giggle was as bad as a gaggle of girls surrounding and laughing at me in my bathing suit.

"Um…" I scrambled to find words. I lit up like a red Christmas bulb of embarrassment.

It was a rare moment when she didn't have any wisecrack. Even though I couldn't see her through the helm I was sure she was looking down and away.

I could just barely see her eyes through the visor as she looked up, recovering faster than me, and responded, "So you just want me because I'm warm-blooded?"

"No, of course not!"

"Oh. You just think I'm hot?"

"No! I mean yes! Or—what I meant to say was, is it hot in the armor?"

"Oh, so I'm not hot. Well." She sat her armored chin on her fist as she thought. "It breathes better than the leather armor. It moves well too."

She totally had me backpedaling. I could always beg for forgiveness, or… "Yes, you are hot. Cute. Attractive. And look amazing… with the armor on."

Getting hit on the arm with steel gauntlets hurts.

"It does look nice, doesn't it?" Her attention was now squarely on testing the armor and not our friendly back and forth. It seemed the joints allowed for almost nimble movements. The only burden was the higher weight, which was partially held up by the frame of the armor itself.

It wasn't the last armor she tried on. She ended up choosing a mix of a few different plate mail pieces. The attribute bonuses were +450 to Con, +100 to Str and +225 to Int. To get the Int she took dark red gloves in place of gauntlets. That wasn't all. Magic resistance was increased by a huge 15% except for water and electrical magic.

Armor rating was far more complicated. Gone was the simple armor rating that I was used to in the games from my past. Instead, there was a breakdown of the material: Steel (Fine Quality). I guess I would have to test the material to get a better idea of how useful it would be.

As for plate armor causing spell failure as in most games to balance things out, here that just wasn't the case. It was only the gauntlets that had the ability to cause any kind of real problem, unless she cast something out of her mouth, like my Flame Thrower. Since things didn't seem balanced like a game, it was a good choice. Steel versus leather, steel wins every time.

In the end, our Wind Mage was decked out in full plate mail with a black cloak with a violet lining, a small steel buckler and new silver wand that looked similar to a dagger, except it had small carved wooden figures up and down each side of the blade-shaped shaft. 700,000 coins later she was newly equipped and had less than 80k left to her name.

Part of me was torn. When the time came to shop myself, should I focus on armor, weapons, and items, or books? Maybe a mix of the two? After seeing how much her rarer drops sold for I was pretty sure I'd end up with 500,000 or more. Why were there so many choices?!

Leaving the merchants, I made a point of telling them I would be back later that night.

Aeris stopped me in the hall. This time her helm was off and in her inventory, but she still wore the rest of her new armor.

"You said earlier that the vampire gave you a spell that allowed you to drain a target's blood to gain stats?"

The way she said it had me worried. I had a feeling I was about to get a stern warning about my safety. It didn't stop me from explaining it to her. More than that I set up my argument as to why it was worth using.

To my surprise, she wasn't concerned for me at all. "Do you think I could learn it?"

"Well." I thought a moment. "If you learn blue magic, I think it's possible I could teach it to you. I was going to purchase a number of books anyway. I'll look for something for you."

Her face lit up. "Oh, this?" she said, fishing such a book out of her inventory: a Blue Magic Compass.

"When did you…"

"You were so infatuated with how hot I am that you were watching me and not what I was buying."

Why exactly had I been worried about telling her about what really happened with the Mistress? It was clear she was going to try and take care of business with or without me, so I might as well tell her.

When I was sure that no one was there with us, I took her by the hand and walked her down the hall into the armory. As I had hoped, it was empty.

"There's something I need to tell you," I said, turning to face her.

She looked up at me with expectant eyes but held her arms across her chest like she wasn't sure about what she thought I was going to do.

"I..." I swallowed to wet my throat, unintentionally finding myself in a romantic situation.

"Aeris. I need someone to know what really happened with Skyler. It's time we had that talk."

She mouthed, "Oh," slowly dropping her gaze as she processed what I had just said. Her shoulders relaxed and her arms fell to her sides. When she looked back up at me I knew the moment had passed.

"What is it?" she said.

"Skyler wasn't released because the Mistress had punished him for his crime. It had nothing to do with right or wrong. She was going to eat him, or whatever she does, and only she let him go because I talked her out of it."

Her head was nodding up and down before I even finished. "I knew it! We can't stay here, can we?"

"No, but we can't just leave, either. Not yet. We just aren't strong enough. But if we can buy enough time... It's time we start planning."

CHAPTER 23 – PLANNING FOR THE LONG TERM

"10,000 coins to identify the sword?!" It must have sounded harsher coming out than it was meant to. 10k was a lot of money to just take a chance with. I hadn't even mentioned the vampire's ring yet.

"If a normal identity scroll doesn't work, then it is more than just a magic item. I can assure you," the goth dwarf encouraged. "Besides just normal magic items, there are much more powerful items that exist. In order of rarity, items are categorized as Normal, Magic, Rare, Unique, Artifact and Legendary. Normally the rarer it is the more powerful. There are exceptions in regard to quality which can blur the lines, but it is a good practical way to look at them."

Taking a step back, I considered it for a moment. Glancing to the closest merchant, I saw both the dark elf and the halfling watching me closely with no objection to what the dwarf was saying. It was just the four of us so I had their undivided attention. The dark elf was even nodding at what was said.

There was another question that had to be asked. "Can I learn to identify such items?"

He sighed heavily. "With enough time and hard work. All craftsmen and tradesmen gain the ability to identify certain items. As an example, blacksmiths can identify armor and weapons, and leatherworkers can identify leather armor, and leather items. Merchants, because of the amount of time we spend with all forms of items, unless we are in a niche market, slowly gain the ability to identify anything. Of course, it all depends on the rank and level of your Identify skill as well."

"I see." Well, there was no fast way for me to get around the 10k cost.

Since the item seemed to garner so much attention, I considered my chances pretty good that it would be worth the cost.

"Very well." I exhaled.

The dwarf took the four foot long sword as delicately as you would handle priceless jewels. He sat it down on a sturdy wooden stand just behind the table he used to display his goods.

Suddenly, his eyes lit up with an azure glow as he scanned the sword from top to bottom at length. It was five minutes before he took his eyes off the blade.

"I think you will be very pleased with what I found. It's not just rare, but a unique item."

Taking the blade back after handing him the coin, I was able to observe its characteristics at will now.

General Cunningham's Bastard Sword

Earth Alignment

Mana channeled through the blade will intensify its damage by one for every two mana used.

Skill granted: Build Momentum (Advanced)

Build Momentum (Advanced)

Grants the blow additional weight the longer the blade is swung in a consistent motion.

Maximum weight added, 200 lbs.

The wielder only bears 10% of the weight that is magically placed behind the blow.

Description: Bastard sword wielded by a leader of thousands through twenty-four victorious battles. Has been used to slay over five hundred men before its master was run through with a spear and then hacked to death by a dozen men. The blood of its enemies and master has given the blade unnatural power.

Staring at the blade's abilities for a long time, I found all three merchants were having a bidding war on the blade when I recovered from the shock. Was it really wise to sell such an item? If I could master using it my blows could impact my target with over two hundred pounds behind the blow at the cost of only adding twenty pounds to the weight of the weapon. With this single weapon, I could mow through an army of mobs and literally cleave and launch the enemies around like a blowtorch through butter. That didn't even account for the ability to add mana to the blade. It was overpowered! If this was just a Unique item than what would an Artifact or Legendary item be like?

Since there were no class, level or strength restrictions, I would have to try to wield it before I would know if it was too much for me.

"Two million!" the dwarf roared, beating the other two merchants by 500k.

They hesitated.

Did he just say two million? I could eat whatever I wanted for a year or ten.

Considering it seriously, it would be possible to change my fighting style to take advantage of the weapon. With some good armor and Health Buffs, I could become a healing tank with an Earth-based sword. The skill the sword carried seemed to be directly related to its alignment.

None of the other merchants seemed to be willing to go higher than two million. A very important question came first. What could I get with two million coins?

I held up my hand and halted the negotiation to not encourage the dwarf until I was sure I would sell. "Sorry, but I'm not sure I'm selling yet. Will the bid stand?" I asked.

"It will." The dwarf nodded.

Not wanting to disappoint, I added, "I just want to see what is available for that kind of money before I trade in such a powerful item. There is no doubt that keeping it would greatly benefit me."

There was an experienced businessman behind the eyes of the dwarf. It was really not necessary to explain myself to him, but I did it out of courtesy. That didn't negate the fact that this might be the only item this powerful that I came across for a long time, if ever. It was foolish to assume this would become a new norm.

Forcing myself to stop imagining what it would be like to use the blade, I looked from one merchant display to the next. Each of them was hurrying to put out new items for display as I looked. They knew me well enough by now to know in detail what I was looking for.

It was overwhelming. I had recently shopped with Aeris, so remembering, the dwarf carried out the most powerful plate mail I had seen. Not just one, but three different suits. The stats were as insane as the prices. +50,000 to HP, 50% Magic Resist, Frozen Aura, +2000 Strength and more looked up at me from his bench.

The dark elf had mage based items he had just put out for me to see. Two different staves, robes, cloaks and four different orbs had stats just as crazy as the armors. +60,000 mana, +1000 Int, +1000 Wisdom, +500 Mana Per Minute, +30% damage to a single element... Not to even mention the bonus skills and spells they gave.

Books, scrolls, and potions were the items the halfling pulled out. One item made all of the other items fade into the background. He had Experience Potions! +50% bonus experience over 24 hours begged me to buy them. At 15k a shot they weren't cheap, but with two million coins I could afford to take advantage of them. Besides the revelation of the amazing potions, the most important thing in my purchase would be knowledge. I needed the books the halfling had, and there were a lot of them. Long-term I expected to outgrow the sword.

I... I became convinced looking at the prices and items available that the two million would be better spent elsewhere than keeping the sword. It was difficult, but I walked up to the dwarf holding it out for him. "Deal."

His eyes lit up like a child's face on Christmas morning.

After collecting a lot of coins, even though he cashed me out in 20 golden leaf bullion worth 100k copper coins each, they all expected me to begin my shopping spree. When I pulled out the vampire's ring with the large blood ruby encased in gold I caught them off guard. If you looked closely there seemed to be something written in an unknown script on the gold encircling the ruby.

"Could you identify this as well?"

The dwarf looked closely. His mouth slowly dropped open. A flash of blue came to his eyes and was gone. "How? You have yourself a master ring."

Master Ring

A sole key that unlocks a nearly impenetrable magic lock.

The lock is only known to its user.

I handed him the 10k for the identification and his eyes never left the item.

"How much is it worth?" I asked as I began studying it.

"We don't carry that kind of coin here."

A chorus of "Mmmms" backed up his reply.

"Depending on the original owner this could be tens of millions or more. It is more of a key than a ring. It unlocks only the most powerful enchanted locks. It takes so much mana to cast the spell to create the lock that just a vault with such a door costs close to a billion coins. People don't spend that much to secure something cheap."

"Did you say vault?"

"Yes. It's popular for only the richest or most powerful people to have master rings in the Underworld."

Quest item! Undead Dance Party with Birthday Cake! Okay, such a cake could never come out pleasant... Immediately I knew it was a key to unlock either the home or treasure vault of the Vampire Lord the Mistress had fought. It might be some time before I was powerful enough to pursue it, but I now had a good incentive to leave the labyrinth besides just being free of the place.

It was almost a big enough revelation that I forgot about spending my 2 million coins. Okay, not quite, but it still nearly caused me to dance in front of them!

It was time to focus. If I wasn't careful I could end up with a lot of great items that wouldn't have the best long term benefit for my character build. The danger of some unknown army attacking us wasn't entirely gone, but I doubted the vampire had told anyone else about us. He was arrogant enough to attack the Mistress because he thought he could take all that she had. I doubted he wanted to share any of the loot. Was I safe? No. Perhaps never again. But this was the best I could hope for in this messed up world. What was here that could help me grow as strong as possible when time wasn't a factor?

The small book collection the halfling possessed was the first thing on my list. I decided to take 20 of them to keep the price under 400k. Some of them were more expensive than the ones I saw before. As much as 50k each. Maps and encyclopedias would be priceless to me this early in the game. There were a number of element and spell class compasses. Also, there were things on fencing, pole weapons, alchemy, blacksmithing, smelting, forging, jewel-smithing, stealth, lockpicking, and trap making and disarming.

Finally the peanut butter and jelly of the crop were the books on magic theory: *How to Get the Most Use out of Elements for the Ogre-brained Among Us*. Learning as much I could about magic was essential.

As I scanned through one of the elemental compasses on Water Magic, it became clear immediately that picking up another element wasn't going to be easy. I had to either find a teacher, or a dungeon of that alignment.

When it came to the rest of my purchases I kept one thing in mind. What would help me survive? Just as Aeris had spent a good portion of her new wealth on defense I would do the same. After the lesson from the succubus, I knew I had to get good armor as soon as possible to guard against my weakness. It was only a band-aid for a long-term problem, but I had a feeling there were some awesome band-aids. I stayed away from any item that added new skills that I didn't already have. I didn't want to become dependent on an item if I could help it.

My Steel Full Plate Mail wasn't terribly ornate except for green runes along the trim of each polished plate. The helm had wings above the ear slits and a flat top. My boots and cloak I kept to help with my stealth. Besides that, the only other thing that remained was my scepter. Even my rings I sold back to them to upgrade.

I bought a pair of trap detecting rings that gave me over 100 to the skill. How it worked or what the 100 translated to in the real world I didn't know yet. The shield I now used wasn't actually one I purchased, but one I got from a zombie.

Here is a breakdown of my new gear:

Durable Full Plate Mail of Life

Quality: Exceptional

Alignment: Nature

Improved Durability

+45,000 HP

Spell Dampening 40% (Lessens spells effectiveness.)

If the suit was a full set including the boots and gauntlets I would have an additional 5,000 HP that I passed up for the cloaking bonus. They were in my inventory so if I needed them I had them. I doubted there was a lot of the nature element in the Underworld. It would be better than facing off against the 80% of dark aligned creatures.

Stone Steel Kite Shield

Quality: Fine

Alignment: Neutral

Spell Dampening 60%

I was hoping that the spell dampening of 60% and 50% of the armor would stack, making it possible to fully block most spells. Though I was pretty sure it wasn't this simple, this was the highest percentage shield I had seen even if it didn't have any special stats or characteristics.

Channeller's Orb

This orb acts as a magnet to arcane forces around you.

+250 Mana Per Minute Mana Regen

The more mana regen the better! In a lot of cases, the additional damage my scepter granted me was overkill in the dungeon now, so I planned on carrying this in one hand and my shield in the other; or possibly just switching out between the two. It wasn't like a game where you could only equip one item per body part. Technically I could hold the shield and orb in the same hand. That would be a little awkward though.

2x Silver Ring of Trap Detection

+50 to Spot Trap

After the purchase of the books, armor, orb and five experience potions, I still had 700k to my name. I had a plan for 500k and the extra 200k was my back up.

Now that I had greatly increased my chances of survival, it was time to turn my attention to base building. If we could get a decent blacksmith and a few other crafters, it might make gearing up a whole lot easier. Having a good blacksmith that could constantly improve my armor and change its alignment could very well save lives. I had no idea how long it would take me until I could change the alignment myself, so it was essential to pursue it.

As a human, my lifespan was short in comparison to some of the monsters of the Underworld. It was likely impossible to grow as powerful as the lords of the underworld unless I found something that would allow me to live forever. Maybe I could count on Light Magic for that? *Another question that needed answers.* Focusing and mastering one alignment was possible though. The Mistress had said as much. It could at least give me a fighting chance in the right situation. What I needed the most was knowledge.

What would I do next? Try to get the forge built for one. After that, I didn't know if I should try to conquer the tower first, maybe leave the Mistress's dungeon and enter the rest of the Underworld. I could seek the Vampire Lord's magic vault. Mastering Light Magic was a given since it was what I was talented in. I had already noticed that it leveled much faster than my Blue Magic spells. Learning other schools of magic would help prepare me to take advantage of any elemental weakness and so would learning more Blue Magic. The Mistress made it all too clear that I needed more than just my Light Magic. I agreed with her.

The first thing on the menu though would be a snack at the cafeteria. Then I would let everyone know my plan about building a forge. I guess I should build a library as well. One thing was for sure. There was no end to what needed to be done.

CHAPTER 24 - STUDY

My lone Skeleton Warrior stood at the ready for any monster that dared approach me as I studied.

This was the fruit of my new Undead Dominance spell. I had beaten this Skeleton Warrior to an inch of its life then took over its mastery with a single cast of my Blue Spell. It leveled up whether I was dominating new mobs or keeping a single one under dominance, so I just kept this one under my control. It was another 100 MPM spell to add to my list.

The Skeleton had leveled from 120 to 132 since I had set up shop here in the last four hours. Unlike other Skeleton Warriors, this one was fully armored in Skeletal Plate Mail and a Skeletal General's Horned Helm. It made the summoned skeleton nearly invincible to creatures even 100 levels higher than it.

It hadn't been as much trouble as it might seem to set up this ornate wooden desk and lay out all my tomes as I studied in my own personal dark corner of a deep side cavern. My inventory coupled with my 350+ Strength made hauling it around easy. This area was good experience for my minion and the drops were decent. Mostly low-end magic weapons that Russ could deconstruct to help with his forging and blacksmithing skills.

I reclined back in a modern steel folding chair with my magical light orb shining bright overhead. The modern chair had been cheaper than any chair that might go better with the desk. The desk itself was something the dwarf merchant was just going to throw out so he had given me a good price.

One of my many tomes sat in my lap tilted against the desk as I read.

Looking up and off to the distance, I pondered the current logic of my book's author. The author, Boris Coddlehead, was a Werecat and just as self-indulgent as any cat you would run across in the world above. He just happened to be a genius with dark magic too.

To unlock the spell tree for Dark Magic would normally take finding a dark magic vein and a very specific process to unlock it. But since I was naturally talented with Light Magic, I would likely never be able to become aligned with Dark Magic, its opposite alignment. Nothing explicitly said I couldn't learn it, but it was clear that it would be much harder because all the alignments had a relationship with each other. As an example, Fire and Water Elements were opposites, so they didn't work together. Fire and earth though did work well together, creating their own sub-elements like Magma, Metal and Explosive magic.

How easily you could learn another alignment depended on the elements you already knew and their synergy to the alignment you were trying to learn. The natural Synergy between Fire and Earth Magic was 50%. This meant a person who possessed Fire magic would have a 50% chance to learn it during the right ritual. They would also have 50% efficiency when using the other element after they learned it. So they could learn to use 50% of the spells in that spell tree. They would also only be 50% effective.

Once they learned the two main alignments of fire and earth they would have had a 75% Synergy with Magma Magic, one of the sub-alignments that were a mix of the two alignments.

Fire's Synergy with the primary elements was as follows: Earth 50%, Air 80%, Water 0%. The sub-elements varied even more. But what was odd was that what you were talented in would affect the synergy between alignments. As an example, if you had a talent in an element you would have 60% Light and 60% Dark Magic efficiency. They could actually use both, but depending on which one they got first, the opposite alignment would immediately change to 40% efficiency. So if someone chose Light Magic, they would only have 40% efficiency in Dark. What you chose to learn first really mattered.

Also, because talents varied so much, synergy efficiency could vary even more. There was often more to it than just having a higher efficiency, just like my ability to heal a person's endurance and health wasn't a normal characteristic of Light Magic.

Personally, I had 0% efficiency with Dark Magic, but a 60% efficiency with all elements. This included all of the sub-elements. The exception was that if I learned one element, then I became less efficient with its opposite. So if I chose Water Magic, I would immediately have only 40% efficiency with its opposite. The advantage was that even though I couldn't ever be considered a master in an element, I could use each element, even if I possessed all of them, regardless of their opposites.

It was rarer to be talented in a sub-element. Olivia was one of the lucky ones to specialize in Nature Magic, a sub of Water and Earth. She had 100% efficiency in Nature, and 80% in Water and Earth. Because of her high degree of specialization, her opposites Fire and Air only allowed her 20% efficiency.

Blue Magic was a different story. Everyone could learn Blue Magic regardless of synergy because the spell cast was considered a monster skill. One problem was that Blue Magic Dungeons were hard to find as Blue Magic Veins were rare in the area surrounding the Head Mistress's dungeon, so even after we got out it would be a while before anyone could learn it.

Being able to pick up every spell alignment would likely take years if not decades. And that was at the best a guess. We had yet to enter a dungeon. The Magic Compasses explained the difficulty of dungeons by giving a recommended level, but these weren't dungeons like you might think of in games. These were living, breathing ecosystems that could be taken over and ruled by more powerful beings. They had the ability to grow and even level up.

I wasn't the only one trying to learn more. I lent my books to the others liberally as long as I had read them already. Every caster had at least read through their own alignment. Some owned their own.

Putting down my book, it was time for some fun.

"Batman!" I yelled just like they do in some anime to cast a skill or spell. Of course, it really was quite unnecessary to say anything, but I was alone and needed to give my brain a break.

Bat Form took hold of me, taking two seconds to fully transform into a three foot tall bat. Currently, I was *In the Buff*, so my size as a bat was more than twice the size of when I cast it without buffs. Sadly, any skeletal armor didn't really work well in bat form. The weight of the bones weighed me down. My regular armor and clothing also didn't stack with the form, so I lost their benefits. I was just thankful my clothing was also transformed with the spell, so I wasn't left naked after I was done, having to redress myself.

Flapping over to my Skeletal Warrior, I perched on top of its head, wrapping my wings comfortably around the horns of my minion's helm. It must have been an interesting sight to see a three foot tall bat with six-foot wingspan chilling on an intimidating, thickly armored skeleton warrior.

"Onward, Betty!" I cried in all squeakiness.

The Skeletal Warrior took a step forward, not really obeying any verbal command, but following my will through the spell.

My desk was hidden in a fairly secure nook of the cave system by the Skeletal Scouts area. It was a side cave off the main, man-made hall system that connected the different difficulties of skeleton mobs. It was the perfect place for my Skeleton Warrior to auto-hunt close by while I read. If there was anything that it spotted getting too close to me then it would protect me first.

Leaving for a few minutes to fight some scout archers wouldn't put my library in danger. Anything that dared to approach my precious books would have to get past me first.

It was possible to put my skeletal minion in different basic modes with general commands. Defend was the one I was using earlier while I was reading. In that mode, you guessed it, he defended against spawns nearby. It also worked like an auto-hunt for him because of the constant spawns in this area. The aggression mode caused him to attack anything I considered an enemy. Dance mode was a work in progress because I had to teach it each dance move. Yeah, I had completely made this one up. Since I couldn't dance myself—at least you probably wouldn't call it dancing—it was slow going. Others also could be used but you get the picture.

There was a completely manual mode that required my full attention. In this case, it was more of a puppet than a minion. Fighting with line of sight was not the same as fighting using my own eyes and body though.

The more detailed the commands I gave it the better it would usually do, but the real trick was giving it a general command like 'attack', then feeding it updated commands as it fought. This way I could manage it without having to fully control it.

Our first Skeleton Scout appeared as we rounded a corner. He was alone. Boring. I could change that.

I flapped my wings enough to pull off of my perch and hover.

"Bullrush, Betty!" I cried, pulling the scout's attention.

An arrow loosed from the scout's bow, giving me a quick challenge. As I flapped harder on one side to shift my bat body to the side, the arrow missed by a foot.

My beloved Betty ran at the scout like a mad rhino, lowering its head at the last moment and completely shattering the scout's rib cage even though the horns had missed their mark. Perhaps he was too strong for this area.

Further in we found a group of three that would give me a bigger challenge.

Lifting off my Hilda's head once again, I issued a new command.

"Dance, boney britches!"

Suddenly my minion was doing a very robotic version of the Carlton and arrows started bouncing off his armor.

Ugly or not I gave a little bat grin.

Opening my mouth, a fireball developed and flew. The three arrows that came at me turned to ash as the fireball rushed at them. The explosion of fire popped one skeleton's head right off its shoulders. I dived as it fell.

Snagging the skull before it hit the ground, I screeched something that was supposed to be a word.

Score! I deserved 100 points each for that one! Not that I really got anything for my little trick except for the satisfaction of pulling it off.

Another group of two Skeleton Scouts joined us during the commotion.

Fireball was a good time, but even that could get repetitive. Ice Shard had a tendency to shatter them. I was looking for something a little different.

Dodging the next volley of arrows, I just flew at them as if I was going to attack. I probably could do some damage to them with my bat form's claws, but it was something I had yet to play around with. Good time to start.

An idea hit me as I was about to make contact with the closest skeleton. Dropping the arrows in my grasp, I fired a couple of quick Alpha Bullets about the size of baseballs to sever the two scouts' bowstrings. With their weapons out of the way, I grabbed at one's head. With a quick twist and hugging my wings to myself, I was able to twist and get my claws in its eye sockets.

With a wicked screech, I launched myself up hard and was easily able to pull the skeleton from the ground. I had overestimated how much it weighed and suddenly found myself 10 meters in the air smacking my head against the solid stone ceiling. Even though it smarted, I was mostly fine. The scout whirlwinded its arms as it found itself in a very unnatural situation for its undead self.

Flying toward the skeletons below, I didn't swoop too terribly low but gained some momentum for what I was about to do. When I was sure my aim was right, I let go of the scout that did a half backflip before it meteored into its archer friends.

"Skeleton Bowling!"

The pile of disconnected bones left scattered in the aftermath gave me a fit of pleasure.

It was moments like these that made the labyrinth and the whole kidnapping thing bearable.

After about half an hour of fun, I headed back to my books. Enough of Mr. Werecat's blabbering on about Dark Magic. I couldn't spend any more time reading. Sadly my time was limited.

I gathered my desk and books, then a few dozen drops that had been left from my skeleton minion's auto-hunt, and headed back to base. I needed to drop off these low-end weapons for Russ.

CHAPTER 25 - CONSTRUCTION

As I entered what used to be the newbie Decrepit Skeleton area, four players, including Russ, were there specializing in crafting instead of being off hunting. Two of the players had picks and were chipping away at the wall near the entrance that led to the cafeteria, our bunks, and armory.

The wall they were chipping away at was shaping up to be the entrance to another room. They had already mined out two others that would eventually act as our personal apartments. It wasn't just construction they were focused on. Their labor had a dual purpose. As they dug out each room they were gathering any ore they ran across. Much of the rock itself was fairly worthless for blacksmithing, but there was some common iron, copper, and bauxite. It didn't hurt that mining was a sub-skill of forging. Their Strength and Endurance attributes were also increasing as they worked.

As I passed I threw them both a Heal.

They both stopped and waved their thanks. The grimaces on their face relaxed a bit before they went back to their work.

Russ was on the opposite end of the stadium-sized room where we had agreed to build all of our crafting stations. Half a dozen dwarves had already dug out an open space twice as high as the apartments. They had also made the ceiling level ten feet higher. They were currently working on the furnace. Why the furnace they were building climbed twenty feet in the air straight up to the ceiling was unclear, but the blue-grained granite they were using made the structure look even more impressive. There were two different sizes of bellows that would be manually worked once the structure was done. The anvil in the center of the room was not made of gray steel as I had always seen in pictures, but a black speckled silvery metal I hadn't known existed. It was orbulist-alloy. Not that I knew what that was.

The furnace for smelting was in a separate room next to the forge. It looked like a giant cauldron. There were actually three of them. The main one nearly reached the ceiling. Another was slightly taller than a person. The last one was about three feet tall and was off the ground on a slab of stone.

While I had been convinced that getting a blacksmith was something we had to do, I don't know what I had imagined it would look like, but this wasn't it. Being here, fighting monsters and constructing a base, made everything seem more real somehow. I almost envied Russ and the two others with talent for blacksmithing and smelting.

I had initially balked at the idea of spending the money, knowing eventually we would have to find a new place to settle. But I had a feeling the armor we could create with it was something we would need before we dared to leave. Also the Mistress wouldn't suspect anything if it looked like we were building a home here.

Lydia, our fourth crafter, had her own room that was already mostly finished. She had almost solely set up her alchemy station herself, except for help from Chris. The equipment was so much cheaper than blacksmithing that it wasn't funny. All the beakers, mixing pots, burners, etc. that she needed had cost less than 200k. It had cost us 2.5 million to construct what we needed for the forge. The construction was also little more than digging out a room for her and giving her some counter space. That didn't mean it would remain cheap. The real cost from Alchemy was the price of ingredients.

Her room came first before I reached Russ closest to the corner. I stopped there because even though I didn't get many crafting ingredients, I had started collecting them again to help her level up.

"Elorion." She nodded, looking up from pouring a glass measuring cup into a boiling liquid on one of her burners. Her blond hair was short and wavy, tucked behind her ears. She pressed her finger up to the bridge of her nose as if to reposition her glasses that she no longer wore as she turned back to her work.

It was good to see her up and doing something. Aeris was doing most of the legwork with keeping an eye on how everyone was doing, but I could at least help keep Lydia busy.

I had been able to restore her vision from low prescription to 20/20. If her vision had been worse, I don't know if I would have been able to heal it. She wasn't very social, but usually stopped what she was doing to acknowledge me. I guessed I had leveled from suspicious stranger to acquaintance...

"Hey, Lydia. Got a handful of ingredients for you."

"Thanks. Go ahead and set them on the table." She pointed to the island counter that was cluttered, but still the cleanest surface in the room. "I'll sort them later. Oh, and if you find any Lizardmen, I need their toenails."

"Uh." Not exactly something I ever thought I would hear her say just by looking at her—or anyone for that matter. "Okay, Lydia... You got it." I saw an open book on a table perpendicular to where she stood now. She must have found a recipe she was interested in.

I shrugged and left after dropping off some, mostly gross, undead leftovers. She was a total geek but had petite features giving her a delicate cuteness. Perhaps that was why it seemed so odd that she played with disgusting things all day.

Honestly, I really didn't buy many of her potions, yet. The ones she was able to produce so far were mainly buffs. +10 to Intelligence and Wisdom for 4 hours. +40 to Dexterity for 2 hours. There were some poisons too, but we didn't have many uses for those, at least not yet. Not bad for only being at it for a few days, though. Healing potions did not have the most common ingredients which made them expensive. Still, she was learning new potions every day. I hoped eventually she would figure out how to make experience potions so that we could mass produce them.

I found Russ out in front of the forge that was still under construction. The dwarves had questioned him like an imp that was caught stealing the Mistress's undergarments. Since he was a newbie that had never touched a forge before, they insisted on building him a small, temporary one to practice on as they built the one we commissioned. It had taken them no more than an hour to build the furnace that came up to his shoulders. He had a normal steel anvil and a rack of tools behind him. He also had three books open on a simple wooden table that I knew he had been pouring over the last two days. The main forge was going to take two weeks to complete.

Stopping, I watched as he struck a once worn sword into something more useful. There was a wooden crate of deconstructed weapons and armor he had been pounding on. What surprised me was that what was once a pile of blades and hilts, plates and leather straps, was now filled with mostly intact items. Another crate on the other side of the forge was filled with the junk we had been dropping off for him to practice with. A few days ago those items would have been considered far from junk, but after the little battle, we were rich in comparison.

His gigantic arm rose and fell at a steady pace. Sweat soaked his brow, chest, and back. He wore no armor, only a smoke colored, long-sleeved shirt covered in small pockmarks from the sparks from his hammering. Even after hours of this he was still going strong and didn't even seem winded. Not only was he talented in blacksmithing, but in Constitution. I had a feeling it was no mistake that he was talented in both.

Earlier he asked me not to heal him except once a day. He explained if I healed him too often he wouldn't get the increase in stats that came from exercise. How many attribute points had I lost out on because I was always healing myself? But would I have hunted and leveled up as much if I hadn't? Perhaps I should look for a middle ground and do both.

When he stopped and raised the short sword to turn it over in his hand and examined it I started emptying my inventory into his crate.

He noticed me then.

"Dude! You've brought me more ladies!" Russ licked his lips.

I almost facepalmed. "Ladies?"

"Yeah. I moved on from just deconstructing them to putting them back together and even repairing them as much as I'm able. It's really amazing what you learn as you work with them. Each one of these beauties divulges their deepest darkest secrets if you give them some love."

I didn't want to encourage him, but I couldn't help myself. "Oh really?"

"Of course! This little lady might be short and a little thick in the waist, but she was forged in a fire dungeon by a novice minotaur. You see the location is important because in element rich environments the magic is literally everywhere and it's impossible for an item being forged not to be affected. And then, minotaurs are naturally of the earth element so any object they make has the chance of bearing earth based enhancements. Now, this minotaur wasn't exactly an enchanter, but there was enough in the circumstance and environment for it to get a hint of fire damage, only +3, but it also has the fire alignment. It gets critical damage against those of the water alignment.

"But that's not the best part. This little beauty is very gracious to its master, giving +60 to strength! She's incredible and was something her crafter really shouldn't have been capable of. It was likely his best work."

"So even though it's not rare generally, it is rare in that it's among the best work that blacksmith ever did?"

"Yes!"

"That's really incredible. How do you know it was a minotaur?" I was genuinely impressed. Not with the item, but he had never struck me as the engineer type. I guess once a person is in their element they blossom, or just get huge as in Russ's case.

"Well first, enchantments aren't a part of the item itself. Most spells don't last more than a short period of time, but for permanent enchantments, there has to be something like a jewel or gemstone to hold the spell. A few rare metals do so as well. This one is without the required adornment, and normal steel doesn't hold magic, so it has to be forged into the steel itself. That happens when the steel is smelted and further as the blacksmith pounds the item into shape.

"I think it's a minotaur just because that's what my books say is most likely. I could be wrong. It could be an earth imp or something, but minotaurs are known to enjoy blacksmithing. They are just the most likely earth aligned species."

By the time he was finished with his explanation, my mouth was drooping open. I closed it quickly. Magic or not, there was definitely a science to it and Russ seemed to be the perfect guy for the job.

"How long until you can forge something like that?"

He looked up as he scratched his chin for a moment. "I'm not really sure. A couple weeks, or maybe a couple months."

My chest deflated a bit. The sword he was holding was okay, but it was little more than a newbie item. I hated to think it, but I couldn't help it. *How long until all this money we've spent will turn into something useful?*

He must have seen the concern on my face. "With better materials and our new forge I should be able to do better in that time, but the results will be sporadic at first. I don't fully understand how the forge works, or how to smelt. The dwarves said it can only be fully understood through experience. There is a connection of some kind that happens between the forge and the blacksmith. When I asked if it was magic, they looked at me like it was a stupid question.

"Also if we can find someone to enchant items, then we could probably double the attribute output. Maybe more."

Even if I was still slightly worried, my fascination overrode all distress. "Good to hear, man, keep it up. I'll look into enchanting and see how easy it is to get started. I don't think anyone was talented in it, but that doesn't mean we can't figure it out."

"That would be great. Will do."

I hadn't told anyone, but since I no longer had to sleep, I was getting bored doing nothing but hunting and studying. The perfect hobby might be learning to do something like enchanting. I was interested more in the long-term kind instead of just casting a spell that might wear off though.

After some bacon and eggs, even though it was lunch time, I headed back out to do a good twelve-hour stint wiping the Skeleton Sentinel room. I was a day or two from getting every level I could out of them. Then it would be time to open the Bone Palace. I still wasn't sure if I would try to climb the tower, or just conquer the first floor then leave for the Underworld. There was so much I needed to do. Getting everyone out of here safely was the number one priority. Exactly how I was going to pull that off was the real question.

My wish list was to hunt down more Blue Magic, find new creatures for bonus experience and try to loot the Vampire Lord's home. *One day.*

Regardless of what I decided, there was no time to relax. As much as I disliked the Mistress, I also respected her power. What she had said to us on the first day had stuck with me. The underworld was something I could have only dreamed of until she brought me here. Being able to level up, to grow stronger, left me in awe. I was now able to use magic, to heal myself, and I would never have to sleep again. It couldn't be denied that part of me was thankful for this opportunity.

Not that I could forget the danger, or the fact that on a whim she could change her mind and would very literally eat me; probably with ranch dressing.

Should I seek to grow powerful enough to destroy her, or just to break the power that she had over me? My freedom was not as confined as I once believed. We had full access to the Underworld, even if that meant never seeing the surface again. But that wasn't out of the question.

I didn't know what I would be doing a week or a year from now, but one thing was clear. I would fight. We were not safe, so the first thing that was necessary was to continue growing stronger. As strong as possible.

THANKS FOR READING!

Besides purchasing the book, nothing helps an indie author more than reviewing their work!

Please take the time to review on Amazon and Goodreads!

Underworld Book 2

Through the Belly of the Beast is Available now on Amazon

And Kindle Unlimited!

Try the author's other Amazon Best Selling Series, Codename: Freedom!

Survive Week One

The Goblin Siege

Looking for Updates?
ApollosThorne.Com

Interested in reading chapters early?
Patreon.com/ApollosThorne

CHARACTER SHEET

(Base stats at the end of book 1)

Name: Elorion Edwards

Race: Human

Age: 17

Level: 260

Health Points: 2500

Mana Points: 5000

Endurance: 800

Attributes

Strength: 64

Dexterity: 100

Constitution: 100

Intelligence: 100

Wisdom: 1003

Stat Points: 15

Attributes Drained

+14,741 HP

+11,277 MP

+66 Str

+37 Dex

+71 Con

+207 Int

+103 Wis

Note: These stats are permanent as long as you use Vampire's Might at least once in the next 7 days and once a week after. If you do not find another creature to drain within the next 7 days these stats will be lost at a rate of 3.33% a day until the end of a full month when your stats will return to normal.

As you drain targets, the benefits you receive will depend primarily on the purity of the source. Once your stats have reached a certain level, you will not be able to drain from low-level creatures to improve stats, only to sustain them.

If no stats are lost in a year's time, they will become yours permanently without having to continue to use Vampire's Might. All attribute gains through use on multiple targets of Vampire's Might stack. The one-year timer does not start over with each gain of more stats. Each creature drained starts a separate timer.

STAT BONUSES

Novice Mana Flow Understanding

Sitting is no longer required for quick mana regeneration.

Total mana multiplied by 2. Your 200 mana has now increased to 400.

All spells cost 20% less mana to cast.

All spells are 20% more powerful when cast.

New skill: Meditation

Mana regeneration rate slowly ramps up the longer you meditate reaching a maximum of 5 times your current regeneration rate reached after 10 minutes of meditation.

Warning. Meditation can be dangerous because it requires your complete focus.

Note: The first minute of meditation is the normal regeneration rate.

Novice Mana Manipulation Understood

You can now charge a spell to cause greater damage.

The amount of mana per point of Intelligence has doubled.

All spells cost 20% less mana to cast.

All spells are 20% more powerful when cast.

Intermediate Meditation

Mana regeneration rate slowly ramps up the longer you meditate reaching a maximum of 10 times current regeneration rate after 5 minutes of meditation.

If you continue meditating after you have reached maximum mana, you will be able to store mana through meditation of up to double your current maximum mana.

Warning. Meditation can be dangerous because it requires your complete concentration.

Note: The first minute of meditation is the normal regeneration rate.

Intermediate Mana Flow Understood

Mana rejuvenation is now calculated by 2 points of mana per minute per point of wisdom.

Total mana multiplied by 5. 1000 base mana is now 5000

All spells cost 40% less mana to cast.

All spells are 40% more powerful when cast.

Novice Spell Mastery

All spells at the Novice level now cost 5 MP/MPM or less regardless of level.

Durable Body

Instead of 10 HP for each point of Con, you will now receive 25.

All damage taken reduced by 5%

Enhanced Endurance

Stamina doubled.

25% less stamina used.

Toughness Synergy

Because of the close relationship between Strength and Constitution, your high Con now reflects this. Every 5 points of Strength acts just as 1 point of Con would.

Light Step

You have surpassed the normal human limit for agile reactions. Due to this, it will seem to others as if you float off the ground when you run.

Speed Increased by 20%

Quick Reflexes Increased by 20%

Speed Synergy

Due to the relationship between fast twitch muscles responsible for Dexterity and how they help when lifting heavy objects, for every 5 points of Strength, it will be as if you have an additional point of Dex.

Heavy Lifter

You are now able to lift things 10% heavier. Because it is so much easier for you to handle lighter weight, all damage with melee weapons is increased by an additional 10%

Intensity

You will now have the ability to increase your focus at will at a cost of double stamina use to add 25% damage and 50% aim to every melee attack.

Full Body Synergy

Strength, Constitution, and Dexterity all work together through muscles, tendon, and bone. Because of this relationship and the improvement of all three, it will be as if you have an additional +25 in all three attributes.

Additional +1 to all three stats for every 5 points put in each attribute equally. Example: 5 Str = 1 Con and 1 Dex.

This +25 is included in all damage and skill calculations but does not apply to Leveling Bonuses.

TALENTS

Light Magic Affinity

Due to a natural affinity with light magic, the user's healing spells will heal health, endurance, and exhaustion. As individual spells level, this can grow to heal status effects as well. Healing spells will level faster than normal.

Blue Magic

You now have access to Blue Magic.

General Magic

Light Orb

This orb will obey your will and light up the path before you. The higher the level the further and brighter the light can extend. This spell can be essential for survival or a power outage.

Mage's Deodorant

When unable to use deodorant because of unavailability, poverty, or strange religious alignment, this spell will keep you from adding smelly funk to your social engagements. The smell is neutral. As this spell levels up you can add special scents for any special occasion.

Mage's Toilet Paper

Never run out of this household essential again! For anywhere you find yourself you will never be without! As the spell levels up lotion can be added to the effects of the spell!

Power Nap

When you sleep, you recover your HP and exhaustion twice as fast. Passive.

Light Magic

Lesser Heal

This is the novice level healing spell for those who have unlocked the Light Magic Alignment.

Base healing of 100 HP

Base cost of 50 MP

Heal

Base Heal of 1000 at level 1

Cost 100 MP per cast.

Advanced Healing

Base Heal of 5000 at level 1

Cost 1000 MP per cast.

Health Bullet

When Healing magic is condensed and fired at a high velocity.

Health Bomb

When Healing magic is gathered at one point and compressed. I can be thrown, but the more magic channeled into the spell the less stable it is.

Mind Buff

When Healing magic is applied to the mine both Intelligence and Wisdom is increased.

The amount depends on the rank of the Healing magic used.

Muscle Buff

When Healing magic is applied to the body's muscular system both Strength and Dexterity is increased.

The amount depends on the rank of the Healing magic used.

Skeletal Buff

When Healing magic is applied to the body's skeletal system the bodies Constitution and endurance is increased.

The amount depends on the rank of the Healing magic used.

Organ Defense

When Healing magic is applied to the body's organs the ability to resist poisons and status effects is increased.

The amount depends on the rank of the Healing magic used.

In the Buff

When Healing magic is applied to every bodily system the buffs are combined into one spell.

The amount depends on the rank of the Healing magic used.

BLUE MAGIC

Creature Observation

This is the basic skill that all blue magic is based upon. It allows you to steal the natural skills of other creatures and mimic their abilities through magic.

Force Learn

Force Learn is the spell form of Creature Observation. By channeling mana into your eyes, you are able to form a magic connection with what you are trying to observe. This works by greatly increasing your focus and giving you a glimpse into the spectrum of magic.

Explosive End

The moment before death you will have the option of directing your remaining mana into a finale of fireworks, injuring the targets you set your sights upon.

Note: After you have used this spell you are dead. There is no way to cheat death and watch the cool effects of Explosive End; dead is dead. If you just so happen to know someone with a resurrection spell, then perhaps, but you will still probably miss the show because of the long cast time of such spells.

Cleanliness

Use mana to clean your body. Its ability to clean and disinfect grows with level. At the highest level, this can even be used to cleanse bacterial diseases.

Pain

This is the intermediate skill that sends waves of pain throughout the nervous system.

Stun of 10 seconds

Lesser Pain Resist

You have a small amount of tolerance to the status effect, Pain.

Decay

Through careful observation, you have understood Blue Magic: Decay. This spell stacks with itself and other corrosives.

Against non-living objects or creatures, this weakens and even destroys the target with enough time.

Against the living, this spell weakens and can cause harm. In time, because of a living creature's ability to self-repair, the spell will be overcome.

Invisibility

Through invisibility you are able to fade into a true ethereal state.

Fades in and out of invisibility depending on your speed of movement, skill and magic use.

Shadow Step

Manipulates shadows to make you difficult to see.

Skeleton Warrior's Shield

You have understood the magic nature of the shield of the Skeleton Warrior. A thick bone shield is summoned at the casting of this spell.

Cost 50 MPM

Skeleton Warrior's Sword

You have understood the magic nature of the sword of the Skeleton Warrior. A sharp bone sword is summoned at the casting of this spell.

Cost 50 MPM

Skeletal Breast Plate

You have understood the magic nature of the sword of the Skeleton Champion. Hardened bone forms over your torso giving you a strong and well-fitting armored shell.

Cost 100 MPM

Skeletal Armor

When Skelton Warrior's Shield, Sword and Skeletal Breast Plate merge they big you a full bodied suit of armor with the shield and sword in combination.

Skeletal General's Defense

Full bone platemail combines with Skeletal General's Helm to form full body and head protection. You also get to look awesome!

Fluid Body

5% resistance to physical damage

Your resistance will grow as the spell levels

Fluid Mentality

5% resistance to magic damage

Your resistance will grow as the spell levels

Blue Magic - Undead Dominance (Novice)

Unlike Raise the Dead, you are able to both bring the dead to life and command those that are already raised unless the being is directly controlled by the necromancer. The level of undead you can control or raise depends on the level and rank of the spell.

Stench

Invited to an undead block party? Here's the latest in aromas to die for! Now is your chance to smell like all the cool corpses!

Teeth Whitening

A passive spell that will ensure your teeth stay healthy and white. This spell costs no mana but will cease to work if the user dies.

Bat Form

Capable of turning into a bat form. All spells and stats remain available in this form, but the stronger you are the larger the bat. Stealth becomes harder the higher the Strength and Constitution, but Invisibility is possible.

Cold Resist (Novice)

The ability to resist cold damage. This skill grows as your spell levels and increases in rank.

Vampire's Might

Novice Blood Drain evolves into its truest form. By draining a creature's blood, the power gain can be applied to Heal, Mana and attribute points. Must continue to consume blood for your power to not fade over time.

Fear

An aura of bloodlust terrifies all of those caught in its influence. Its effects grow with level. Does not affect those with a strong will, rage, bloodlust or high focus.

Alpha Bolt

A sphere of neutral magical energy with the force to knockback a target when cast.

True alignment neutral base damage 500

Cost 500 MP

Alpha Bullet

Neutral magical energy compressed into a small bullet and launched at high velocity.

True alignment neutral base damage 400

Cost 200 MP

Alpha Bomb

Neutral magical energy is gathered at one point and compressed. I can be thrown, but the more magic channeled into the spell the less stable it is.

Flamethrower

A stream of flame is propelled magically from the casters mouth. The range is 5 meters and the span is 5 meters.

Fireball

An explosive ball of flame is propelled magically from the casters mouth.

Lesser Wail of the Banshee

Sonic damage expelled through one's cry. Dead mages who are resurrected for whatever unknown evil become ghouls and have this ability naturally.

Ice Shard (Novice)

A large ice shard is propelled at your enemy. The number of shards and your ability to manipulate them grows as it levels. One additional shard for each 10 levels while in novice rank.

Apollos Thorne is the Amazon Best-Selling Author of the Underworld and Codename: Freedom series. He resides in Orlando, Florida, with his wife and two children. To learn more about Apollos, visit his Web site at ApollosThorne.com.

Made in the USA
Monee, IL
25 November 2019

17457443R00203